C000088655

PENGUIN BOOKS

# LOVE BEGINS WITH AN

Jeana Vithoulkas was born and raised in Melbourne and currently lives there. She was educated at Melbourne University and has worked as an interpreter, a union official, a university tutor and a freelance writer, among other things. This is her first novel.

# LOVE BEGINS WITH AN A

## JEANA VITHOULKAS

PENGUIN BOOKS

Penguin Books

Published by the Penguin Group
Penguin Books Australia Ltd
250 Camberwell Road, Camberwell, Victoria 3124, Australia
Penguin Books Ltd
80 Strand, London WC2R 0RL, England
Penguin Putnam Inc.
375 Hudson Street, New York, New York 10014, USA
Penguin Books, a division of Pearson Canada
10 Alcorn Avenue, Toronto, Ontario, Canada M4V 3B2
Penguin Books (NZ) Ltd
Cnr Rosedale and Airborne Roads, Albany, Auckland, New Zealand
Penguin Books (South Africa) (Pty) Ltd
24 Sturdee Avenue, Rosebank, Johannesburg 2196, South Africa
Penguin Books India (P) Ltd
11, Community Centre, Panchsheel Park, New Delhi 110 017, India

First published by Penguin Books Australia Ltd 2003

10 9 8 7 6 5 4 3 2 1

Designed by Marina Messiha, Penguin Design Studio
Front cover photograph by Chris Kapa
Author photograph by Ponch Hawkes
Typeset in 11/16.5pt Minion by Post Pre-press Group, Brisbane, Queensland
Printed and bound in Australia by McPherson's Printing Group, Maryborough, Victoria

National Library of Australia
Cataloguing-in-Publication data:

    Love begins with an A.
    ISBN 0 14 300144 2.

    1. Greek Australians – Fiction.  2. Man–woman relationships
    – Fiction.  I. Title.

A823.4

This project has been assisted by the Commonwealth Government through the
Australia Council, its arts funding and advisory body.

www.penguin.com.au

*In memory of*
*Bettina Piskopos*
*and*
*Mitsoula Vithoulkas*

## ACKNOWLEDGEMENTS

Many thanks to Martin Flanagan and Christos Tsiolkas for their encouragement and faith, to Jess Migotto and Nicole Karidis for their assistance, to my cousins Akis Soulis in Zakynthos and Kostas Georgoudakis in Athens for their support and counsel. And to Michael Rizzo for his eternal optimism.

# CHAPTER ONE

Love begins with an A in Greek. It is the first entry in the dream dictionary, our family's most consulted book. 'Love' followed by 'Arab'. A very long entry with many cross-references, followed by a very short one with none. Rather like my life: a long entry for unrequited love with cross-references I could have done without, followed by short entries that died natural deaths.

In recent times the entries had been blank, a situation my mother was keen to remedy. She rang me to tell me about her dream, in which she saw horses.

'What does that mean?' I asked.

'A wedding, of course.'

Of course.

I was sitting in the garden on a Sunday afternoon while the sun dried my hair, which was in curlers.

'And you know what?' she continued. 'I saw Tony's

mother the other day and she was asking about you with great enthusiasm.'

'Mum, I'd forget Tony's mother if I were you. I'm pretty sure he's gay.'

'What? Him too?' She gasped in disbelief. 'What is this, some sort of epidemic? When I was young there was one, maybe two men of whom it was said . . .'

'Does that include Uncle Emilios?'

A pause. 'No.'

'So that makes three. That you know of,' I reminded her.

Another pause, before she abandoned her evidence altogether.

'Well, the point I'm trying to make is that every second man you come across is gay. What's to become of all the women in the world who want men?'

She sighed noisily, before adding, 'Are you sure?'

'Yes, Mum, I'm pretty sure.'

'Fuck it,' she said. 'Unbelievable.'

I could hear someone making their way down the side of the house, and as I was wearing nothing but my underwear I said goodbye as quickly as possible and bolted inside. I put on my dressing-gown, a vampish creation in sky-blue satin that had been made by my sister Elendina and resembled something Greta Garbo might have worn. It always made me look out of place in my various dwellings, places with little ornamentation in desperate need of a paint job. And I shared houses with smart young middle-class girls who thought wearing lipstick was risque. I loved dressing-gowns and wore them around the house simply for comfort. It was a family thing, and I didn't think it was unusual or different until I left home and people told me it was glamorous.

Coming into the kitchen, I saw, of all people, Bruce Stewart standing near the door. Tall and broad-shouldered but otherwise thin, he had a body built up by adolescent exercise but run down in later years by long nights and too many good drugs. He turned to me, cigarette in mouth, green eyes full of cheek. I was unsure how to greet him. It had been a fortnight since our last meeting, when I'd turned down his proposition for sex. He'd put the offer to me the night of Matthew Muldeary's party, having spent the better part of the evening putting me down. Apparently this is a feature of Australian men's mating habits. He'd had an awful lot to drink, like most of the people there, and was getting on my nerves with his goading, so I wandered off to talk with Matthew's brother Patrick. After a few rounds of 'The Boys Of The Old Brigade' and 'The Foggy Dew', all led by Patrick's mother, a singer if there ever was one, I said my goodbyes and headed home on foot. Outside on the foot-path, a block away from the Muldearys', Bruce was standing with his back to me having a piss. He was zipping up as I passed him.

'So, you off home then?' he said, and started to walk with me. 'Where abouts?'

'I don't live far. Just the other side of Brunswick Road.'

3

We walked on. 'Where do you live?' I asked, thinking he must also be close by.

'St Kilda.'

That was miles away. 'Are you going to walk all the way home?'

'Dunno,' he said, scratching his head. 'Where are we again?'

'Brunswick.'

'Might hail a cab,' he mumbled to himself. He pulled some coins out of his pocket and began to count, but dropped them. As he crouched down to pick them up, he lost his balance and fell backwards.

'Are you all right?' I offered him a hand. It was after one in the morning, in the middle of winter. His chances of hailing a taxi were slim and he was pitifully drunk. 'Come back to my house and we can call for a taxi from there.'

As soon as we got home he plonked himself on the couch and I offered him a cup of tea. While he drank it, I rang for a cab and was on hold for twenty minutes. There was a feeble attempt at small talk.

'So this is where you live. Nice house. You live alone?'

'No, I live with a girl called Jane. She's away in Benalla visiting her parents.' I gave up holding on and put the phone down. 'Since Jane's away, you're welcome to sleep here the night. There's too much of a wait.' I wanted to go to bed. I'd been up late the night before and was having trouble staying awake. In my late twenties, partying hard all night then doing it again with little sleep was becoming a thing of the past.

'Yeah, okay,' he muttered. I pointed out Jane's room, told him where the bathroom was and rose to go.

'Why don't we go to bed together?' he asked, out of the blue.

Somewhat stupidly, I asked why.

'Why not?' He made an attempt at a seductive smile.

Why not? Because you've been rude to me all night and if this is the best you can do to woo me, you can't want me that much. This wasn't the first time I'd had such an indifferent request for sex from an Australian man, but I'd been told I should appreciate them because at least they were honest. As if there were inherent value in honesty in all situations.

I laughed to cover my awkwardness and said sorry, as women tend to do even when it's not their fault.

'Go on,' he insisted, as if challenging me to a dare. Then, when I made to leave, he asked me again, 'Why not?'

Hadn't he ever been turned down before? He sounded like a two-year-old constantly asking why things are the way they are. Given his intoxicated state, I didn't think there was any point getting into a discussion with him.

'I'm going to bed and I'll see you in the morning, Bruce.' I took my cup and headed for the kitchen.

'It would be nice,' he called after me. 'Much nicer than being on your own.'

I stopped, took one look at the smirk on his face as he

fumbled to place his cup on the table, and imagined his beer breath all over me, the possibility that he might throw up. I decided that being on my own wasn't a bad option.

'Goodnight,' I said firmly, 'and remember, the toilet is the first door on the right.'

'Don't be such a Greek girl!' I heard him say. The last gasp of the desperate. Yeah right, I thought, shutting the door of my bedroom. What other reason could I possibly have to turn him down?

Greek girls don't fuck. I get told this all the time. Even after I've been to bed with someone. Greek girls want relationships. They want to get married. And other girls just want to fuck, of course, they don't want relationships and they never want to get married. So don't make the effort with Greek girls because you won't get anywhere. Such big efforts!

It's not that I object to sex on a whim. Some of the best sex can be had on a whim. What I don't like are the rules that go with it. As my housemate Jane explains, they go something like this: you go to a party or a pub where a great deal of alcohol is consumed and end up in bed with someone you may or may not know. You may or may not see them again, but if you do see them again you pretend it hasn't happened. You're supposed to pretend that you don't even know them. Just to show that you're not hung up on them or anything. That it was just a fuck to you.

But I've been with men who don't have to pretend. They don't remember whether it happened or not. My sister

6

Bettina says they get so drunk they don't remember who *they* are, let alone who you are.

I find these rules very difficult. In the first place, it's hard for me to get drunk. Three glasses of anything and I'm dying to go to sleep. And I mean sleep in the literal sense. In the second place, I need to feel some measure of excitement and desire to have sex with someone. So I'm usually already 'hung up' on them and can't see the point of hiding it. I would have thought that sleeping with someone you desire is the very time and place to show your interest.

In accordance with these rules, I didn't expect Bruce to come knocking on my door again. He was gone before I was up that day and I didn't really give him another thought.

'Would you like tea or coffee?' I asked him now. I wondered if he had left something behind.

'Yeah, thanks.'

I made tea and he rolled a joint with some dope he had and we smoked and talked. Or tried to talk. He wasn't exactly the talkative type. Stoned, I become garrulous and I was off and running with all sorts of stories. I forgot about the curlers in my hair and being in my dressing-gown with no bra, even though Bruce personified cool in his black jeans, unironed black cotton shirt, and a haircut straight out of a hip magazine. A style which looked anti-fashion but which was a fashion of its own.

'What do you do?' he asked, interrupting my account of a funny incident at work.

'I'm a lawyer.'

'Oh yeah.' He looked around the room. 'Do you go out?'

'Out?' Of course I got out.

'I mean, to see bands and that,' he added, realising the inadequacy of his question.

'If I like them.'

Silence. Then, 'I play in a band,' he said.

'Which one?'

'The Sub Urbans.'

I'd never heard of them.

'We're playing on the fourteenth at the Prince of Wales. Do you want to come?'

The Prince of Wales was a Melbourne institution. It being the early 1990s, the Wales was one of the few inner-city pubs that had managed to escape renovation and still feature live music.

'Well, I don't think I'm doing anything. I'll see if anyone wants to come with me.'

'Yeah, I'll put your name on the door.' He pulled the sleeves of his shirt down, then pushed them up again. 'You could come with me. I mean, we could go and get something to eat, maybe, first. We're not playing till late.'

I think he was asking me out.


The fact that I had never heard of Bruce's band was not unusual. Melbourne is a band town. Bands play in pubs all over Melbourne all the time. Some are well known, some are suburb famous, some become city famous. Not even the most dedicated music enthusiast could know all of them, least of all me whose taste in music is very eclectic: Greek, world music, and some black American artists from the fifties and sixties. A few days later at work, I asked Nick, who has an expansive knowledge of the local music scene, if he knew the Sub Urbans.

'The Sub Urbans, are you kidding?'

'So you know them?'

'Of course I know them,' he said, astonished at my ignorance. 'Why do you want to know?' He was munching on a sandwich and perusing the newspaper at the same time.

'I'm going to see them play.'

'At the Prince of Wales?'

I nodded. 'One of the band members asked me to go. He's put my name on the door.'

'Which band member?' Nick abandoned the newspaper and looked at me with interest.

'Bruce Stewart.'

'You know Bruce Stewart?' he said, his eyes widening.

'Well, I've met him a few times and he came round to my house yesterday.'

'No! When did you meet him? How come you never said anything? How could you keep a thing like this a secret?'

I explained that I wasn't keeping anything secret, that

Bruce was just someone I'd met through friends. But Bruce Stewart wasn't just anyone, I learnt.

'I can't believe you, Fiore. Don't you know anything? I've told you before, you need a crash course in popular culture.'

'Just because I don't know this band doesn't mean I'm out of touch with the whole world.'

Nick came into my office three times that afternoon. Bruce Stewart was a wanted man, according to Nick. Wanted by him and many others, men and women. He was gorgeous. Delicious. I was so lucky. Nick looked me up and down and said I had to go to this gig in something that didn't look like a Jane Austen outfit.

'Whatever you do, don't wear any of those hats your sister made for you. Especially not that one from *1900*. Or that Mary Poppins thing.'

Nick was with my sisters and me one cold winter night when we went to see *1900* for the first time. It was freezing in the cinema and we sat huddled together with our coats over us to keep warm. In among the sea of emotions we experienced watching the film, Elendina fell in love with a hat worn by Dominique Sanda. Elendina makes clothes and hats and bags, and would probably make shoes if she had the equipment. She takes her inspiration from movies, and that night, between weeping for the old women being killed by the fascists in the rain and cheering when Donald Sutherland was mauled by the peasants, she lusted after that hat. She sketched it roughly in the interval and made it for me afterwards. She made me others as well, including one inspired by *Howards End*. The Mary Poppins one, as Nick called it.

I told him I was grateful for his advice but wasn't sure how interested I was in Bruce. 'He looks bored in my company and I don't really know why he's asked me out,' I said.

Nick looked at me as if I were mad. 'Well, give the guy a chance. He might be nervous.' Nick had complained before that my standards in men were too high, but then he'd tell me not to settle for second best. 'It might surprise you, Fiore, but not a lot of people feel passionate about the Irish question. Or know much about Ugandan musicians living in Belgium.'

Nick was more excited than I was about my date with Bruce. He told everyone at work. He told his friends. He told his neighbour. He even told one of his clients. For months afterwards, I saw people who would ask me, 'I heard you were going out with Bruce Stewart. Is it true?'

A good friend who loved me to bits, Nick wanted me to be happy. He was always on the lookout for a decent man who might be of interest to me, but given that he was gay he didn't run into a lot of straight men socially. And when he did, they weren't always too sure they were straight. He gave me advice, often contradictory, about how to have better success with men.

'The thing is, Fiore, you intimidate a lot of men. I've seen them trying to impress you with something, and if you're not

11

interested you look bored. Or worse, you get up and leave. Not exactly encouraging. Men have fragile egos.'

'Why should I act interested in something if I'm not? It'll just give the wrong impression.'

My boss Victoria was a woman who never gave any man the wrong impression by looking interested. Although she had a man, you'd be forgiven for thinking she could easily have done without. She made it clear she preferred women to men and never missed an opportunity to point out the latter's inadequacies. Men were a necessary but often irritating fact of life. It was hard to disagree with her, but I marvelled at how she never let her feelings interfere in her unwavering mission to fight sexual inequality wherever she found it. She was a professional woman with very firm views about the salvation of the female sex through work, and she did her best to promote capable young women who were prepared to put in the hard yards.

'He looks like a drugged-out boy who hasn't washed for a week,' Victoria said when Nick showed her a photo of Bruce in a music magazine. She shook her head in disapproval. She never seemed to be moved by men physically. It just never figured in her approach to them. They didn't have that sort of power over her at all. I understood it, but thought it rather strange.

'Don't you find any man attractive, Vic?' I asked.

'Why should I be attracted to a member of the sex that starts wars, rapes women, kills their wives and destroys the planet?'

12

'Well, I'll just go and organise my sex change,' Nick said sarcastically.

'Haven't you ever felt something that you can't control?' I asked her. 'You know, looked across a room and seen someone and your knees weaken –' This was the wrong word to use with Victoria.

'No,' she said firmly.

In a way I envied her and wished I could be more like her. I could have avoided a lot of dramas in my life and saved my tears for worthier causes.

'Don't you ever just crave sex?' Nick asked.

'Well, my sexual urges do not translate into a quest for power over everything. And I think all this business about the natural rampant sexuality of men is total crap, a convenient excuse for their obsession with their dicks. For heaven's sake, why can't they learn to deal with their infantile urges in a mature way?'

Victoria was absolutely right, but when I fall in love I find it very hard to remember all the terrible things men have done to the world. Perhaps that's the point. Love makes you weak, blurs your judgement, and is an unreliable indicator of a good relationship. Mihalis was the first man I fell in love with – he was handsome and political and could sing with a voice that made me want to cut my heart out and give it to him on a plate. And he turned out to be a womaniser. Definitely not relationship material. Victoria, despite her intense feminism, shared my parents' belief that people

13

should be partnered according to the compatibility of their family, education and cultural values: a system where romantic love is not a priority. This might sound like a logical way to organise your life, but in the meantime, what do you do with your heart?

# CHAPTER TWO

That night, my sister Bettina woke me with a phone call from Greece. She had never learnt to calculate the time difference, and it took me a while to realise that the phone was not ringing in my dream. After a brief conversation during which I grunted incoherently, she asked me to send her some money, which she'd pay back when I got to Greece.

'You are coming, aren't you?' she said.

'Yes, I think so,' I yawned.

'What do you mean, you think so?'

'I don't know whether I can take the time off work. We're busy at the moment.'

Bettina, who had no interest in work apart from the fact that it gave her a means to enjoy her life, couldn't see a problem. 'For God's sake,' she said, 'you couldn't come last year for the same reason. Just come. Forget about work. It will always be there when you want it.'

I didn't see it that way. I was always insecure about work and fretted over doing the right thing as far as my career was concerned. Taking off on an extended holiday right in the middle of a government review into community legal centres didn't seem like a good idea. Explaining this to Bettina, however, was like talking to myself. It was a subject she didn't want to know about. Instead I inquired after our younger sister Elendina, who was also living in Greece.

'I haven't seen her since summer. She stayed in Zakynthos,' Bettina said with disapproval. She thought the island of Zakynthos, our parents' homeland, was a backwater, invaded every summer by cashed-up hicks and drunken English tourists.

Bettina's decision to move to Greece had been an unexpected one. She simply packed up and went, without wasting time talking about it. She was followed a year later by Elendina. Both of them went boldly into the unknown, leaving me alone and envious. My parents were bemused at first, convinced their daughters would be back within a year. But three years on, they showed no signs of homesickness. Their phone calls and letters were full of parties and laughter and interesting times. I'd started to toy with the idea of going too, but I always came back to the issue of work. What would I do for money? I couldn't work as a lawyer. Even though I didn't love the job, at least it gave me an income. My sisters didn't mind what they did. They worked in bars or nightclubs or cafés. This upset my parents no end.

'We came all this way and took on the worst jobs so that our children could get an education and have a decent quality of life. And what do they do? Leave good positions to go and work in bars in Greece,' they said time and time again. 'What did we have children for when they abandon us?'

My parents were the other reason I hesitated to leave. Being the oldest, most successful daughter, I was the proof of their hard labours. Their feelings about my sisters' decision to live in Greece were a mixed bag. Mostly they were in denial and didn't think it would last. As children and teenagers, all three of us had hated anything to do with Greece. Several years later, it was Mum and Dad doing all the talking about what a bad place Greece was in an attempt to dislodge this crazy idea that had taken hold of Bettina. When Elendina followed, I thought my mother would die of a broken heart.

This whole Greece thing baffled my parents, the memory of savage arguments about going to Greek school still fresh in their minds. It was Bettina who had flown the flag on her sisters' behalf on this one. In fact, it was Bettina who led the charge in most of the battles.

'I don't want to go to Greek school any more,' she would announce every so often.

'And how are you going to learn to read and write and speak properly?' my mother asked.

'Why do we have to? We already go to school, I don't want to learn Greek,' Bettina insisted.

'Don't say stupid things,' Grandmother Phaedra put in. 'Of course you want to learn Greek. What if one day they kick us out of this country? Like poor Nina – her family had been in Egypt for over a hundred years. And all the poor Pontians, who had to return after thousands of years.'

The Pontian Greeks had lived in the Black Sea area for three thousand years before being forced 'back' to Greece at the end of the war between Greece and Turkey in 1922. Their story fuelled the idea among migrant Greeks that they might one day be forced to return to the homeland.

'We are foreigners here,' my grandmother continued. 'One day we might have to go back. What do you want? You want people in Greece to laugh at you? They'll say, Look at those stupid people, they can't even talk properly.'

But Bettina was recalcitrant. 'I'm never going to Greece. Even if they do kick us out of here. All the people there are poor and there's no television and no-one's got toys.'

'And in Greece,' Elendina joined in, 'they only eat fish and chips.'

'Fish and chips! There's no such thing over there,' my grandmother laughed. 'It's the Greeks here who work in fish and chip shops.'

'Well, I don't care. I'm not going. Lots of people are in jail in Greece and democracy is dead. Dad says so.'

My grandmother was not amused. She looked accusingly at my father, who was eating his salad, trying to pretend he hadn't heard.

'This is what happens when you talk politics in front of the children,' she scolded him. 'Listen to them! Saying all these terrible things about their country.'

'Well, they need to know what's going on,' my father said defensively. He was still his mother's son.

'Your grandmother's right,' he told us. 'You must go to Greek school. This dictatorship won't always rule Greece. People will fight and change will come. And of course there's television and toys. Where do you get such ideas?'

'You, Dad, you said so. You didn't even have a ball to play with.' Bettina was crying now. She'd lost the battle. Elendina and I watched from the sidelines.

Funny how things change. Who could have foreseen that our grandmother was right? That Bettina would choose Greece as her home and that Greek school might prove to be of some use? Listening to her on the phone, though, as she dropped the occasional Greek phrase, she sounded like a girl from the back streets of Piraeus. We sure didn't learn that kind of talk at Greek school.

I had trouble getting back to sleep again and was not in a good way at work the next morning. And it was a busy day. First up was Jeff, who came to see me about a drink-driving charge. He had been to us with the same problem a year before. He'd lost his licence for a few months, got it back and was now set to lose it again. Jeff lived in the Housing Commission flats across the road from the legal centre and was an itinerant worker in the building industry. He needed his licence to start a new job in Dandenong.

'When does the job begin?' I asked.

'In a fortnight.'

'We'll try and postpone the hearing so you can get a start on the job and make some friends. By that time you might be able to organise a lift with a workmate.'

He nodded indifferently.

'How's that?' I asked him.

'Whatever.' He shrugged and rose to leave. 'The thing is, I wasn't drunk. I'd only had a few. It was me mate's fortieth. I might have been over the limit, but I wasn't drunk.'

'I believe you, Jeff, but that's the law.'

'Well, it's fucked.'

After Jeff, I had an appointment with a woman who'd been caught shoplifting. She'd also been in before. The first time it was Italian stockings, this time cosmetics. She was on a disability pension due to some type of anxiety disorder brought about by stress in her last job. Barely making ends meet, she'd decided to steal the luxuries she could no longer afford. She went into upmarket boutiques and helped herself to the finest quality money could buy. The magistrate had reprimanded her two years before, saying he had little sympathy for someone in her position stealing things that were clearly not basic necessities. I had a private chuckle at this, as there weren't too many people who came before the courts for stealing the necessities of life. I liked this woman's attitude. She'd worked out that it's the same crime whether you steal cheap or expensive. But, like it or not, I didn't run the system and she could get herself into serious trouble. It was my job to prevent that as far as I could.

The people who came to us for help were all different but in similar situations. They had no money. They couldn't afford a private practitioner and we were all they had. And we weren't enough. Nowhere near enough. Just when I thought we couldn't stretch our resources any further, a special staff meeting was called, where we learnt that things would get even worse. The government had decided to amalgamate community legal centres in order to cut costs.

'This will ultimately mean shedding staff and those remaining taking on even bigger workloads,' Victoria explained. 'Since most of you are flat out trying to keep up with your present caseloads, I'm appalled at the idea of fitting in even more cases.'

There were cries of despondency and groans of frustration from the staff.

'We don't have to accept this,' Victoria said, trying to rally her exhausted troops. 'Some of us from the Northern Region got together after the last regional meeting and we want to mount a campaign. I will do everything I can to save the centre and stop further cuts to our funding.'

When people ask me what I do and I say law, they think

money. Most times they're right. A lot of lawyers make a lot of money. Some people conclude that doing my job means I have radical politics, because I spend my time defending the poor, and that I'm not in it for the money.

'I really admire you,' they'll say, as if I'm a saint doing charity work. There's definitely an upper-class attitude towards working for the community. Everybody thinks this is good, meaningful work that is beyond a monetary value. In other words, the pay is lousy. But we're not doing charity work and we're anything but saints. We're always complaining about being underfunded and not having enough money to do a proper job, and the ones who leave do so for jobs with better pay.

When I applied for the job in the centre, friends commented that the money wasn't good but that it didn't matter. This always intrigued me. I wasn't a high-society lady looking to do volunteer work to add meaning to my affluent and boring life. I became a lawyer because I liked the American courtroom dramas I watched on television. I didn't have any other role model. And my parents wanted me to be a lawyer because where they came from the educated people were the doctor, lawyer and teacher. I'm not sure I ever liked my job. I was often frustrated by an inability to make a difference, but I trudged on, thinking – hoping, perhaps – that something or someone might come along to make things interesting. I couldn't imagine leaving the law altogether, because I couldn't think of anything else I wanted to do.

As for representing big companies and helping the rich get richer, I had enough problems trying to sleep at night.

I left work an hour early and went home to bed. I slept for nearly two hours, until Jane woke me with the phone in her hand.

'It's your mum.'

I yawned and took it. 'Hi, Mum.'

'What are you doing tonight?'

'Nothing.'

'Then come over for dinner. Nina's coming too.'

'Okay,' I said sleepily.

'I had a dream,' she went on. 'I saw guns.'

'Guns? What does that signify?'

'A wedding!'

'Again a wedding?'

'Yes, of course. I looked it up in the dream dictionary. Here, I'll read it to you . . .'

The dream dictionary used to be consulted every morning at breakfast time in my family's house. Our neighbour Nina would come to our kitchen and join us for a coffee, help my grandmother braid our hair and talk about her dreams.

'I saw Victor last night,' she'd say. She was always seeing Victor, her husband, long since dead. 'He was walking in the street here, wearing his fine blue suit.'

Inevitably, my mother's worn-out dream dictionary would be consulted. The cover was long gone and its pages had been resewn with red thread by my grandmother, who had never discovered sticky tape. My first Greek reader had been set out in alphabetical order, just like the dictionary. As I learnt the alphabet, acquiring a new word for each letter, I found another word in the dictionary. A for Anna in one, A for *agapi* – love – in the other. In learning Greek, I learnt the meaning of dreams.

One night when I was six, I dreamt of crocodiles. I woke frightened and went to my parents' door. I wanted to tell them, but I stood there in the dead quiet of night, not daring to wake them up. I leant against their door for a while before going into the kitchen to look up the dream dictionary – there was no entry for crocodiles. My grandmother, whose bedroom was off the kitchen, heard me.

'What are you doing?' she asked. When I told her that the dream dictionary had no reference for the crocodiles that had frightened me, she said, 'Come to bed with me,' and pulled me into her arms. 'I'll make them go away and then you can have sweet dreams.'

'Can I choose the dream I want?'

'Maybe,' she sighed. 'But they're only dreams, my little partridge. You must remember that. Whether they're good or bad, they're only dreams.'

'But dreams come true,' I insisted. 'You said so.'

'Yes, sometimes. But most of the time you also need to

24

work and struggle, and even then your dream might not come true.'

'Why not?' I asked, immensely confused.

'Because I may dream of being Gina Lollobrigida, but if I'm an ugly hunchback it will never come true.'

I tried to understand. I looked down at the book. It was open at the letter K. My eyes fell on the entry for *kordelles* (ribbons). 'If you see ribbons,' my grandmother read aloud, my finger following the words, 'it means your kin are pursuing a match between you and a rich old bachelor.' My grandmother laughed. So many of the dreams were about love, sex and marriage. And so much of our lives.

Throughout my childhood, marriage was never off the agenda. My grandmother and Nina, who both played a major role in my upbringing, had something to say about it on every occasion. If I made them an exceptionally good cup of coffee, they promised to dance till dawn at my wedding. If I took too long to get ready, they'd remind me that I wasn't going anywhere to meet my prospective groom. My grandmother spent the bulk of her pension cheques building up our trousseaus. The travelling manchester man did good business at our house. Every birthday, every name day meant a new tablecloth, double-bed sheets, his and hers towels, and more tablecloths. It made show-and-tell at school a bit tricky. I finally complained that I wanted proper presents. Toys and books.

'But these are proper presents,' my mother explained. 'They're for when you get married.'

'But what if I don't get married?' A reasonable question, I thought.

'What a thing to say!' was her response.

'Touch wood, my child,' said Grandmother Phaedra, hitting the table to shoo away bad luck. 'Of course you'll get married. You're not crippled or blind or ugly. Nothing of the sort.'

Yet my grandmother had never wanted to get married herself and put it off until she was thirty, when her parents finally said that time was getting on and she couldn't stay single forever. She often likened married life to slavery and talked with pleasure and longing of her life as a single girl, when she'd spent her time reading books, helping her mother and going out with her brothers. But her dreams and wishes for her granddaughters were always entwined with marriage. When we didn't want to eat, she would say that skinny girls did not have good marriage prospects.

'Eat,' she insisted. 'Men want something to grab onto.'

'Phaedra, things have changed from the days you were young,' Nina would say, forgetting that she was the same age as my grandmother. Catching a man, Nina argued, had nothing to do with eating a lot, but involved other, complicated rules.

'The game of love,' she maintained, 'requires strategy and tact. Otherwise you'll never get what you want.' She had plenty of anecdotes from balls and operas to explain the rules, but I had trouble grasping them. The eating option seemed a lot easier.

Nina had had a life of operas and balls because she was an Egyptian Greek. They were set apart from other Greeks by one major factor: they had money. In their heyday they lived an aristocratic life. Nina had never been poor. She didn't ever talk about doing without shoes or going hungry. Her stories were plucked from a decadent life indulgently lived. Although they were the same age, she and my grandmother had grown up worlds apart. While my grandmother had fed her five children by working as a servant in the house of a countess, Nina could have been that countess. Rich, beautiful and spirited in a libertine kind of way, in her youth she was the stuff of romance novels.

Nina was the only woman I ever saw sit and play cards with the men. Cigarette in mouth, dealing a hand of Manila, she was all concentration. Her house was different from any other I knew. It had high ceilings, French antique furniture, and the main room was dominated by a huge portrait of her as a young lady, a painting commissioned by her father when she reached the age of twenty-one. As children, we would be invited for afternoon tea, served in delicate china. She taught us graces and manners and let us scavenge through her old boxes full of clothes and finery from bygone eras. Only Bettina escaped Nina's influence as far as clothes were concerned. Elendina made them and I wore them. Unlike my grandmother, Nina never wore black. She favoured bright colours, jewellery and lipstick and had short dyed curly hair that she wore like Edith Piaf. When she pulled her hair back into a bun and put on her black Ray Ban sunglasses she looked like Oum Kalsoum, an Arabic singer whose voice was often heard in the rooms of Nina's tastefully furnished house.

Whenever she told stories about the suitors of her youth who were desperate and foolish for her, we hung on her every word. Nina never came out a loser in any of these tales. Nobody ever broke her heart, nobody took her for a ride, and nobody slept with her and ignored her the next time he saw her. How was this?

'You just have to learn to play men,' she declared. 'They are not very complicated creatures. Most of them would follow their dicks to the end of a cliff.'

Learning to play men: I had a good teacher but I was a poor student.


I was rummaging through my wardrobe looking for something to wear to dinner. Nina always expected certain standards. I picked a red dress with a low-cut top and an A-line skirt. She liked me in red and would complain if she saw me in dark colours.

'What are you, a widow? Wear another colour and brighten yourself up a bit,' was a common greeting from her.

I had just finished getting dressed when Jane came in again. 'Oh, you look nice,' she said. 'Listen, a guy called Bruce is at the door. He's not the singer from the Sub Urbans, is he?'

'Yeah, that's him,' I said.

'Wow, how do you know him?'

'He's a friend of the Muldeary boys. He slept in your bed one night when you were away.'

'Wow, Fiore!' she said again.

'Sshh, he'll hear you.'

'I thought you were going to your mother's.' Jane gave my outfit a once-over. She reacted like this, no matter where I was going, if I wasn't wearing a pair of jeans and the plainest jumper in the world. 'Oh, that looks good, but you can get away with it,' she'd say.

I could never understand this. Jane was tall and had a fabulous figure and could have got away with a lot more than I did, but she had a puritan attitude to ornamentation. I understood better when she told me her parents were Baptists. She saw me dancing around the sitting room one day and commented that she wished she could do the same. When I inquired why she couldn't, since she was athletic enough to jog and cycle and God knows what else, she told me dancing was forbidden in her parents' house because they were Baptists. I hadn't known there were religions in the world that forbade you to dance. Then it all made sense. When she'd say that she didn't have the guts to wear a nice pair of shoes, I knew it was the Baptist thing again.

If I had the guts to wear most of the things I did, it was due to Elendina, a style queen if there ever was one, who encouraged me to wear what I liked. This was easier said than done in the milieu of the law, where women have to do their utmost to repress their femininity in order to be taken seriously by the men – and by the women who want to be like the men. Try as I might, I was always off the mark. A shoe with too much detail, a lipstick too dark, an ornate bow in my hair – these were my undoing.

I put on my shoes and went out into the hallway, where Bruce was waiting for me. Again he was just passing by. Again I was surprised. This guy must have a problem with the phone, I concluded. He mumbled something about getting food, which I took to be a dinner invitation.

'I'm sorry, I can't,' I said. 'I'm going to my parents' for dinner.'

He mumbled something else and there was another pause between us as he shuffled uncomfortably. Without thinking, I told him he was very welcome to come with me. Surprised, he hesitated, but when I reiterated the invitation he accepted.

'Your dad doesn't have a shotgun, does he?' Bruce asked as soon as we got into the car.

'No, he does not,' I said, regretting immediately the night ahead. 'And stop this ridiculous Greek-girl routine.'

'Geez, calm down. You're easily ribbed. I'm only joking.'

'Well, I don't find it funny.'

'All right,' he said, without conviction.

My mother answered the front door and made a big fuss over Bruce, as she did with any guest to our house. My father was absorbed in the newspaper and greeted us distractedly. Nina rose and greeted me in French, which she always did because I'd studied it at university.

Bruce was intrigued. 'What language are you speaking?' he asked.

'French,' replied Nina, asking him for a cigarette. She waited for him to light it, but when he didn't take the hint I did it for her.

'You don't know it?' she asked him with some disdain in her voice.

'No. I was never one for languages,' he professed with some kind of satisfaction. Nina just looked at him, then turned and said something in Greek for my ears only.

My father, hearing her, looked up. He studied Bruce for half a minute before ignoring him again to show me the newspaper. 'Have a read of this,' he said, pointing to an article about migrants from former communist countries pouring into Greece. 'Albanians, Russians, Poles. Just like us thirty years ago. Except they're looking to Greece for their salvation. How the world turns!'

Once we were seated and eating and the small talk was over, Nina got down to business.

'So. Bruce. Bruce – that's your name, yes? And your surname?'

'Stewart.'

'Ah, a Scot.' She said this as if she had uncovered something of consequence.

'Ah,' said my parents almost simultaneously, 'you're Scottish.'

'Well, I'm Australian,' Bruce said. 'I could have a Scottish background, probably do.'

My father, who knew about revolutionaries in every culture, began to talk about Robert Bruce. I asked him in Greek to stop. He often told stories he had plucked from history, and they were often incorrect. He ignored me and looked to Bruce for confirmation of what he was saying, but Bruce just shrugged. Poor Bruce. I felt sorry for him. My parents always wanted to know where people came from, who their people were. It was a reference point for them. Being 'Australian' didn't mean anything to them. According to them we were all migrants here, apart from the Aborigines, and the fact that so many people had no idea about their ancestry was a bit of a worry. How could these people not know their past? they'd wonder. It's not as if we're talking a thousand years. Didn't their parents and their parents' parents tell them where they came from, how they came to be in this land?

My father had probably written Bruce off by now. His mistrust of my boyfriends had started with the first boy I dated and the discovery that his parents were monarchists. My father had nearly choked on his whisky. A royalist! A Greek one at that! He made his opinions known to my date and hassled me about it ever after. 'In this day and age,' he'd say, shaking his head, 'to believe in the royal family. It's ridiculous. Stupid. The most stupid people believe in the concept of royalty.'

'But Dad, it's not his fault his parents think like that,' I protested.

'It shows an inferior intelligence in his family. The boy himself might be all right, but it takes a very special person to go against the grain of their family at the end of the day. Believe me.' My father was of the belief that one's politics were inherited.

'What do you do?' my mother asked Bruce, pouring him another whisky.

'I, ah . . . I sing in a band,' he answered, by now not too sure of himself at all.

This impressed my mother and she insisted he sing for us. He laughed it off.

'Mmm. A singer,' Nina mused. 'My husband Victor was a beautiful singer. The Caruso of Alexandria, people called him.'

'Come on, Bruce,' my mother said, 'sing for us. We'll sing together.'

Bruce thought this was a great joke and refused outright. As a form of encouragement, my mother sang instead. She got her guitar and played 'Your Eyes'. I sat there mesmerised, as I always am by her voice, imagining her as a young girl when she first learnt to sing it. When she was full of hope for the promises that love could deliver. Before my father, before motherhood, before the disappointments that took hold of her endless optimism. Then Nina sang, apologising just before each verse for her frail voice; then my mother and father sang, and then I sang with my mother.

33

Singing with my mother, or any Zakynthian, is a difficult task. They take their singing very seriously and most of them have an ability to sing natural harmony that often leaves me lost, trying to find the melody line in one of their voices.

'Oh, you've ruined it,' my mother said as I once again followed her into secondo and went completely out of tune. 'Just stick to your voice,' she ordered.

Easier said than done. I tried to keep the tune but was quickly distracted. I didn't have a strong enough voice to hold my own and was easily misled. She gave up after two attempts, sticking to the melody line so we could finish the song.

'Fiore! If that young man is representative of what's available out there, then I'm not at all surprised so many young women are becoming lesbian,' Nina said as I walked her home.

'He doesn't say much, so it's hard to know what he thinks,' I said, feeling the need to defend my association with him.

'Maybe he doesn't think. He sat there the whole night and didn't say anything worth recalling. No charm, no wit, no sense of fun at all. Is it that hard to make a little bit of an effort? Terrible,' she said, shaking her head.

In Nina's view of the world, there are thousands of charming, intelligent men out there – engaging conversationalists and skilled dancers who know how to be with a woman.

'Look, he's not my lover or anything,' I said. I couldn't argue with her and I was keen to distance myself from him.

'I suppose,' she said, doubting me. 'But a flirt every now and then is important and necessary, and he doesn't know the first thing about it. He was almost asleep at the table.'

'Nina, I don't want to flirt with all the men I know. It *is* possible to have different relationships with men.'

'Yes, yes, I know about your platonic friendships, but once in a while you need someone who's going to make you feel special. Even if it's for one night. And besides,' Nina said, holding my hand and looking up at my face under the light of her verandah, 'what's the point of looking so beautiful and getting so dressed up if there's no interest from a man?'

The fact of the matter was that Bruce was the first man to show me any interest in two years. He didn't have to be a dazzling catch for me to consider him. One part of me knew Nina was talking sense, but I quietened it. I was sick of being alone and was trying to be optimistic. I focused on what I liked, or rather what I thought I should like. His looks, his creativity. He was a musician, after all. I assumed he had some intelligence and depth. Underneath all that awkwardness and cool exterior there must be a world that he would eventually reveal. Still waters run deep, they say. There were possibilities in Bruce, I thought, but more to the point, if not him, then who else?

When I got back to the house I found Bruce already gone and my father washing the dishes.

'Have you heard the news?' my mother said. 'My dreams turned out to be right after all. Not with regard to you, but your sister. This is what happens when people close to you are far away.' She sighed, looking into an abstract distance.

'What are you talking about?'

'Elendina is living with a man in Zakynthos. Dionysis Zougras. Apparently you know him. Looks like they'll be getting married.'

I remembered Dionysis. He was one of my cousin's gang. It took me a minute to reconcile this information with what I knew of Dionysis and what I knew of my sister. It seemed a strange match. He played at being bohemian but was running a successful tourist business on the island. An actor by training, he was given to speaking as if delivering soliloquies, and quoted philosophers and poets by the dozen, all the while using his hands in grand gestures to accentuate his words. He was from an old Zakynthian family – very upper-middle class, perhaps even aristocratic – who had lost their money, and he carried with him all the graces and airs of that tradition.

Elendina, on the other hand, while she had a strong creative side and a bohemian style, was an unworldly goody-two-shoes who'd lived at home with my parents until she left for Greece. She'd insisted on keeping her virginity for the right man, despite a united effort from Bettina and me to make her see sense and live life to the fullest. It was hard to imagine her with Dionysis.

'They're getting married?' I asked. Was she still a virgin? Surely not.

'Well, obviously it's on the cards if they're living together. What's he like?' my mother asked.

'He's a nice man. He's an actor, but I don't think he's doing that any more.'

'An actor. That's all we need. I hope your sister doesn't have to rein him in all the time. Actors are notorious womanisers.'


As soon as I got home I rang Bettina to learn more. Elendina was still waiting for a phone connection and was uncontactable. Bettina wasn't in. I left a message on her answering machine and fell to thinking about my first meeting with Dionysis.

It was the same afternoon I met Mihalis. I was newly arrived in Zakynthos and overwhelmed by the affectionate welcome from family who had come from all over the island to meet me – family I didn't even know I had. They showered me with love, my cousins Fioroula and Petros committing themselves to showing me a good time. Two days into my stay, Petros fell ill with the flu and I was keeping him company in his bedroom. Dionysis was the first visitor, followed by Mihalis and a friend, Aristotle, who stood leaning against the bookcase. Petros and Dionysis were describing to me the different political parties on the Greek left, with interventions from Aristotle. I watched

Mihalis pull a book of poetry out of the case and begin to leaf through it.

'I'm in the Greek Communist Party,' my cousin confessed with pride, giving me his reasons. Mihalis, bearded and tall, had a red highlight in his hair that was only visible with the sun coming through the window. He looked like Che Guevara, only much better dressed. Eventually he looked up and interrupted Petros' account of the party's years in exile. 'Are you up to going out tonight?' he asked him.

'I think so,' Petros answered. 'Come over at ten.'

'Okay. Nice to meet you,' he said, reaching over to shake my hand. And he gazed straight into my eyes, not for a second hiding his desire to take a good long look at me, nor his pleasure at what he saw. I was surprised at his fearless display of sensuality, having never experienced it before, but I was to see it many more times. I noticed he had green eyes set deeply and surrounded by dark circles, as if he'd had too many late nights. I forgot to take my hand back. Despite the dark circles, which gave him a pained look, I thought him very handsome and hoped he wasn't another cousin. Dionysis and Aristotle got up to leave with him.

'And Mihalis?' I asked my cousin after they'd gone. 'What political party is he in?'

Mihalis had a charm and confidence that I'd never known. It was in the way he raised his voice in a song of desire and loss. He walked upright, looked me in the eye, and used all his body when he talked to me. He had that Venetian singsong lilt in his voice that characterises the Zakynthian accent, and a cheeky attitude to match. Before Mihalis, it was the last thing I considered sexy. When I first heard him speak, my inclination was to laugh, especially when he addressed me as 'my lady'. I thought he was sending me up, or sending himself up. But he wasn't putting on the accent, he was a Zakynthian and this was how he spoke. It took me a while to overcome the weird feeling of being attracted to a man a few years older than me, with rugged good looks and dashing style, who when he opened his mouth sounded like my father.

He noticed what I wore and his attention to detail was impressive, if disconcerting – I was not used to this in men.

'That green is very becoming on you,' he said on one of our first outings, with my cousin and others. 'The buttons on that dress would be complemented by a tortoiseshell comb. There's one in my house, passed down by my grandmother, from the days when there was no environmental shame in making things from the turtles on the island.' He commented if I wore my hair differently or a darker shade of lipstick or a new dress. He was a Eurocommunist, or 'soft left' as my cousin Petros said when he finally answered my question, as opposed to the doctrinaire 'hard left'. The implication being that they didn't quite have the balls to do whatever was required of the proper left, but if this was meant to dissuade me it had the opposite effect.

I liked the Eurocommunists. They were a small left party

39

that embraced socialist economics and progressive social policies. They had denounced Stalin, adopted policies for homosexuals' rights and produced groovy posters. All my cousins and their friends were various shades of red, the majority supporting the populist mainstream communist party which was pro-Soviet, macho and into lots of flag waving. They would get together and argue their differences and similarities into the early hours of the morning, in among their partying and work. I was delighted by the passion they had for ideas, and they had a profound influence on me. They made me believe you could do something with your life besides just exist in the system. Each of them impressed in me different ways, but the star of them all was, without a doubt, Mihalis.

I spent the better part of a month with Mihalis, two weeks of which fell in the middle of the Carnivale. There were parties every night, and when there wasn't we would create one. All we needed was four or five people and a guitar. An accordion was a bonus. I remember that time like one long song, sung by Mihalis. One night, a few of us walked for two hours from a tavern in Vasiliko back to the town of Zakynthos at four in the morning. We were in total darkness and I was unnerved by the fact that I could not see a foot in front of me. Several times on the journey back, my heart stopped beating at the sound of barking dogs. I imagined them running out to attack us and I let out a cry of fear. Mihalis took my hand.

'It's all right,' he laughed. 'Why are you so frightened?'

'I can't see anything. There're no lights,' I said.

'No, this is a village. We don't have streetlights.'

Another night, Mihalis and I and a friend of his meandered around in the dark looking for a house where the object of the friend's affection lived. We were on a serenading expedition and Mihalis was required for his guitar-playing skills, and because he knew the area. I went along for the ride.

'I thought serenading was over in the last century,' I said after half an hour of wandering through olive groves, mud all over my shoes.

'You mean you've never been serenaded?' Mihalis asked in mock surprise. 'What manner of men live in those Antipodes, anyway?'

Men who don't go looking for a girl's house in the dead of night hoping to rouse her with a song in order to make a pass. Some might consider it stalking.


On the final night of the Carnivale there was a big dance at the Casino. I got all dressed up in a black evening dress and Mihalis wore a suit. I hadn't imagined him in a suit. He got around in jeans and thick shirts, woollen pullovers and long jackets and boots. But he wore a suit like Cary Grant, despite the freedom-fighter beard. There was a big band, almost an orchestra, and we waltzed all night long. Most people had come in fancy dress. I felt like I was in one of those old films where the characters dress up in their finery and go out to an opulent-looking place where there's a band and sit around drinking and lighting each other's cigarettes. I watched those films when I was young and I couldn't wait to grow up and go to places like that. But it didn't happen, because they didn't exist. So that night I soaked it all up. I had the best time of my whole life. At four in the morning, a group of us went to Mallias' restaurant in town where people ordered tripe and I ate a crème caramel.

At six in the morning, Dionysis, who had a car, offered us a lift home. But first he took a detour and we went up to the lookout at Bohali. There, with the first faint light of day, we saw the harbour and town of Zakynthos, perfectly still.

'I always come up here and have a good look before leaving for Athens,' Mihalis said, dragging on his cigarette, and he and Dionysis sat in silence for a few minutes as if paying homage.

'"Beautiful and alone Zakynthos rules over me,"' Mihalis said, quoting a poem by Andreas Kalvos. 'I couldn't relate to Kalvos until I'd been away from here for a long time.'

'Now that you mention it, I wonder what the precise meaning of that line is,' Dionysis said. 'Do you think he means that only beautiful Zakynthos rules over me, as in Zakynthos and nowhere else? Or is it the sense that Zakynthos is alone?'

'I don't know. It could be either. There's ambiguity there. What do you think, Fiore?' Mihalis asked, turning to me.

I had no idea. I had seen that inscription a thousand times on the base of the little bust of Kalvos that sat on the mantelpiece at my parents' house. I'm certain my father must have recited the poem in its entirety to me; I had heard him go on about Kalvos, but had never paid much attention. He was just another poet from Zakynthos to me. That morning in Bohali I felt seriously deficient.

When they dropped me off, I floated into my uncle's house, where I was staying, and into bed. Mihalis had said something to me while we were dancing. Something about my eyes. I said it to myself many times. *Sayineftika*. I had no idea what it meant, but I liked the way the word filled my mouth. I liked the sound of it. I carried that word halfway around the world with me before finally discovering its meaning. I looked it up in my dictionary when I returned to Australia and it said: 'enticing, enthralling, enchanting, bewitching'. These were my eyes according to Mihalis.

I knew in my bones that something would happen between us. This was a courtship and I was enjoying it immensely. I was happy to be with him and I showed it. When he told me he was returning to Athens for his studies, I wasn't concerned. I would catch up with him there. I fantasised about our romance and thought that it would be better in Athens, away from the watchful eyes of all my relations.

I was on top of the world on one of his last nights in Zakynthos as I walked into the bar in Vasiliko with my cousins. I greeted Mihalis with the open affection that was now established between us, only to find two very disapproving eyes on me, eyes that belonged to a woman who sat possessively close to him. I smiled at her, about to introduce myself in order to diffuse her glaring scrutiny, but Mihalis beat me to it.

'Fiore, this is Julia. And Julia, this is Fiore, Fioroula's little cousin from Australia.'

She grunted a 'pleased to meet you' to the little-cousin tag, which was obviously intended to denote innocence and not danger, and then proceeded to ignore me for the rest of the night. Fair enough. She was quite right to be disapproving of me. I had shamelessly thrown myself at her boyfriend. She was a stunning girl, with short bobbed hair, smouldering eyes and an arty sophistication that left me jealous.

So Mihalis had a girlfriend. It was the last thing I'd expected. He hadn't said a thing. So many nights, so many conversations, so many laughs and he never mentioned her once. And of course he would have such a beautiful girl; it was hopeless thinking I could ever compete.

I was furious with him, but I calmed down and thought that, at the end of the day, he hadn't done anything wrong. He had been a perfect companion. He had not been dishonest with me. It wasn't as if he'd told me he didn't have a girlfriend – I'd never thought to ask him. He didn't really act as if he didn't have one either. Nothing remotely physical had occurred between us, except for the odd brotherly

44

kiss. Even the way he occasionally stroked my hair or gently placed his hand on my shoulder could now be seen in another light. Hadn't Petros done the same thing? And Dionysis? And didn't Fioroula and Artemis walk arm in arm with me? I wasn't used to the tactile way these people related to each other. The reason Julia hadn't surfaced before now? She'd been in Athens and had just arrived that afternoon. So, I reasoned, I had no right to be furious. Disappointed, yes; but annoyed, no. Very disappointed, in fact. Mihalis should have been the great love affair. Instead he was the very good friend.

Another four years passed before I laid eyes on him again. I received the odd card or book through the mail and that always brought a smile to my face. I planned to return the following year and said so, but life got in the way. In the meantime Zakynthos changed and it seemed Mihalis changed along with it. Bettina went to Greece three years after me, when the tourist boom had just taken off there, and returned with a suitcase full of stories about the men. According to her, they were all disreputable low-lifes who cheated on their wives, girlfriends and lovers and chased the tourist girls relentlessly. Petros, Dionysis, all of them.

'I had a good time with them all,' she claimed, 'but I wouldn't trust them as far as I could throw them.'

What had happened to the cultured, political young men I met? Since Mihalis' name had not been mentioned, I asked after him, eager for news.

45

'Mihalis?' Bettina paused for a second to recall him. 'Oh, that arrogant guy. I couldn't believe he was the one you'd told me about. Slept with him once, but nothing to write home about.'

It took me a while to recover from the fact that Mihalis was not the person I'd thought he was. My feelings were confused, and out of that confusion I concluded I had made a gross misjudgement of character. Was it possible for such a transformation to have occurred in such a short space of time, or had I been wrong about him in the first place? I decided on the latter and kicked myself for my stupidity and naivety. Although upset that Mihalis had slept with my sister, I was grateful I'd found out. I wanted to know the details but didn't want to ask the questions. With the passing of time, it ceased to matter and I didn't want to know any more, but it sealed forever any fanciful notions that one day something might materialise between Mihalis and me. Really, Bettina had done me a favour.

But in the four years since then, Mihalis had always been in the background, a point of comparison that no other man could reach.

# CHAPTER THREE

The day of my date with Bruce was a bad one at work. The secretaries were in a terrible mood and spitting poison all day. They were negotiating a pay rise with Victoria, who wanted them to give up their rostered days off in return. Feeling themselves pushed into a corner, they retaliated by making our life hell, slamming doors and phones, huddling together with dark expressions on their faces, muttering, 'Hypocrites,' in loud whispers.

'She's got all these posters about women's rights and equal pay all over the place, and look at the way she treats her own staff,' one of them said.

Victoria did not deal very well with being challenged, particularly by those she considered underlings. 'I can't believe that at a time like this, with all the funding problems, they want a pay rise *and* to keep their rostered days,' she said to me on our way to a lunch organised by a women lawyers group of which Victoria was president. She'd insisted I come with her to do some networking. Men do it all the time, she explained to me, and we women had to do it too so we could get ahead.

The speaker was a woman from one of the richest families in Melbourne who also happened to have a law degree. She gave a long speech about overcoming obstacles on your way to the top, a common theme at these lunches. She talked about working within the patriarchy to get more women into positions of power. It was important, she said, because women worked differently from men, being more cooperative and not as competitive. She concluded by saying that elevating women into influential positions was good because it set role models for others to follow.

I chuckled at the thought that the secretaries in our office would regard Victoria as a role model. That didn't seem to be part of the vocabulary they were cursing her with that morning. I wanted to ask Victoria why she wasn't prepared to listen to the staff on this issue. They were all women and they wanted their rostered days off because the majority of them had children. What was the point of having strong women like Victoria in positions of power if they couldn't, or wouldn't, understand the importance of time for the women they worked with? I liked Victoria; she was smart and capable and it was good that she ran the place and encouraged women. But it seemed she was only interested in encouraging women who were prepared to play by a particular set of rules – the very rules that most women found to be the problem in the first place. I wanted to say all this to her, but didn't know how.

In the taxi on the way back to the office she was in better spirits, and I thought it might be a good time to say something.

'Victoria, I think the admin staff are really upset about this rostered days business,' I began.

'Well, there's nothing we can do about it. They have to go and that's that. I don't get them, why should they?'

'But you get paid three times what they do.'

She looked at me accusingly. 'Who's complaining about it and what did they say?'

'No-one said anything directly to me,' I said. The last thing I wanted was to get anyone into trouble, but Victoria was not giving up.

'I won't have this talk around the office. If they've got something to say, they can say it to my face,' she insisted. 'I don't talk behind their backs.'

But you're the boss, Victoria, I wanted to say. Of course you don't talk behind their backs. You don't have to.


I'd arranged to meet Bruce in a pub that night, and I regretted the arrangement as soon as I arrived. No matter how hard I've tried to like pubs, I can't. I have a deep feeling of unease being in one, despite the fact that I spent years hanging out in them because that's what everybody did. I remember clearly the first day I was taken to one, by Matthew Muldeary, after a history lecture in my first year at university. It was four in the afternoon and I wanted a Sambuca and a cup of coffee. The bar attendant didn't know what I was talking about. She asked the manager and they found a bottle that she needed a ladder to retrieve. I sensed she was pissed off that I'd put her to all this trouble, and Matthew and his friends made fun of my fancy tastes. They drank beer steadily for over two hours while I grew increasingly bored with their conversation, which seemed to get sillier as their intoxication increased.

I spotted Bruce leaning against the bar with a cigarette in his mouth, talking to someone. I kissed him hello and his body stiffened. He didn't introduce me to the other man.

'So what's happening?' Bruce said, giving me the once-over.

I talked about work and how busy we were and the proposed budget cuts. This didn't seem to interest him. Apart from a few meagre responses, we were back to silence again. I tried to engage him by saying I was thinking of going to Greece, and he looked at me directly for the first time.

'Hey, great,' he said, 'I'd love to spend some time on the islands. Your mum was saying that your sisters live there. How come?'

'Oh, they both went on a holiday at different times and then returned a few years later for good.'

'Yeah,' he nodded as if taking this idea in. 'We might be going to Greece.'

'Who's we?' I asked.

'The band.'

'Really?' The Sub Urbans were known in Greece?

'Yeah, there's a possibility we might be supporting Nick Cave. Apparently we've got a bit of a following over there. Our agent's trying to organise something. What's it like? Greece, I mean.'

'It's hard for me to say. I see it from a different perspective because I speak the language and I have family there. I'm not exactly a tourist. But I like it.'

This was followed by another episode of silence, from which we were saved by Bruce's acquaintance. He was a tall man with melancholy eyes and was wearing a black leather jacket and a beret. He was completely whacked and looked like he'd just got out of bed. Swaying a bit in an attempt to keep his balance, he stood close to Bruce and spoke in a barely audible voice, mainly gossip about people in the music business, none of whom I knew. This went on for half an hour or so, and I was wondering what the fuck he'd invited me out for if he was going to spend the whole night ignoring me. What was I supposed to do with myself, ignore him back? They'd drunk about five bourbons apiece by the time I decided I wanted something to eat, but by then Bruce wasn't hungry.

At about ten o'clock we set off: me, Bruce, and the guy in the beret. I drove, as I was the only one who hadn't drunk a lot. We smoked a joint on the way to the pub where the Sub Urbans were playing. I sat around on my own for a while, waiting for the band to come on. I can't say I thought they were brilliant. They were all right. Bruce was screaming and moaning into the microphone for a few of the songs, which didn't enhance them very much from what I could tell. There were all these blonde thin girls with sullen expressions on their faces hanging around at the back of the stage at the end of the gig. No-one introduced anyone to anyone. I introduced myself to someone who sat me near me and got a nod in reply.

I was finally rescued from this riveting company by Matthew. He was working that night and when I saw him through the curtains I rushed over to the bar.

'What are you doing here?' he asked, surprised.

'I'm here with Bruce Stewart.'

'Yeah? I thought he liked you, by the way he was carrying on at my party.'

'So I'm led to believe, but you could be forgiven for thinking he didn't even know me. He's hardly paid any attention to me all night long.'

'Come on, Fiore, give the bloke a chance. He's probably nervous.'

At last Bruce came over and asked me if I could take him home. We left his mate with a bunch of blondes. Matthew gave me an encouraging wink on my way out.

'What did you think?' Bruce asked once we were in the car.

'Yeah, I thought you were good,' I lied.

We got to his house and I made a cup of tea while he

rolled a few joints. I shared one with him and got so out of it I had to lie down on the couch and take deep breaths. Bruce had another two bongs and talked about music. He said he found the Greek music he'd heard at my house a bit over the top. 'The music's all right, but the lyrics are full on. Depressing, you know.' This from a so-called grunge musician. 'Anyway,' he joked, 'I thought Greeks were happy people. Why don't they sing about souvlakis and that?'

I let that one go by as well. Besides, I was too stoned to respond. My head and heart were spinning. Fuck, what had he put in that joint?

'You all right?' he asked.

I took a deep breath. 'Yes.' He got me some water and I sat up to drink it.

The next thing I knew we were rolling around on the couch and he was kissing me. After a while, he suggested we go to bed. I don't know why I acquiesced. I suppose that's what the night had been all about. I suppose I assumed he was interested in me and everything had been leading to this. I stepped over some dirty cups and plates on his bedroom floor and got into bed. Bruce returned with another glass of water that he also put on the floor. He climbed in beside me, taking his jeans off at the same time, and he kissed me and we eventually had sex. Half comatose from the joint, I could remember little about it later.

'You're very intense,' he said to me, smiling, stroking my face.

Was that good or bad? I wondered for a while, before I fell asleep.

I woke up in the middle of the night with the urge to go to the toilet. There was no toilet paper, and after looking around for some I went back into the house, running smack bang into a spiderweb in the back yard, and woke Bruce. Half asleep, he seemed surprised I wanted such a thing and told me there wasn't any. He turned over and I went rummaging in the kitchen for a tissue or a napkin, finally settling for newspaper. It did the job but I couldn't get back to sleep after that. Bruce's snoring and the smell of a full ashtray some-where close to my nose were keeping me awake, so I crept out of bed, got dressed in the dark, scribbled a see-you-later note and drove home.

Nick wanted every detail. He hassled me to tell him what happened. I told him everything except the part about sleep-ing together. He asked me every day for an update, and when nothing happened he pressed me to ring Bruce. I should take the initiative, he said.

'He might not have your phone number. And besides, what is this, the 1950s? Why should he ring you?'

But I'd already rung. A few days after our date I left a message on Bruce's answering machine, which he didn't return. I was a bit insulted by that. Another one bites the dust, I thought, and after going over everything to reassure myself that he was no great loss, I walked into him three weeks later in a café. He was with a tall blonde I remembered from the gig who was smoking and drinking black coffee while he ate. Our conversation was awkward, to say the least. But when had it ever been otherwise? When I got back to the table I was sharing with Nick, I was surprised to find Bruce right behind me.

'Fiore, I meant to call you but I lost your phone number,' he said hurriedly and my eyebrows shot up in disbelief. 'It's true,' he insisted.

'It never stopped you before,' I said, thinking of his unannounced visits.

Nick stood up and put out a hand that Bruce didn't see. 'Hello,' he said. 'I'm Nick. A friend of Fiore's.' He preceeded to compliment Bruce on the band and I thought he was going to ask for an autograph.

Bruce turned his attention back to me. 'Fiore, I was on tour with the band in Western Australia. Look, can I see you later?'

'Later, when?' I looked at my watch. It was nine-thirty. What did he have in mind, dumping the blonde and then meeting me?

'In about an hour,' he said.

Nick kicked me under the table and I agreed.

I had planned things differently. I told myself I wasn't going to sleep with him that night, but it just happened. He was sexy in his own way, there was no denying that. Afterwards, there was another period of no contact for about two weeks, then he reappeared out of the blue and after some preliminary awkwardness we ended up in bed again. This went on for two months. I never knew whether I would see him again after each encounter. I was so keen to ensure there would be another time that I didn't stop to think about what was going on, or even whether I was enjoying myself or not. I was desperate for some intimacy and I hoped it would flourish into something else. But I wasn't sure I was going about it the right way. I needed Bettina. When it came to men, Bettina knew her stuff. Although younger than me, she had years on me in experience.

Boyfriends had been forbidden when we were in school, but Bettina paid no attention. Our grandmother gave stern warnings of consequences that 'no Christian could imagine' if my father caught us doing anything with boys. Fearing such consequences, I naturally obeyed. Bettina, naturally, did not. My father, who left soaked bread for the birds in our back yard, took food to the drunks at Ozanam House, and cried his eyes out when our dog died, was not going to do anything that no Christian could imagine to anyone. Bettina could see through our grandmother's propaganda and was prepared to take risks for the sake of a good time.

Then, when I was sixteen, Grandmother Phaedra left permanently for Greece and a new era of freedom dawned in our house. My parents always arrived home late from working in the shop and this left the three of us to fend for ourselves. Bettina saw this as an opportunity not to be squandered.

There were rendezvous in the park with boyfriends and lots of cavorting with the Lebanese neighbours' boys. Elendina often accompanied her and I would guard the home front in case of an unexpected visit from one of our parents. How were these decisions made among us? They just happened, because Bettina had the boyfriends and I didn't. As far as Elendina was concerned, hanging out with boys was preferable to keeping watch with me, and who could blame her? If our parents dropped in without warning, I'd tell them my sisters had taken our new dog Zorro for a walk.

But winter came, the weather became colder and Bettina bolder. She began bringing visitors home, and before we knew it we were hosting parties for whatever boyfriend was Bettina's flavour of the month, and their assorted companions – and they always had companions. I kept watch by the sitting-room window for our parents' car, and there were a few hasty exits through the kitchen door while we tackled Zorro to keep him off the escaping boys. It never occurred to me to refuse to play a part in this. We were all in it together. Trouble for one meant trouble for all. Or rather, trouble for my sisters meant trouble for me. I was after all the oldest and the buck stopped with me, so I had my own interests to protect.

There were a few close calls, but one episode left me with the shakes for days. I was reading a book and didn't notice my father's car until he was at the front door, already turning the key in the lock. I could hear him whistling from the other side of the door. I have never been an athlete, but I managed in a single jump to move from the front room to the bed-room where Bettina was holding court with a young man called Gavin. I called out that Dad was home and ran to the kitchen to warn Elendina, who was watching television with Gavin's friend Tim. In no time Tim was out the back door and making a run for the fence, with Zorro in hot pursuit. My father came whistling down the hallway to the kitchen, in blissful ignorance of goings-on behind bedroom doors, and planted a kiss on my fearful cheek. He looked in the fridge for some food and asked absently where my sisters were. Bettina appeared on cue, red-cheeked and sleepy-eyed, saying she was just having an afternoon nap. Bettina never had after-noon naps, but before Dad could comment, our attention was seized by Zorro's growling.

'What's going on with Zorro?' My father cast a look towards the kitchen window.

'Elendina's just playing with him, Dad. I'll run out and check.' I was gone before the last word was out of my mouth.

Zorro had his teeth into the jeans of the escapee and would not let go. Elendina was making a valiant attempt to pull him off, which only made Zorro even more determined. Making a quick calculation that his life was worth more than his trousers, Tim slipped out of them and dashed for the back fence in nothing but his Y-fronts. In among this chaos, I recalled that the only person Zorro obeyed without question was my grandmother. I picked up a twig from the ground and did the best imitation of her I could manage. With my legs apart, one hand on my hip and the other waving the twig threateningly in the dog's direction, I yelled at him in Greek. Zorro cowered immediately and disappeared into his kennel. Tim was over the fence and halfway up the street when I threw his jeans over and yelled for him to get them, but he didn't look back. I have no idea how he got home half naked because we never saw him again. Meanwhile Gavin lay quietly under the bed, rediscovering his Catholicism as he said his prayers. We never saw him again either.

In the wash-up, the finger was pointed at me. It was my fault for not noticing the car sooner, for having my nose in a book, for being asleep on the job. Bettina was initially hurt by Gavin's disappearance, but he was soon written off as a guy with no guts.

'Good riddance to him,' she said. 'What do I want with a guy who's going to be put off by a little thing like that?'

I made a feeble attempt to defend him, but Bettina shook her head at my ignorance.

'Fiore, don't you know anything? A man who runs at the first sign of trouble isn't worth crying over.'

Not for the first time, Elendina took her cue from Bettina. 'Yeah, Fiore,' she said.

My little sisters considered me a naive fool. As much as I tried to appear the worldly oldest sibling, in things that mattered I knew nothing. I had no boyfriend until I was twenty and I could do nothing but listen when they shared their adventures of the physical delights of doing things with boys. Or even on their own.

'You mean you don't know how to do it?' Elendina asked me one day as they talked about masturbation. I shook my head.

'You put your finger there and twirl,' Bettina said, as if giving knitting instructions.

Put your finger where? I wanted to ask, but they gave me a book to read instead. *Him*, by the anonymous author of *Her*. It came from one of the Lebanese girls in the neighbourhood. Her father had found it in the back of his taxi. Without giving it more than a cursory glance and with his minimal English, he thought it was a novel that his daughter might want to read. *Him* referred to a man's dick and the story was based on this dick's sexual adventures. After the first twenty pages, the shock value wore off and I was bored. I struggled on for another twenty pages, but it was the same story told over and over: the ups and downs of Him. I preferred D.H. Lawrence. I was reading him intensely in those years and believed that love would come to me in a mystical, wordless union of two souls who just knew there was a special connection between them. I was sucked in by the writings of a man from the northern English working class who had big issues with his background but who idealised the men from it in his books, making their severe repression poetic and erotic. Bettina was right, I didn't know anything.

By the time I got to first base with a man, Bettina had been at it for some years, and Elendina, despite her insistence on keeping her virginity for someone special, also had a respectable number of boyfriends under her belt. Far from being the oldest, wisest sister whose word they considered in times of doubt, I was the one asking for advice and looking for reassurance when my insecurities took over.

Finding myself once more in this situation with Bruce, I rang Bettina, but again the answering machine greeted me. I was sitting on the couch feeling glum, with no light on, when Jane came home.

'What's the matter? Why are you sitting there in the dark?'

'I miss my sisters,' I said, not knowing how to tell the whole story.

Jane knew me well enough to know that something else was afoot.

'You don't look very happy to me,' she observed and I responded with a sigh. 'I hope you don't mind my being forward about this, but I think you should stop seeing Bruce,' she said with the relief that comes with frankness.

'Really? I thought you thought he was all right.'

'I did. I do. He's gorgeous, there's no denying that, but I don't like the way he treats you.'

'I know, I don't like it either, but what should I do? I don't want to say anything to put him off, or come across too heavy with him.'

'Why not? What's the point of continuing with the thing if you're not happy?'

I listened open-mouthed to this revelation. Jane was right.

'Next time you see him,' she went on, 'tell him what bugs you. Say something about his disappearing acts. He goes off and then turns up whenever it suits him and you're always here to welcome him with open arms.'

'What should I say to him?'

'Tell him you're not prepared to put up with it any more, and then leave it to him. If he wants you, he'll be interested in making you happy. If he doesn't want you, you're better off finding out now.'

Did I really want to find out that he didn't want me? Yes, I did. I preferred that to a slow death.

So the next time Bruce turned up unannounced with a ready-rolled joint and an erection in the making, I told him what was on my mind. 'I don't like this,' I said. 'We sleep together and you disappear for a while and then reappear as if it's the next day. This hot and cold business doesn't appeal to me.'

'What do you want?' he asked.

'What do you mean, what do I want? Don't you know how to treat women? For one thing, call me –'

'Look, I don't call people.'

'I'm not people,' I said, exasperated at his laconic response. 'I'm your –' I stopped, searching for the right word. What was I exactly? 'We're going out together,' I stated.

'Listen, Fiore, I'm not interested in anything heavy. Maybe you've got the wrong idea.'

There was very little I could say to that, and after he left I never heard from him again.

Nick said it was for the best and it was a good thing I'd stood up to him. 'That's what I like about you, Fiore. You don't take any shit.'

I wished that's what I could have liked about myself. Deep down I was, as always in matters pertaining to men, plagued by doubts. Maybe I should have said nothing. Maybe I shouldn't have been so touchy about the Greek stuff when he was having a lend of me. I wasn't so much upset about losing Bruce as I was disappointed in myself. I saw it as another failure in my long line of failures with men.

'Put it down to experience,' was Jane's advice.

Another one for experience! When was this rich and varied experience of mine going to come into use? When might I meet someone I connected with, who wanted to share a life with me? I'd had experience with drug addicts, jealous psychopaths masquerading as lawyers, and comatose accountants. Now I could add unreliable rock musician to the list and move forward. At times like this, when I was sure I would spend forever going from one failure to the next, it was always my fault. I knew Bruce wasn't the man for me but I'd made the effort because what spurred me on was the fear of ending up alone.

# CHAPTER FOUR

Things became progressively worse at work over the next few months and I became more and more morose. Victoria was busy lobbying and campaigning to keep the centre funded, and her workload was divided up amongst the rest of us. I was coming in earlier and leaving later. The secretaries lost their rostered days off when Victoria dug her heels in and told them that unless they gave them up there'd be no pay increase, and if they didn't like it she would happily show them the door. Two of the staff retaliated by resigning on the spot, and the ones who remained were bitter and resentful. Asking them to do something prompted a verbal assault or a slammed door. In the middle of all of this, I quit.

Everyone thought it was a spontaneous act, but my unrest had been a long time festering. It was a typical day at work that brought everything to a head. I had an appointment with a repeat offender who had psychological problems and a junk addiction to match. Nothing unusual, but every now and then people like him got to me. What he needed was treatment and care, and what he was likely to get was jail. I spent an hour in Nick's office complaining about the state of the world. I felt self-indulgent, but there were times I couldn't cope and thought myself inadequate to deal with the job.

That night, after a drink and a smoke with Nick, I found myself in front of the television, listlessly watching whatever was on. I flicked the channel and was alerted by the distinctive sound of a Xarhakos bouzouki. A Greek movie was starting. Aliki Vouyouklaki and Dimitris Papamihail, who were husband and wife in real life, played a husband and wife who ended up singing together in a nightclub in Athens. The film was full of scenes of people dancing in the streets, and I remembered seeing it as a young girl at the cinema with my parents and thinking in my own grown-up way that people didn't really dance in the streets in Greece. But Greece was to prove me wrong.

I watched the whole film, despite its predictable storyline and its very politically incorrect message, and went to bed, my head full of Greece. I lay awake caressing memories of the Greece of my two visits, which had been sharpened by the film. Those images hung around as I drifted into sleep and then they appeared in a dream. I was on a wintry Piraeus street where a homesick Cretan was dancing the pentozali. The Cretan morphed into Mihalis, who was dancing and looking at me with laughter, urging me to get up with him. I was shaking my head.

'I don't know how to do this dance,' I said by way of explanation to all the people, and they nodded without believing me. They were looking at me with pity and asking me what was wrong with my eyes. 'Nothing,' I said. 'There's nothing wrong with my eyes.' Yet the question continued. 'What's wrong with your eyes, *koritsi mou*?' 'Nothing,' I maintained. 'Why are you asking me these questions?' I ran from the crowd while Mihalis danced on, still beckoning me to join him. Away from everyone, I saw that there in my face were the sunken, lifeless eyes of the junky client I'd seen that morning.

I woke upset and shaken. It's just a dream, I told myself. I looked at the clock; it was four a.m. I got under the covers again and willed myself to go back to sleep. But I couldn't, my brain was ticking over. It was obvious I was suffering from stress and needed a break. The despair I saw in my office week in, week out was taking its toll. Who was I to think I could make a difference? I decided to quit and go to Greece. What the fuck was I doing with my life anyway? My career meant nothing, my love life was non-existent. I was in a rut and needed a change.

But Victoria would not accept my resignation. 'Do you know what you're doing?'

Probably not. 'I've decided I'm going, Victoria. I have two sisters over there I want to see and I just need to get away. Maybe I'll end up staying.'

'Stay in Greece? Where has this come from? I've never heard you say anything about that before.'

66

I didn't have an answer to this. Both times I'd left Greece it was with an uneasy feeling that I wasn't doing the right thing. It had taken months to wear off and it felt like prolonged jetlag.

'Fiore, why don't you just take some time off? Although we're snowed under at the moment, I think it's probably a better idea if you take a month's holiday before making any major decisions. You're probably well overdue for leave, anyway.'

'I need more than a month,' I said. 'I want to go for at least three months.'

'Three months! I don't know whether that would be such a good thing for your career.'

If this was meant to alarm me, it didn't. I'd been seduced into thinking a career would give meaning to my life. After all, it's what defines who we are. But when all's said and done, it's work. It's eight or nine or ten hours a day in a sterile office with people you have to tolerate or pretend to get along with. And it's no longer enough to simply work, or work hard, we now have to *love* work. Protestants have a lot to answer for. But rather than say all this to Victoria, who would think me completely mad, I told her I wasn't sure if I wanted to work in the law any more.

'What do you want to do instead?'

'I don't know,' I answered, and before she could give me further advice I told her I appreciated her concern but that I was really in need of a break.

In the end I left work with Victoria still refusing to accept my resignation. 'We'll all still be here whenever you get over this,' were her parting words. 'Three months. I'm replacing you temporarily and I'm keeping your job open for three months.'

My parents were convinced I wouldn't be coming back.

'Are we to lose you as well, then?' my mother asked sadly.

'I'm just going for a holiday.' I had to say this to avoid the litany of tears and complaints I knew would be coming my way if I confirmed their worst fears.

'That's what your sisters said.' She could sense I wasn't telling the whole truth.

'Well, so what if she decides to stay there?' Nina broke in. 'Don't put pressure on the girl. Let her do what she wants.'

'I'm not putting pressure on her. I just never expected to be abandoned by all my daughters in my old age and left alone. Why did I bother to have children?'

'Mum, you're fifty, not eighty. Besides, I'm only going for a holiday,' I repeated. 'I've been to Greece twice before and I came back. Don't worry.'

A second migration, my mother called my sisters' departure. 'All the pain and tears of parting when I left my family to come here,' she would say, 'and I have to go through it all again with my children.' My father was more stoical. Or at least that's how he acted, trying to tone down my mother's dramatics.

Some children of migrants are told stories of their parents' homeland that give a glowing account of the place. When they finally go themselves, they're disappointed with what they find. That was the case with Matthew Muldeary. After years of growing up with a particular image of Ireland, he went there in his early twenties and found an Ireland not up to his ideals. He got the shock of his life. To him it was cold, wet and conservative. The opposite happened with me. The Greece I grew up hearing about was poor, miserable and hungry, but the Greece I found was vibrant, interesting and merry. Not that there wasn't poverty and misery and probably hunger, but these were not in my face. The question that was constantly in my head at the start of my first trip was directed at my parents: 'Why did you leave?'

But then, in Zakynthos, my mother's oldest brother Xenophon took me to the house where my mother was born and reared. I was curious to see the landmarks she'd referred to in the tales of her youth, but when I saw the house itself I was speechless and almost in tears. It was one room.

'You all lived here?' I asked, stunned.

'This house was built after the earthquake, the old one was smaller.'

I never asked my parents that question.

My father had been the first to leave. He was born to a couple whose marriage was an attempt to mend a feud between two families that had been going on for as far back as memory could take them. The attempt failed not least because his mother, Phaedra, had not wanted to marry at all. At seventeen she had fallen in love with a young man who died fighting in the Asia Minor wars. Unbeknownst to anyone else, she had given him her heart and it was buried with him. But it was not done for a woman to remain single, so at the age of twenty-eight she was hitched to my grandfather, a man I never met. Phaedra, with no romantic inclinations towards her husband in any case, grew to hate him for his drinking and violence, and in all the years I knew her she never said a kind word about him.

My father, who they called Caesar, was an only child. When Caesar Foskolos was nineteen his father died, and in those few years before emigrating, Caesar made a name for himself. A name I only discovered on my first trip to Zakynthos. 'Your father the nightclub owner,' people would say to me. With precious few resources, Caesar opened a nightclub that became the place to be seen; he started the football team on the island and worked a day job in some kind of manual trade. Despite all this, money was hard to come by and so he left for Australia.

As a young man, he was thin and handsome and he dressed with care and style. A photograph of him taken just before he emigrated hangs on my parents' kitchen wall, above the bookcase containing my mother's translated French and Russian classics. Sometimes he would take it down and dust it carefully, handing his youth around so others could share it. Taken on a slight angle, the photograph shows him looking seriously into the camera lens, almost stern and with intent. The image is shirty, a bit like Robert Mitchum. It says, 'Don't you fuck with me.'

In reality he was not at all stern – I have never known anyone to pursue fun and laughter like my father. But people who visited our home in his absence saw only the tough-man image above the serious books. To his wife, it was sexy. To the boys his daughters brought illegally into the house, it was fearsome.

He never felt at home in Melbourne. The first Sunday after he arrived, he put on his only suit, combed his hair, trimmed his fine moustache, polished his shoes and set out by tram. He returned earlier than expected, in a state of agitation and stumbling over his words, to deliver a disturbing piece of news: there was no sign of life in the city. It was almost completely empty. Something had happened. There must have been a military coup or something, and the army had declared a curfew.

'I walked up and down, round and round, and nothing. A few old drunk men in the park, poor souls. Nothing was open either. No cafés, no clubs, no nothing. What's going on?' he asked.

The people in whose house he was a guest laughed. 'Well, nothing,' they declared. 'That's what it's like all the time.'

My father protested. How was it possible for the centre of the city to be empty? Where did all the people go on Sundays, where did they congregate and socialise?

I only appreciated this story fully after I made my first visit to Greece. Athens rocks all day and all night. The city that never sleeps, they call it. Every time I stepped out in Athens I felt that something was going on, that an event of some importance was bringing people out in hordes. Zakynthos was quiet in comparison, but there was still more street life there than I had ever seen in Melbourne. There were always places to go at any time of the day or night – except for the afternoon, when everybody slept. It took me a long time to get used to the deadness of Melbourne when I returned, and I had lived there all my life. I can only imagine the shock my father must have experienced.

But although he never felt at home in Melbourne, he never went back to Greece. He always said he would go, but it never happened. I was surprised that his desire to return was not stronger, as each time I visited Zakynthos, people every-where asked after him. It was the same with my mother. People stopped me in the street in her village to ask me if I was Mariza's daughter. It was only in Zakynthos that I learnt that my parents were striking individuals. They had both made strong impressions in their community for very differ-ent reasons. Being Caesar and Mariza's daughter meant something I hadn't known before. In learning things about them I learnt something new about myself. I also learnt my mother's reason for leaving.

Mariza was the sole sister of four brothers. Her father died in the Second World War when she was three years old and she had no memory of him. But much was known about him. He was very beautiful; Valentino was nothing compared to him. My maternal grandmother was madly in love with him and forgave him every infidelity, of which there were plenty. She was five years his senior and my mother remembers her justifying his skirt-chasing by saying he was too beautiful to be enjoyed by just one woman. When he died, they took the coffin around the village square one more time.

'What a shame for such beauty to be eaten by the earth,' the villagers mourned. At barely forty, my grandmother was left a widow.

Mariza's brothers had inherited their father's looks and his left politics. They were also excellent singers, dancers and musicians, with a reputation throughout the island. Fathers tried to keep their daughters hidden from these lads, who could make any decent girl's head turn with their bewitching looks and their serenading. There was no doubt they had a lot going for them, but they were dirt poor and on the wrong side of the political fence. Definitely not husband material. Two of them had already been in and out of jail for various political misdemeanours, and my grandmother too had been jailed briefly after the Second World War for housing a communist fugitive. The whole family, like everyone on the left, were hounded by the quasi-military governments who ruled Greece for an eternity after the war. Both my parents grew up poor, but my mother's family were destitute and their persecution by the authorities made it worse.

Mariza, the youngest, had all the qualities of her brothers and was the diamond of the family. As the only girl, she was adored by her brothers and fiercely protected by them as well. Much admired and desired by many suitors, she was out of reach, like a doomed siren, with no dowry and marred by the family's political curse. As if that wasn't enough, doubt was also cast on her honour due to her 'secret' liaison with Markos Kallinikos, a man from the town.

I knew nothing about Markos until my first trip to Greece. Mihalis, thinking I should learn more about my culture, took me to Markos' tavern one night to hear Markos sing. He specialised in traditional Zakynthian seranades.

It was a cold night at the end of the Carnivale season, when both Zakynthos and Mihalis had me under their spell. We entered the tavern and as soon as Markos saw me he stopped mid-song, staring at me as if in shock. He flustered his way through the rest of the song without taking his eyes off me, then came over to the table where we were seated.

'Pinch me,' he said to Mihalis, while looking at me. 'I'm in a dream.'

'No, you're not,' Mihalis laughed, and introduced us.

'Yes, I know who you are,' Markos said, taking my hand and holding onto it. 'The image of your mother.' A huge tear splashed off his cheek onto the tablecloth. I looked around the room, thinking all eyes must be on me and this bearded stranger with the build of a construction worker who was still holding my hand. But everyone was eating their food and talking.

'You knew my mother,' I said, stating the obvious for something to say.

He nodded, and then in a hoarse, shaky voice, said, 'A long time ago. A lifetime ago.' He sat down to regain his composure and began the usual questions regarding the length of my stay and the health of my parents. He differed from everyone else in not following up with his own anecdotes about them, but motioned to the waiter to deliver some wine and bread.

When he'd returned to his ensemble to do some more songs, Mihalis remarked, 'Markos obviously had a thing about your mother.'

I shrugged my shoulders. It was the first I'd heard of it.

The following day, before I could ask anyone about it, my uncle Xenophon appeared at his brother Yannis' house, where I was staying. He got straight to the point with me.

'Where were you last night?'

'I went to Markos' taverna with Mihalis Xenitos. Why?'

Yannis rose from his chair immediately and gave me a fierce look. Suddenly I felt like I'd done something wrong.

'Don't you know who he is?' Xenophon demanded.

'No. Only that he knows my mother and was very upset when he saw me.'

'I bet he was,' Yannis scoffed. He and Xenophon looked at me, their faces weather-beaten from years of working in the sun, and told me the story.

'They were madly in love,' Xenophon began. 'He was crazy about your mother. Who wasn't in those days? It was pretty much given that they would marry. The when and how were mere details, but he gave us his word and we took it as the word of a comrade and an honourable man. He was one of us, you see. Then he got caught with some leaflets.' Xenophon finished rolling his cigarette and paused to put it in his mouth and light it.

'No, it was a newspaper,' Yannis corrected him, and took up where his brother had left off. 'The case blew out of proportion before it even got to court. Markos was in jail awaiting trial for nearly a year. In that time his father – who had connections everywhere in the government, and the money to buy them off – licked every arse there was to lick from Zakynthos to Athens to get him released. When he got out of jail, his father said to him, "Right, pull your head in, because next time I won't be able to help you. And by the way you're getting married. A girl from a respectable family –"'

'And with a respectable dowry,' Xenophon put in.

'He threatened him,' Yannis continued. 'Probably said something like, "If you think I made all these sacrifices so that you can go off and marry Mariza Andreola, who doesn't have a drachma to her name, you can leave this house immediately." And Markos did exactly what his father told him. So much for the great revolutionary!' Yannis spat on the floor.

'He never even had the guts to come and tell us,' Xenophon said bitterly. 'He got out of jail and he never came to see us, never saw your mother, never spoke to her, not even a letter. That was the worse thing. After that, your mother was heartbroken. That's why, when your father's uncles came to ask for her, she said yes immediately. She wanted to get as far away from here as possible.'

They were both silent for a while as they recollected the sadness of that event.

'And as you know, it wasn't long after she left that our mother died,' Yannis said at length, and not for the first time since my arrival Uncle Xenophon started to cry. On this small island, where everyone knows what time you go to the toilet, they never spoke to Markos again. If they saw him in the street, they crossed to the other side.

I only knew the last part of this story. The part about my mother saying yes straight away. I had heard it so many times, but every time I asked her there was some other detail or nuance that I hadn't heard before. My mother had come to Australia due to a shortage of Greek women. Most of them arrived already betrothed to someone else, and the vast majority of Australians were not interested in foreigners. After considering the situation for a year or so, and suffering failures in his pursuit of female companionship, my father realised action was needed. He wrote to his uncles with an instruction to find him a girl, and they found my mother. When word came her way that my father's uncles were about to visit with a certain intention, she borrowed a pair of nice shoes from her neighbour to go with a dress a distant cousin had sent her from

America. She thought the uncles rather ugly and was worried that Caesar might be too. She had seen him only once and couldn't remember him very well, but they brought a photograph and she was relieved to see that he looked nothing like them. For their part, the uncles were so taken with her that halfway back to their village they wanted to turn around and confirm that they wanted her for their nephew. They were worried someone else might make a better offer. But it was not the custom to do this while the family were considering their options, so they continued on home and waited until the next day before sending word that they approved.

Mariza's brothers did not want her to go. Sending their jewel of a sister to the other end of the earth, to a man she barely knew, was a hell of a decision. They knew Caesar, they had worked at his nightclub as musicians and singers. He was a man of honour who always treated them with respect. That much they told her. The rest was up to her to decide.

This was not difficult for Mariza. 'As if I'm going to hang around here,' she announced, 'waiting for the honourable knight who'll take me without a single drachma. Caesar it is. Australia it is.'

It was amazing that she made it at all as she was initially refused a passport due to her father's political activities. This was common practice for all communists and fellow travellers, who could be thrown in jail on any pretext, but a distant cousin who was in favour with the governor argued her case.

Caesar and Mariza finally met in the early summer at

Station Pier in Port Melbourne. She got off the boat wearing a pale green floral dress she had made herself, and my father greeted her with a bouquet of flowers. They married five months later, by which time my father had brought out his mother, and my mother had brought out her oldest brother. The photos of the wedding attest to a party and a half. They were party animals, my parents, always going out.

In time, they got out of the car factories by going to work for themselves in a series of businesses, none of which brought lots of money. The last one, in which they settled for a long time, was a small grocery store that meant they worked long hours for the bulk of our childhood and adolescence, so that we saw little of them. They had three daughters, much to the disappointment of everyone, but they got over it eventually. Just as they were coming to terms with Australia as the place where they would stay for good, two of their children packed up and moved to Greece. Never in their wildest dreams had they imagined they would lose two daughters in the same way their families had lost them.

Markos Kallinikos died from a heart attack a week after I met him. His funeral took place the day I was leaving, and the whole island mourned him.

'What a beautiful man, with a beautiful voice, and he is lost to us forever,' people everywhere said.

My uncles had their own explanation. 'He saw you and died,' they said. 'It brought everything back and he died of his own shame and a broken heart.'

My cousin Fioroula reminded her father that Markos had been a heavy smoker with a weight problem whose mother had also died of a heart attack.

'Bah, I'm as scientific as the next man,' Xenophon argued. 'But you can't discount matters of the soul.'

'May God forgive him,' muttered Yannis.

I told Mihalis the whole story and he listened in disbelief. I recounted what my uncles had said about Markos dying of shame and a broken heart that could never be mended.

'There *was* a lot of grief about the man,' Mihalis said, deep in thought. We were standing at the port in front of the ferry that was about to depart with me on it. 'Poor Markos,' he muttered.

'Poor Markos!' I spluttered. 'It was his decision to abandon my mother and marry someone else,' I reminded him.

Mihalis shrugged his shoulders. 'Perhaps, but put yourself in his shoes. Think of all the guilt he carried around with him. It's sometimes easier to be the virtuous one, even if you are hurt, because you never did anything wrong, you never compromised yourself.'

I let out a barrage of disagreement, some of it no doubt due to having had my pride wounded by Mihalis myself. 'I can't have any sympathy for a man who betrayed my mother in the way he did. He surely was not stupid. He knew what this place was like for women who were known to "belong" to someone and then dumped. But he didn't give a fuck because she was lower class, and in the end he succumbed to the expectations of his class. It's one thing to go to jail, but it's another thing to marry beneath you.'

Mihalis stepped back in surprise at my onslaught. 'Oh, Saint Dionysis,' he said. 'You may be right, but can't I feel sorry for the man? He just died, and according to your uncles, you played a part in his death.' He shook his head. 'I'd better watch myself around you,' he said, smiling, and I couldn't help but think that it was me who should have watched myself around him.

# CHAPTER FIVE

A cheap deal with KLM meant a night in Amsterdam. I thought this would be a good way to arrive in Athens refreshed and relaxed for once, but my one night in Amsterdam produced one hell of a hangover.

I was eating alone in the dining room of the swanky hotel in which the airline had arranged for us to stay, when an impeccably mannered and fabulously dressed Italian man approached and asked if he could join me. It was an effort. What with his bad English and my worse Italian, there wasn't much to say after his initial surprise that I was single and travelling alone. 'Such beautiful that you are, why?'

He didn't believe I wasn't Italian when he heard my name. Ugo Foscolo was a famous Italian poet who was born in Zakynthos. I had the Greek version of his surname – Zakynthos was a Venetian colonial outpost for a number of centuries and before that it had belonged to the Sicilian Normans, so the Italian influence ran deep.

'*Ma tu sei Italiana,*' he insisted. '*Veneziana.*'

Perhaps I was.

We went wandering around the city and ended up in a bar, where the Italian bought me a very expensive drink. Some Dutch people were arguing with an American about US foreign policy and I joined them. The American complained about how unfair it was to be constantly questioned about his country's doings around the world.

'I'm just a regular guy, you know. I'm living in Egypt for a year and I come to Europe for a holiday and I'm always hassled about politics.' The eternal defence of the right wing.

'What are you doing in Egypt?' I asked him, curious.

'Learning Arabic.'

'Really?' You had to see this guy. He was blond with a straight Mormon haircut and he was from one of those midwestern bible-belt states where they think the Republicans are too liberal. Everyone around the bar was thinking the same thing: What was he doing learning Arabic?

'You like it?' the Italian asked him.

'Like what?'

'Egypt. Cairo.'

'You gotta be joking. The place is filthy. Egyptians are the pits. And there's no place to get a decent hamburger.'

'You can't get a decent hamburger?' I asked. 'Well, why are you there? It seems ridiculous to stay somewhere if you can't get a decent hamburger. You Americans,' I said, shaking my head, and I launched into an attack on their attitude to the rest of the world.

A young Mexican who was sitting near us also got stuck into him. He objected to that fact that whenever a North American is asked where they're from they always say Montana or California or Seattle or Chicago, never the USA. 'They think the USA is the whole world and South and Central America is their toilet where they can do all their dirty business,' he said. 'Fidel did the best thing to kick you out of his country. Here's to Fidel Castro,' he said and we all drank to Fidel, despite his faults.

To give credit where credit's due, the American stayed put and took us all on. With the charm of those well-suited Mormons he talked about America as the saviour of democracy and reminded us that it was his country that had saved Europe from the Nazis. The Dutch at the bar responded with dark faces and a few historical facts, and the Italian said that the Americans had liberated the Italians all right. They liberated the Mafia who had been in jail during the war and restored them to their rightful place in Italian society, and then worked hard to ensure that the communists didn't win an election. There's nothing like the joy of watching a bunch of pissed-off Europeans getting stuck into an arrogant American.

'He's look like spy,' the Italian said to me in an aside, and I stepped forward about to say exactly that when he took my arm, ever so gently.

'Come, Fiore. We go. I'm becoming angry and you too. Is no good.'

He was right. I go on the attack without thinking sometimes. But who can help themselves around ignoramuses? An old lover once told me I was like the anarchist who shot the Archduke in Sarajevo. 'He was right to do it, the Archduke was an arsehole, but look at the consequences of his actions: the First World War.'

My father said this was nonsense and the war would have happened anyway. 'You could be more strategic, though, sometimes, Fiore,' he said, 'and consider the impact of your utterances on those around you. But you take after your mother – and mine. You've got the fiery blood of the women on both sides of the family. Besides,' he added, 'you shouldn't listen to inadequate men.'


We landed in Athens. Any minute now I would be seeing Bettina. I put my novel away and watched out the window, full of excitement. But when I was finally out of customs and in the waiting area, she wasn't there. I scanned the room carefully, dragging my suitcase along with me. Damn. My heart sank.

I changed some money and headed off to the phones. A man with some kind of accent answered Bettina's phone and I thought I had dialled the wrong number.

'Who's this?' I asked.

'Who are you?' was the response.

'I'm Bettina's sister. I've just arrived in Athens and she was supposed to come and pick me up.'

'Right,' said the man.

'Well, where is she?' I demanded to know.

'I wouldn't have a clue,' he yawned.

'So, what should I do? I suppose I'll catch a taxi,' I said, thinking out loud. 'I'll see you when I get there.'

'Ah, no you won't, because I'm just about to leave.'

'You can wait half an hour for me, surely.' I heard him chuckle, but hung up before he could refuse.

Outside, I wrapped my coat tightly around me. The Athens wind in December is a fierce one. My initial excitement about seeing Bettina had dissipated and the feelings of anxiety that only surface around my sisters greeted me again. I have very little memory of life without my sisters, since we were all born within two years of each other. And from as far back as I can remember I was saddled with the curse of the oldest child: responsibility. Look after your sisters, I was told constantly. Never mind that my sisters didn't want to be looked after. Where did our parents get the notion that younger siblings listened to older ones as a natural occurrence?

Bloody Bettina. She never was reliable. I'll never forget the Friday night in Melbourne when the two of us ended up at some nightclub and without warning she disappeared. She was supposed to spend the night at my house but she never showed up. Nor did she ring. By Sunday night, after no-one I asked had seen or heard from her, my fury had turned to panic. Various scenarios featuring violent, unstable men and bad endings started to play in my mind and I took up smoking again in a big way. She didn't turn up for work the next day, but she finally surfaced the day after. By then I was so relieved she was alive that I forgot my anger. Bettina did things like this from time to time, mainly to her family. She liked to make us suffer. What sort of psychological disposition does that sort of behaviour come from? I wondered.

I thought about the last time I'd seen her. We'd had a huge argument just prior to her departure. She had come back from working in a construction camp up north and was living at our parental home for a few weeks. One night after a party, she carelessly left some dope on the chest of drawers in her room, where my mother discovered it the next morning. My mother hit the roof and woke me at a ridiculous hour with a phone call.

'Bettina's on drugs,' she sobbed.

Oh great, I thought. She must have found her dope. I knew this meant calamity for my mother. There was no distinguishing between hard and soft drugs for her. They were all the same and meant the worst imaginable: the gutter, prostitution and death. I got Bettina on the phone and told her what to do.

'Say it isn't yours, say you tried it once and you won't do it again. Say anything, just calm her down.'

But she had other ideas. 'I think we should come clean

and tell Mum and Dad that we smoke,' she said serenely. 'What's the big deal? They can handle it.'

'Forget it, I can't be bothered. And haven't we put them through enough already?' I could not delight in the thought of a family conference about the pros and cons of marijuana use, but Bettina insisted.

'I think it'd be good if it came from you. Being a lawyer and that. They might not think it's so bad if you tell 'em you smoke,' she said.

'I don't smoke that much.'

'Bull-fuckin'-shit!' Bettina raised her voice. 'You don't *buy* any dope but you smoke plenty. Especially mine.'

'That's another issue altogether. We're not telling Mum and Dad,' I said, wondering where this desire for openness had come from all of a sudden.

'Then I'll tell them,' she said.

'Are you fucking crazy or something?' I snapped in the big-sister bossy voice I used, without much success, from time to time with my sisters. 'Forget it. They don't need to be educated about drugs. Particularly now that you're about to take off indefinitely. I want some peace in my life. She'll be ringing me every second day, worried to death about you. Imagining you shooting up in some Athenian alleyway. Do you understand?'

She grunted glumly and hung up.

On the day she was leaving, Bettina sat me down and gave me a litany of complaints about my performance as her sister. How she expected better and how disappointed she was in me. How everything had to be done my way, about the pressures she had to endure from Mum and Dad, about how she was glad to be going and getting away from it all.

'I want to have an adult relationship with Mum and Dad,' she said. 'I don't want to be something they want me to be.'

I thought the days of fighting for our independence were behind us and I had no interest in revisiting them. I told Bettina that our parents had already accepted we'd diverged far from their expected path. Was it necessary for them to know every detail of what we did in order for us to have a proper relationship? Bettina accused me of protecting my parents from the reality of life.

'They're not children,' she said. 'Why should I have to be so cautious about what I say and don't say in front of them? And anyway, it's all right for you. You're a lawyer. Their dream come true. They haven't stopped hassling me about getting a proper job since I finished university and I'm sick of being compared to you.'

I was surprised by her words. It was true that our parents had wished for a more conventional life for their daughters, and that out of the three of us I fitted the bill best, by virtue of my occupation. Bettina had done an Arts degree, Elendina studied fashion. By the time they left for Greece, neither of them had worked in a full-time, nine-to-five, regular job. Elendina worked for herself, making clothes. She worked at her leisure and, although very skilled, was choosy about what she made. I once commissioned her to make me a plain skirt and she told me to buy one as it was not artistically challenging for her. Bettina worked only when she needed money for something. She worked in an abattoir, waited on tables, pulled beers behind a bar to buy her car, and when she decided she was going to Greece she went up north to work as a cook in a construction camp. To my horrified parents she explained that it was her chance to see the bush, the outback, the 'real' Australia, while being paid for it. And it put her off Australia, real and unreal, for good.

What surprised me was her anger towards me. The assumption that I was also to blame for her woes. I took exception to this. I was always going in to bat for Bettina when my mother and father complained about her aimless life. I told my unsympathetic parents that Bettina was still searching and it might take time for her to find her feet. Obviously this wasn't enough. Perhaps she expected me to defend her right to do nothing, full stop. Perhaps she wanted me to be more like her so that she wasn't the only one who copped it. I told her all this and we had an argument that ended in tears, with no resolution. Is there ever a resolution to these things?

I was finally at the front of the taxi queue, and was about to load my suitcase into the boot when I heard my name. I turned to see a trendy, thin young woman with a haircut straight out of French *Vogue* running towards me in a short black skirt. She threw herself at me, crying out my name, and I realised it was Bettina.

'It's great to see you too, darling. Just as I had given up on you.' I stood back to look at her. 'You look great.'

'When in Greece,' she shrugged.

She was even wearing heels, something she never wore except under sufferance as a bridesmaid. Bettina's previous style could be best described as indifferent, in contrast to me and, even more so, Elendina, who paid more attention to her personal grooming than anyone I knew.

We talked nonstop all the way to Bettina's apartment in Kipseli, where she negotiated the fare while I was getting my luggage. A tall man with dark curly hair was standing at the door to the building. Legs apart, in jeans, with a denim shirt and a black jacket, he dragged on his cigarette, and I could feel his eyes on me while I struggled with my cumbersome bags and hatbox. I looked up at him and his gaze was entirely fixed on me. When I got to the door he greeted me in English.

'Hello,' he said, not taking his eyes off me.

I felt self-conscious all of a sudden under his brazen gaze. Ah, back in Greece, where men make it perfectly clear that they're looking at you.

'Alex,' Bettina called out as she approached us, 'I thought you would have gone by now.'

'I'm waiting to be picked up.' His eyes darted back to me.

'Well, I think there might be better trade in the square,' Bettina laughed. 'This is my sister, Fiore.'

'Yes, we spoke on the phone,' he said.

'Oh, that was you. I see you were kind enough to wait after all.'

He considered me for a moment, but before he could answer a dark blue Mercedes pulled up in front of us and he put out his cigarette and got in.

'Who was that?' I asked Bettina as soon as we were inside the building.

'That's Alex. He's a friend of Stelios'. He just got in from Thessaloniki and needs somewhere to stay.'

'Who's Stelios?' I asked. She dropped these names as if I was expected to know who they were.

'A friend,' she said, out of breath as she lugged one of my bags up the stairs. There was no lift in her apartment building and she was two flights up. 'What the fuck is in these bags?'

We dumped my things in the front room of her tiny apartment and I fished out gifts for her from Mum and Dad while answering questions about everyone in Australia. I filled her in on gossip relating to family and friends, and after changing into some warm clothes I sat down opposite the sofa where Bettina was sprawled out.

'Are you having a good time in your life?' she asked me.

'Yes.' I paused. 'I suppose.'

'What's new? Tell me,' she said, taking a sip of the duty-free whisky I'd bought her.

'Nothing. Work. You know.'

'What are you doing again?' she asked absently.

'Working at the community legal centre.'

She nodded.

'It's good,' I said, deciding to tell her about resigning later. I perused the apartment, which was painted in colours you'd see in an Almodóvar film. 'I want to know more about Elendina and Dionysis Zougras.'

'Well, they moved in together two months ago. She's getting the phone on this week. She says she's very happy. I think they're suited.'

'Have they had sex?'

'Yes, thank God.' Bettina threw a cushion up in the air.

'Thank God for that,' I echoed, and felt a little hurt that I didn't know any of this. Why hadn't Elendina written to me?

'It happened on their fourth date,' Bettina said. 'Which is just as well because I was ready to have a chat to Dionysis, you know.'

'To say what?'

'To tell him to get a move on and fuck her, for her own sake. Put something in her drink, anything. She's twenty-five years old and getting into dangerous territory.'

'Bettina!' I shrieked with laughter, but I could see her point. Elendina had a wise sensibility about her that appeared to come from loads of life experience. Her sexual innocence seemed unmatched to her chic, bohemian style and her penchant for partying. She insisted that her virginity was merely accidental. She wasn't ready as a teenager and hadn't met anyone that interested her enough since then. She dismissed our suggestion that she might be a lesbian, and when we hinted at a possible hang-up, she became indignant and told us to stop sticking our noses into her affairs. Bettina and I had spent hours speculating on her reluctance to have sex, trying to find a psychological basis for her disorder, but we could never reach a satisfactory explanation.

The phone rang loudly, startling me. I looked at my watch. It was nearly midnight. Bettina began making arrangements that involved me and I waited for her to end her conversation before saying I was too exhausted to go anywhere. But she waved my objections aside, insisting that people were looking forward to meeting me and that it had all been pre-arranged. She threw some clothes at me, saying we didn't have time to iron any of mine, and despite my preference for a cup of tea and an early night, I was dressed in minutes and ready to go. We threw on our coats, applied our lipstick, and walked out into the December night chill, in quick steps along the steep narrow streets, watching Athens unfold in our path.

Athens is a crazy place. You can lose yourself easily and find parts of you you didn't know were there. Whether you want it to or not, Athens happens to you. It always feels like it's on the verge of some catastrophe, as if the entire city will just break down and everything come to a grinding halt. Many Westerners dislike Athens. It's a difficult place if you don't speak Greek, and there isn't anything much to look at, apart from the Acropolis. Tourists who go for the sun and beaches, or whatever they write about in the travel brochures, are dismayed and sometimes disgusted at the place. The traffic, the dirt, the pollution, the beggars, the ugly buildings, the motorbikes, the noise, the queues, they tell you. They're absolutely right. Corruption and right-wing governments ensured that there was no town planning or aesthetic consideration when the boom went through Athens.

But there is beauty in Athens. It's in the poetry of those cafés in the basements where people talk politics and drink the house wine and the cook comes out to sing with the band. And the woman by the cash register in the green satin dress who has her parrot in a cage perched on the counter next to her. It's in those smoke-filled nightclubs where you dance on the table at four in the morning and no-one's going home tonight, the owner says, getting you another half a litre of wine. And the bouzouki player slips you his phone number, but you wish it was the violinist. It's in those motorbike rides to Lycavitos, the arguments outside the meat market, the arguments at Omonia, the arguments everywhere. It's the boy sitting on his Vespa who is young enough to be your very younger brother never taking his eyes off you as you take the steep road down to the Kipseli square. It's the distant sound of the mournful clarinet and the songs of unfulfilled longing that burn in all of us, especially at three o'clock in the afternoon while everyone sleeps. Everyone except you and the writer across the road whose slow typing is keeping you awake. You either take to Athens or you don't.

Our designated spot was a nightclub in Exarhia that played Rembetika, otherwise known as Greek blues. It was already in full swing when we got there and I remembered the place from an earlier trip, but it had changed. It was more of a student hangout then. There was nowhere for us to sit, so we stood at the bar and several people came to greet my sister and me. The band consisted of five musicians and a well-endowed female singer in a very tight dress. She had long, permed dyed-red hair and the diamonds on the rings of her fingers sparkled in the lights as she moved the microphone. Our cousin Sophie from Sydney, who was also living in Athens, met us there with two men called Mario and Fotis. The music was loud and it was hard to talk, so we danced on the crowded dancefloor. Fotis invited me out the back for a joint and we chatted eventually about the poetry of Edgar Allan Poe. He had been reading him in translation and was very taken with him. I nodded. I couldn't do much else. I had never read Edgar Allan Poe. The smoke made me quiet and tired. I looked up at Fotis, who was trying to keep me entertained, and I smiled.

'You feeling okay?' he asked. I nodded. 'Come on then.' He took me by the hand. 'Let's go dance.'

I took to the dancefloor with Fotis. After a moment, he went down on one knee with his arms outstretched, as if to give me a space all my own. I danced within it, on the edge and around him. For me, for the song, for him, but mostly for me. I loved to dance and the smoke was transporting me through the song. Dancing like this was a feeling better than sex, but then again, my recent sexual escapades had left a lot to be desired. Fotis eventually rose and danced with me. I love it when men dance, especially when they do it like this, with pleasure and passion. Watching men dance in Greece makes you forgive their sex for all its failings. It doesn't matter what they look like or how old they are, or even whether they can dance. Nothing matters except that they are alive at this moment in this dance, and sharing their yearning or grief or happiness in this place. Never, says an Irish proverb, give a sword to a man who doesn't know how to dance.

The song was the last one for the night. I don't remember getting home or how I got into bed, but when I regained consciousness I was lying alone on a soft double mattress on the floor of Bettina's apartment, wrapped in blankets and with nothing on but a pair of underpants. My own coughing woke me. Ah yes, back in cigarette country, where you're a bad sport if you don't smoke. The sharp winter sun was coming through the gaps in the shutters and I shut my eyes again. I turned in my half-sleep away from the light, opened my eyes again and looked straight into Alex's gaze. Although it took me a few seconds to register who he was. He was lying on the sofa with his shirt unbuttoned to his navel, a gold cross around his neck and his curly hair all over the place.

'Hello,' he said.

'What are you doing in here?' I pulled the bedclothes protectively around me.

97

'I was sleeping, until you woke me.'

'Where's Bettina?'

He shrugged and yawned. 'How would I know, I just woke up.'

I found my pyjamas at the end of the bed and hurriedly put them on, then made my way to the kitchen.

A woman turned to greet me as I opened the door. 'Good morning,' she chirped. She was plump, with curlers in her hair, and was smoking. 'Come and sit down and I'll make you a coffee,' she smiled. 'I'm Antonia. Bettina's neighbour. And of course we know who you are. The big sister. She's been very excited about you coming.'

Antonia was an actress who lived in the apartment directly below. She was around during the day, she told me, usually in a dark blue dressing-gown just like the one she was wearing now.

'Did you sleep well?' she asked, but before I could answer, Alex came in. Pulling a low stool from under the table he sat open-legged, rubbing his stomach and yawning. In that tiny kitchen, he took over the whole room. As if it were his to take. I declined Antonia's offer of a coffee and decided to have a shower first.

I ran the hot water and got under it, only to find it was stone cold. I screamed, put on a towel and went out to the kitchen, wondering loudly why there was no hot water.

'Did you turn the thermosiphon on?' Alex asked, annoyed. 'Well, how do you expect there to be hot water?

Hey?' He turned a dial on the wall and ordered me to wait half an hour before getting in. 'And listen, don't do anything stupid like forgetting to turn it off.'

I folded my arms across my chest and tightened the towel around me. 'You don't have to talk to me like that. I didn't know about the thermosiphon. Well, I did know, but I'd forgotten,' I added sheepishly.

'Talk to you like what?'

'Calling me stupid.'

'I didn't call you stupid.' He frowned again in annoyance. 'I said don't *do* anything stupid.'

The front door shut behind us and Bettina came bounding in with shopping bags. She kissed me. 'Hi everyone. You up too, Alex?'

'I didn't really have a choice in the matter,' he said, and threw me a look. I thought I could sense a suppressed smile.


That morning, Bettina had a job interview. She had been out of work since October and some friend of a friend had suggested she try a bar in Glyfada. She wasn't particularly enthusiastic about the prospect of working in yet another bar.

'With your qualifications, surely you could get a better job,' I suggested.

'I've got an Arts degree, Fiore. You know what you can do with an Arts degree here? Teach English. I did it for two months and I hated it.'

'Isn't it better than working in a bar?' I said carefully.

'The pay's better in a bar. You get tips.' Bettina was applying her makeup as I sat watching her. 'If you haven't got anything to do, you want to meet me for lunch?'

I looked at my watch. It was already midday and I'd just had breakfast.

'At about three,' she said. 'At the Meat Market. Alex will bring you. Won't you, Alex?'

Before I could answer, he had already acquiesced and Bettina had trudged out the door as if going to a sentencing.

I wanted to buy a pair of shoes before we met Bettina. I got dressed and wore one of my hats.

'What's that?' Alex laughed.

'It's a hat. You don't like it?'

'Well, for the Carnivale maybe, but not for everyday. It's very fancy.'

I paid no attention. We were about to leave when Sophie rang, saying she wanted to join us.

'But we're going shoe shopping.'

'That's okay. I'll meet you in the square.'

Our cousin Sophie was a fashion victim who packed on the makeup and was always in high-heels that made a hell of a noise on the Athenian pavements. She spoke in a loud western-Sydney twang, accompanied by the jangle of her bracelets as she toyed with her cigarette. She was tall and had big hair dyed blonde that made her look even dizzier than she was. Leafing through *Vogue* was her idea of reading a book; she knew the names of all the supermodels and could tell a dress's designer without looking at the label. On the trolley ride into the centre she complained incessantly about how all Greek hairdressers were butchers, about how rude all shop assistants were, about how rude everybody was, really. She ranted on in English and I was conscious that Alex would feel out of place or ignored. I looked at him a few times, trying to draw him into the conversation in Greek, but he was preoccupied by his own thoughts.

I wondered what had motivated Sophie to come and live in Greece and I asked her.

'I had to get away from my parents,' she said matter-of-factly. 'They drove me crazy.'

She hadn't worked since the end of the tourist season and was broke, but she was optimistic. She took me to several shops that specialised in exclusively priced French and Italian shoes. By the third shop I had bought nothing while she had acquired a pair of red suede Dior heels that cost an obscene amount. Alex's eyes met mine in a united look of disbelief and bemusement.

The Meat Market eateries were brimming with trade, as usual. Just outside, a man was selling cassettes from a trestle table. Distracted by the music, Alex gave an involuntary quiver of his chest and shoulders. Do that again, I thought.

The music was Pontian, something I'd first heard as a teenager. At a concert I'd been to there were ten male dancers dressed in black with gold trimming, long black boots, and pointed hats that would have looked ridiculous in any other context. The shimmying movement of their dancing was electrifying, accompanied by a shaking of chests and punctuated by a complex refrain of stomping.

'Do you know these dances?' I asked him.

'No, I'm not really a dancer,' he said, with a coyness that seemed uncharacteristic.

'Are you Pontian?'

'Yes, from Russia.' He turned away to look behind him.

I wanted to ask Alex more about Russia, but we were interrupted. 'What sort of shit music is this?' said a short man in a loud voice with a shirt to match. He slapped Alex on the back. 'Do we have to sit right next to this guy?' he asked, nodding to the music-seller.

'Hello, Stelios,' Sophie said.

'Hello, girls. Sorry, I'm a bit distracted. Do me a favour, give him five thousand and ask him to move.' He pulled the money out of his pocket and handed it to Sophie, saying, 'Too many whiskies last night.' He focused his attention on me. 'You must be the big sister.'

'I am that. And I like this music.'

'Really?' he asked in honest disbelief, taking off his jacket and folding up the sleeves of his floral shirt. 'I'm more of a popular-music man myself. Give me Kazantzidis any day. Speaking of music, where's your sister?'

'She's gone for a job interview,' I told him.

'Yeah?' He seemed impressed. 'Where?'

'Some bar in Glyfada.'

He rolled his eyes. 'Anyway,' he said, rubbing his hands together, 'we're going to see Papakonstantinou tonight.'

Vasilis Papakonstantinou was a hot act at the time and a seat for his show was not cheap. I looked at Stelios' haircut, which looked like a mid-seventies job, the ostentatious ring on his finger. He didn't look with it.

'Oh, Stelios.' Sophie clapped her hands excitedly. 'Can I come too? *Please.*'

Stelios laughed. 'Of course you can come. We're all going. Now, what are we eating?'

Bettina didn't show up at all, so we ate without her. Meat and peas soaked in olive oil and more bread than I'd normally eat in a week. Stelios and Alex joked and baited each other, and Sophie filled me in on her life over the past year, with more complaints about the foibles of the Greeks. After lunch, the others were going home to sleep but I wanted to walk around.

'Only the mad tourists are out at this time of the day,' Stelios said. 'You're better off sleeping so you won't be tired tonight.'

I knew that my body would eventually succumb to the afternoon sleeps. The late nights would make them essential. But I felt an excitement and an anticipation that could only be quelled by tracking old routes and seeing landmarks again. And there was something I liked about the stillness of Athens in the afternoon. I walked around an increasingly gentrified

Plaka, where the shops and buildings had been done up to look self-consciously pretty. Then I walked slowly back to Kipseli, stopping for a coffee on the way. It was cold but sunny, and outside in the square the only traffic was a few birds, a boy on a scooter, and the odd person moving quietly, as if taking care not to wake anybody up. I took a sip of my coffee, put the cup down and took stock of myself. Why wasn't I here all the time? I *wanted* to be here. I took a deep breath and a calmness descended within me. It felt good. Really good.

# CHAPTER SIX

I spent the next day seeing relatives, giving out the gifts I'd brought with me and having dinner, and arrived back at the apartment just after ten. Bettina was disapproving when I told her where I'd been. She'd been in Greece for a year and had found no reason to visit boring old relatives, as she put it. I found myself justifying my day – they'd known I was in Athens with presents for them. But the truth was I wanted to see them.

Fotis and Mario had arranged a night at the Odeon, where a famous Cretan musician was playing.

The entire Cretan community of Athens must have come to see Psarantoni play with his sons that night. The audience listened respectfully for a few numbers before the dancing began in earnest. People threw money at the musicians as they requested songs and I was swept away by the exuberance of the crowd. We didn't have the guts to dance ourselves since, not being Cretans, we didn't know the steps.

Mario leant over to me. 'Good, huh?' he smiled.

'Fantastic,' I nodded. 'This is something we definitely don't get in Melbourne.'

'Ah, but you have your own music. Nick Cave, the Dirty Three, the Sub Urbans.'

I pulled a face at the mention of Bruce's band. Bruce himself was a long-lost memory, and any disappointment I felt was at my own behaviour. He hadn't set me up, I had. I'd built something out of nothing and had only myself to blame, for being desperate and weak. As I sat watching Psarantoni, his head thrown back in ecstasy while he played the lyra, I thought about how much stronger I should have been. Then I pushed the thought away. That me was somewhere else now.

The next morning the phone woke us. It was the man from the bar in Glyfada to say they didn't need Bettina right now, but would keep her in mind. Bettina was pissed off at being woken up to be told she didn't get the job. I made sympathetic noises and told her I'd take her out for breakfast. She threw a coat over the Indian pyjamas she wore to bed, put on a pair of boots and we went out. With her uncombed hair and unwashed face, she shuffled down Fokionos Negri with me to a place with good coffee.

Once we'd sat down, she sighed with exhaustion and sat in silence, watching the people traffic in the street. I tried again to be sympathetic but she cut me off.

'Yeah, it's a real shame I didn't get the job. I was really looking forward to working my arse off in a bar in Glyfada.'

Bettina had plenty of dark moods in the few weeks I was in Athens and I spent a lot of time tiptoeing around them. She was not in a good way and I seemed to bear the brunt of it. She was particularly glum during the day but would brighten up as night approached, especially if a group of us went out together. Stelios was a regular. He felt sorry for my sister and Sophie having no money and would often come to take them out to dinner. When I mentioned I was leaving for Zakynthos soon, Stelios insisted on taking us to a doghouse in Kaisariani.

The place didn't get going until well after midnight and a bottle of whisky cost half the average weekly wage. The extravagant prices seemed at odds with the patrons, who all appeared to have seen better days. The band consisted of five men and a forty-plus singer in a red shirt that looked like something Tom Jones wore in his heyday. All the songs were about heartbreak and bad women who double-crossed men and made them suffer, and how they should be made to suffer in revenge. Two scantily dressed female singers were also part of the show. Their performance was interrupted occasionally by waiters delivering champagne on trays, courtesy of the customers. Towards the end of the night, a man burnt whisky on the dancefloor after requesting a song. What a ridiculous waste of money, I thought, then saw Stelios do the same thing.

'What does Stelios do for a living?' I asked Bettina as I watched him manoeuvre his way around the dancefloor.

'Oh, he's a bit of a dark horse,' she said flippantly.

'Meaning?'

'He dabbles in things.'

'What sort of things?'

'Business, some of it legal, some not, probably. I don't ask him and I don't care.' She gave me a look, putting an end to my questions.

The nightclub closed at two a.m. since it was a weeknight, but Stelios was drunk and in the mood to party on. He tried to convince the owner to keep the band playing, but to no avail.

'Sorry, friend, it's the law,' said the owner apologetically, referring to recent legislation enforcing closing times, which was aimed at getting Greeks to sleep more so they could perform better at work.

'Total dictatorship by the government,' was Stelios' view. It was the first time I'd heard him say anything political. 'Greeks are social people and if you want to party after two in the morning, this fucking government won't allow you to do it. Whoever heard of such a breach of human rights? I'm only allowed to go out now till two. I have to put limitations on myself to fit in with the system. After all those years of marching for freedom, of struggle and jail and exile, this is the result: a law that says we have to stop enjoying ourselves at two in the morning. To think that I voted for this government! Fascists! That's it, next time I'm voting for the ecological people, just like your sister tells me.'

Stelios didn't strike me as a man who'd been on marches for freedom, or suffered time in jail for democracy. For other things, maybe.

Bettina yawned, looked at her watch and said an early night wouldn't do any of us any harm. She mumbled something about going to see someone about a job the next day on the other side of Athens. Stelios didn't like the idea and told her she was wasting her time.

'I'm telling you, wait. Something will turn up. You're an educated girl. No need to run around like a desperate Albanian.'

'What's that supposed to mean?' I asked.

'It means, what's the point of going from one shit job to another? There's no urgent need for her to work. It's not as if she'll starve.'

How had he concluded that there was no urgent need for her to work? I wondered. 'Stelios, we all need to make a living. We're not aristocrats, you know.'

'Aren't you? But you're from Zakynthos,' he said, making an implicit reference to Zakynthos' Venetian colonial past and its titled class.

'Not everyone from Zakynthos is an aristocrat,' I laughed.

'But you have that way about you,' he insisted.

'What way is that?' I asked, thinking about the hovel in the village that was my mother's home.

Stelios took a handful of walnuts from the table and

stuffed them into his mouth, chewing while thinking for an answer. 'You're civilised. Unlike the rest of us, who are a bunch of Turks.'

'I don't know about that,' I began, but Bettina interrupted me before I could go on.

'I do,' she said sharply. 'Why don't you go and live on one of the islands over the other side for a while and then talk. You'll see a world of difference. Especially where the women are concerned.'

'You see,' Stelios said to Bettina. 'I tell you, you shouldn't go and get that job in Santorini.'

Stelios' belief that my sister ought not get a job that might offend her aristocratic sensibilities was an angle I hadn't considered. What was the story with this guy and my sister? He was different to the other men I'd seen her with. For one thing, he was older. And married. Was she having an affair with him? I saw no evidence of it. Still, if there was nothing going on, why was he doing all these things for us? He must be after something. I didn't trust him and decided to ask Sophie about him. The next time I saw her I quizzed her about Bettina's unhappiness and her bad moods.

'What do you mean?' Sophie asked. We were taking a stroll down Patission and Sophie stopped to look at a dress in a window display.

'She hasn't seemed very happy to me since I arrived and I can't work her out. If she's upset that she's broke, why doesn't she try to find a job? And what's she doing hanging out with Stelios? I can't say anything to her without her biting my head off.'

Sophie was distracted by the dress and wanted to get a better look at it. We entered the shop, where the sales assistant was on the phone. Sophie waited until she'd finished.

'I want to try that dress in the window,' she said when the assistant put down the phone.

'Which one?' It was a funny question. There was only one dress in the window.

'The purple one,' Sophie said.

'Oh, I'm afraid it won't fit you.' The woman picked up the phone and began dialling. 'And that's the last one we have,' she added.

'I think it might,' Sophie insisted.

'My girl, you're too big around the thighs,' the assistant said, looking her up and down as she waited for her call to be answered.

'Well, it's a stretch material so I think it might fit me.' Sophie was not one to give up easily. 'I'd like to try it on anyway.'

'This is a total waste of time.' The woman slammed down the phone and went to get the dress off the dummy, shaking her head.

'She's not sleeping with him, is she?' I asked Sophie from the other side of the change room.

'With who?' Sophie panted as she struggled with the dress.

'With Stelios.'

'No,' she said, as if this were a ridiculous idea, then paused

111

for a moment to have a think about it. 'I mean, I hope not. I doubt it.'

'Then how come he takes her out all the time and spends all that money on her?'

'Well, why shouldn't he? He probably likes her company, and he's bored with his wife and she's probably bored with him.'

'Do you know what sort of job he does?'

'Listen, Fiore, one thing about Greeks, they don't talk about work much. I've met so many people socially and I haven't got a clue what they do.'

'Bettina hinted that he's involved in something illegal. I don't like the sound of it,' I said, becoming annoyed that Sophie was missing the point.

'Oh, people do things like that all the time here. My uncle does something illegal with his sheep to get more money from the EU or something. Could you please zip me up?'

'Sophie, that's different,' I sighed, beginning to regret raising this with her at all. 'Stelios does not get subsidised by the EU.'

'I know he's a bit rough around the edges,' she offered. 'But he's got a heart of gold.'

The kind of comment you make about someone who has little else going for them.

Sophie came out of the cubicle. The dress was too tight around the thighs. The sales assistant shook her head, but Sophie ignored her.

'What do you think?' she asked me, admiring herself in the mirror.

'Well, it's not really my kind of thing,' I said, then added in a whisper that it was too tight.

'I like it,' she said, turning to one side as she studied herself in the mirror. 'I'll take it,' she said to the shop assistant, who threw her hands up.

'Whatever you like,' she responded.

'There're a few things you need to understand, Fiore,' Sophie said once we were seated on a bench in a park with the sun on us. 'Bettina came here with a dream about living in Greece, and I know because I had the same dream. You think it's going to be really great and all that, but it's also really hard. It's not just the work thing, it's that you're completely on your own.' She stopped to look at me and gauge whether I understood. 'I was sick with the flu for a week once and I had no-one to look out for me. I sat in my flat until I had the strength to go out and get food and medicine. There's no social security. The support system here is your family, and if you don't have that you're fucked.'

I was about to interrupt but Sophie put her hand up to stop me.

'It's the kind of thing you can't understand unless you live it, you know,' she said. 'So forget about trying to see Bettina with your Australian eyes, it doesn't work.'

Perhaps Sophie was right, because I couldn't for the life of me see the point of Bettina staying on here if things were so hard for her, if life was so miserable. She had a home and a family, if that's what she missed. What was she trying to prove, and to whom?

I tried to convince Bettina to come to Zakynthos with me but she wasn't interested. I knew our grandmother would appreciate all three of us being together for Christmas and I thought it might lift Bettina's spirits. She sighed with effort at the idea and said that Zakynthos in the winter was a graveyard.

I took her out to dinner the night before I left. I felt sorry thinking of her alone at Christmas. We went to a tavern in a basement with wine barrels against the wall where the cook, looking more like a butcher in his blood-stained apron, cut the meat of your choosing on a chopping board in the middle of the restaurant.

'Madam,' said the waistcoated waiter when he delivered the wine and poured it into my glass. His sense of ceremony seemed at odds with the rough-and-tumble of the place. Bettina was in a good mood. We giggled at the waiter and his change of persona as he argued with the cook before switching back to haughtiness to serve the customers. The conversation drifted to me. I confessed at last that I had left my job. Bettina was shocked and interested.

'Really? Why? You've said nothing about this.'

'It's a long story,' I said.

'So, what are you saying? That you're here indefinitely?'

'No. Let's just say I have no definite plans for the moment.'

'Do Mum and Dad know you left your job?'

'No.' I took another sip of wine. 'I didn't have the guts to tell them.'

The musicians began to play a beautiful tsifteteli and Bettina got up to dance. Every eye on the place was on her. She had become an even better dancer in Greece, moving with confidence and grace, her sensuality unashamedly on display. A handsome young man rose to join her, throwing his arms open as if inviting her into his imaginary circle. There were cheers and whistles when they finished, and he shook her hand and smiled.

When we were ready to leave, he appeared outside on the pavement beside us, straddling his motorbike. He offered us a lift and I laughed. Three of us on a bike?

'We'll fit,' he said, reading my mind.

'No, it's too dangerous.'

'I've done it before.' Bettina took my hand. 'Come on, it's a big bike.'

'Oh my God, this is madness,' I said.

'Stop carrying on, Fiore, and get on the bike. You can go in the middle.'

The man took my hand. 'I'm Laki,' he said. 'And your names?'

'Fiore, and my sister Bettina.'

'Where are you from?' Bettina asked, suspicion creeping into her voice.

'From Ipiros,' he replied.

'Are you Greek?'

'Yes, I'm Greek,' he said, helping me onto the bike.

Bettina got on behind me. 'I think he's an Albanian,' she said quietly so he couldn't hear.

'How can you tell?' I asked.

'His accent.'

'But he just told you he was Greek.' And why does it matter? I wondered.

At the apartment we dismounted and I shook Laki's hand, thanking him for the ride.

'Is this where you live?' he asked, looking at the door.

'Yes, but we're leaving for Zakynthos tomorrow,' Bettina said quickly.

'Good night, Laki,' I said as cheerily as I could. 'Have a good Christmas.'

I opened the door and marched up the stairs with Bettina at my heels.

'You shouldn't have encouraged him, Fiore. I'm telling you he's an Albanian.'

I swung around. 'What does it matter, Bettina?'

'I don't want him coming around here.'

I was confused and suddenly afraid of what else she might say.

'Fiore,' she said, as we reached her door, 'don't look at me

116

like that. You don't know anything about these people. A lot of the Albanians in Greece were let out of jail and came straight here. They're unsavoury types and I don't want them coming around.'

I waited until we were inside and the door was shut and then we fought. It started with the Albanians and what I didn't know about them, and ended up being about us. Bettina accused me of being uncaring, ignorant, selfish and judgemental. She stood over me, pacing backwards and forwards, while I sat listening. She told me she was going through a bad time and that instead of offering sympathy I kept telling her what to do. When I said that I'd known nothing of these difficulties until I arrived and that if things were so bad she could always return to Australia, she said that was indicative of how little I really knew her.

'That's exactly what Mum and Dad say,' she cried. 'I have no interest in doing that. I want to live here, and if I try and talk to you about what I'm going through I don't want a lecture about how fucked up my life is and what I should and shouldn't be doing. You come here completely ignorant of how things are, thinking you can teach me to suck eggs.'

I sighed. It seemed I could never work out what it was Bettina wanted from me.

# CHAPTER SEVEN

Nothing I've seen touches me like the sight of Zakynthos as you approach it by sea. It looks so small as you come in on the ferry that you feel you could put it in the palm of your hand. And that sense of fragility is not just a feeling. Zakynthos has a history of earthquakes. The last one occurred in 1953 and was so devastating that old Zakynthos and its buildings, part of the Venetian grandeur, were gone in a day. Just like that.

At the last minute Sophie had decided to come with me. The upper deck of the ferry gave the best view, and as we got closer the white houses appeared in clusters among the green hills. Closer still and I could read the inscription in large bold letters on the Town Hall: ΘΕΛΕΙ ΑΡΕΤΗ ΚΑΙ ΤΟΛΜΗ Η ΕΛΕΥΘΕΡΙΑ. It translated as 'You must have virtue and daring to achieve freedom.' This epic statement, taken from a Kalvos poem, welcomes everyone who enters Zakynthos by boat. The first time I saw it, I felt I was getting ready to fight the revolution. Instead I spent the month partying aggressively like I'd never done before. It was a revolution of sorts.

Of course I had known much about Zakynthos before seeing it for the first time. The Zakynthos of family stories, of poets represented in busts and ashtrays all over our house, Grandmother Phaedra's violent fairytales, and a nougat called mandolato. We had books by Solomos, the poet who wrote the Greek national anthem and who was persuaded to write in Greek and not Italian in order to furnish the newly formed independent Greek state with poetry; we had books by Kalvos, and something by the Italian poet Foscolo, because we shared the same name. While the rest of Greece was enslaved to the dark Ottoman forces of Islam, the Italian presence in Zakynthos meant that the island was part of the supposedly enlightened, cultured Latin West.

Zakynthos had a middle class that produced doctors, lawyers and teachers, who until unification with Greece were educated in the West, mainly in Italy. Their struggle with the aristocracy, the Venetian ruling class, was the subject of a 1970s film called *Revolutionary Plebeian* in which Contessina di Mara, the sassy daughter of an aristocrat, falls in love with impetuous Zeppo, the son of a raisin merchant. Being a mere bourgeois puts him out of the contessina's league, even if he is rich and studying medicine, but Zeppo doesn't care for the rules. He takes the titled class on, and despite the threat of death eventually wins the hand of the contessina. Like a true macho Greek, he arrives at the church on a white horse to save his love from a marriage to an English nobleman called Mr Brown, who, in stark comparison to Zeppo, is a polite wimp.

My parents loved this film. They thought it was their story, although the only peasants in it were the extras, like the woman carrying the flour sack. That would have been my grandmother; that's my ancestry. But my parents sympathised with Zeppo, despite the fact that he was rich and educated, because he was not considered good enough for the contessina. They identified with his disadvantage at the hands of the ruling class over which he had no control.

Saying you're from Zakynthos often impresses Greeks from elsewhere. The island has a liberal and progressive reputation that means different things to different people. Eyebrows are raised at the mention of the place, followed inevitably by a story. Some talk about the revolt of the populace against the tyranny of the nobility in the seventeenth century – Zakynthos' own French Revolution. Some cite the prolific literary talent produced by the island – the poets and novelists. Those who visited Zakynthos in earlier times talk about the beautiful women, who, unlike their covered sisters in other parts of rural Greece, walked around in public with their hair flowing in the breeze, their skirts cut at the knee and scooping necklines. In Zakynthos they danced the foxtrot and the tango, where a man could take a woman who was not a relative and hold her close to his body. Such was anecdotal Zakynthos.

Then there was the Zakynthos I half knew, typified by the story of the mayor and the bishop who, during the Second World War, refused to tell the Germans where the Jews were living on the island. They gave the occupying forces a piece of paper with just two names on it: their own. Those men risked their lives to save the Jewish community. And there was the Zakynthos I hadn't known about at all – that of Elizabeth Martinengo, a feminist, the first to write about Greek women's oppression. Her work, the pioneer feminist text in the Greek language, was written in the nineteenth century but didn't see the light of day until forty years later. Even then it was a heavily censored version of the original, published by her son to honour her memory but stripped of any content he found offensive. And finally there was the Zakynthos I had chosen for myself, ignoring what I didn't like in order to keep my image alive – something that's impossible to do when you're there. I took a deep breath and got ready to confront this place again, full of expectations of what I might find this time.

I was relieved when we neared the shore. It had been an exhausting day and I'd been on the go since seven that morning when Sophie picked me up in a taxi. I was preoccupied, still nursing wounds from my battle with Bettina and trying to make sense of the tension between us. While the fighting wasn't new, this time it seemed to have shifted to a higher gear and it gnawed at me. Sophie thought I was making too much of it, saying Bettina and I had been apart for a long time and had forgotten those interactions you only have with family.

'My parents came over last year,' she told me. 'I thought they were going to be different with me, you know, because I'd changed. I was independent and all that, but the first thing Mum said was, "Why is your hair that colour?" And my old man was freaking out about the nose-ring, and they were having heart attacks about me swearing in Greek. They were just the way they've always been. But I wasn't used to it.'

I considered this, and decided that the next time I saw Bettina I would start again, tread with care and be more considerate. I would call her as soon as I could and apologise. It wasn't good to let bad blood stew.

The ferry docked and down below I could see Grand-mother Phaedra striding determinedly towards the gangplank. With her head bent and clutching the perennial black handbag, she nodded a greeting to people around her but had no time for small talk. She had business to attend to. A tall young woman was with her – Elendina. She was wrapped in a purple cape, and her long hair, which she always used to wear loose to her waist, was tied up in a bun. She looked different from her usual glamorous self. Elendina was the sort of girl who wore high-heels on protest marches. It was her black stiletto that had gone over the head of a policeman during a rally to protest against the *USS Rathburne*, which was carrying nuclear arms.

Elendina ran to me as soon as my foot touched the

ground, kissing and hugging me and dancing around with excitement. My grandmother stepped back to take stock of me, to see that I was all there, then burst into tears before falling on me in an embrace. With Sophie in tow we managed to load the suitcases on the back of Elendina's utility, and we drove off with my sister waving goodbye to the garbage collectors who were greeting her flirtatiously from their truck.

'Yeah, yeah, in your dreams, mate,' she muttered as she started the car, a cigarette between her lips. She wound her window down and called out to them. 'Will you ever stop pulling yourselves and come and collect the garbage from Skoulikado once in a while? The place stinks.'

'For you anything, contessina,' they declared, undeterred by my grandmother's stare.

'Where do you know them from to be talking to them with such familiarity?' she demanded of Elendina.

After dropping Sophie off at her aunt's in town, we headed for the hills. The ditches everywhere and the poor lighting on the narrow road to Skoulikado worried me. We were going hell for leather in the old car and every time we hit something on the road the front passenger door flew open. Some stretches were no wider than a driveway, yet we tore through them as if they were major highways. Neither my sister nor my grandmother seemed concerned about this. At one stage I saw my grandmother cross herself, but it was not to ask God to help us, but because we'd passed a church. Every time I looked behind me, my grandmother broke into a smile. Several conversations were going on at once. Information was being conveyed to me and sought from me and an argument was surfacing about where I would stay. The decision was postponed temporarily as we stopped at Elendina's to unload my luggage. She pulled up abruptly outside an old house that looked like it had seen better days.

It was freezing inside. The wind swept with ease through the large gap between the door and the floor and the only warmth came from an old kerosene heater. The rooms needed painting and Elendina had hung faded family photos to cover the cracks in the walls.

'They're all Dionysis' people,' she said as I was trying to recognise them.

I sat with my coat on the whole afternoon, answering hundreds of questions and handing out gifts. Eventually a truce was reached – I would spend a few days at Elendina's, then go to Grandmother Phaedra's house. Elendina was excited and happy.

'I'll just take Grandma home,' she said, throwing on her purple cape. 'I'll be back in forty minutes. Don't go anywhere.'

Dionysis came home before Elendina returned. He greeted me with a hug and asked me how I was several times, all the while nodding at me as if to say, Well, well, look who's here. The last time I had seen him his hair was cut in the manner of an eighties boy band, but now he had grown it long and wore it tied back, a little like Mozart. In the year of my first visit he'd been helping rebuild the theatrical and cultural life of Zakynthos. I remembered the excitement of that time, the rehearsals and the productions. Zakynthos had a rich history of theatre and Dionysis had dreams of reviving it. In the intervening years he'd opened up a cultural centre that had now become a nightclub, and he also owned a hotel with his family that accommodated several planeloads of British tourists every summer.

'Business,' he said, nodding with dramatic regret. 'I'm involved in business. I don't recommend it to you.'

He draped his lanky frame on the sofa and filled me in on everyone. Who was alive, dead, married, still single, divorced, still living in Zakynthos; who had gone mad or gone conservative. He omitted Mihalis, and after hearing about everyone else, I had to ask. As soon as I uttered his name a sly smile crept onto Dionysis' face, and the word hung in the air for a few seconds without a response.

'He's fine,' Dionysis said, with none of the detail he had provided on everyone else, teasing me into asking more questions. But I left it at that.

When Elendina returned she threw herself on Dionysis as if she were greeting him after a long absence. He rearranged his body in order to make room for her on the sofa and she lay next to him, stroking his face and looking adoringly at him. After opening the presents sent for him, Dionysis offered to cook dinner.

'You seem very happy together,' I said to my sister when he'd left the room.

'We are,' she cooed. 'It's heaven. I've never been happier in my life. It's just perfect.'

I was about to say how happy I was for her when a dark look overtook her face. 'Except for his mother,' she said.

Ah, the little matter of the mother. I asked the obvious question. 'She doesn't approve?'

'Does any Greek mother like the girl her son is in love with?'

Before I could answer, she was standing up to tell me everything. 'I'm taking her little boy away, you see. Even though her little boy is thirty-two. According to her, I don't come from a respectable enough family, I don't have a large dowry, and because I worked in a nightclub over the summer I'm no better than a prostitute. They think I'm after their money. But unlike a lot of other chicks here, I couldn't give a fuck about his money, or more to the point, his family's money.'

'What's the problem with working in the nightclub?' I asked her.

'Only certain types of girls work as waiters and bar attendants. The proper thing to do is take about ten years to do a four-year degree and then sit around and wait to get a job – like working in a bank or some boring shit like that. Or work for yourself. That's how it is here. You either live off your family or you wait to get posted to some secure job. Greeks are real snobs about things like this, you know.'

Elendina told me she had been set to go back to Athens with Bettina at the end of the tourist season, where she had a good job offer in the fashion industry, but love changed her plans. 'He begged me to stay,' she said, then lowered her voice to add, 'not that it took much to talk me into it. But I said, "If I stay, we move in together. Otherwise, see you later, mate." And that's how we ended up here,' she said, waving her arm about.

Before leaving Australia, Elendina had never lived away from our parents' home and she was very used to all her comforts. She used to say she saw no reason to rent a rundown, inner-suburban house without central heating and with dubious plumbing for the sake of independence. But for the sake of love, comfort had flown out the window. I wondered how long it would last.

Elendina and I stayed in and talked that night while Dionysis went off to Yesterday, his club. He complained for about half an hour before leaving about having to go to work and bade us a regretful farewell. Elendina made up a bed for me, but I had a lot of difficulty getting to sleep. It was freezing and the blankets and quilts I piled on top of myself were not very effective. In the middle of the night, loud noises woke me up. At first I tried to ignore them but they seemed to get louder, and as I came into full wakefulness I realised I was listening to Elendina and Dionysis having sex in the next room. The whole house seemed to be vibrating. Too embarrassed to let them know I could hear, I lay still till it was over. It sounded like my little sister was making up for lost time.

Dionysis left early for work the next day and Elendina called me to her bed where I slept like a baby. By the light of morning I could see that the house was perched on top of a hill looking down at the village. I went outside to the toilet and came back in through the kitchen, where I found Elendina and her neighbour Angeliki, the cheesemaker. Elendina was sketching patterns on a piece of paper, with Angeliki paying close attention.

'I don't think there should be any ruffles on the sleeve, Angeliki,' Elendina was saying. 'It's too much. You'll have ruffles around the neckline, you don't want to overdo it. And not navy,' she added, but Angeliki looked doubtful.

I reheated the porridge that had been left for me in a saucepan; it was one of the items I had brought with me at Elendina's request. I poured it into a bowl, added some milk and sat at the table.

'What do you think?' Elendina asked me as Angeliki eyed my breakfast with a mixture of curiosity and horror. 'About navy for an evening dress.'

I shook my head. 'Maybe in velvet,' I suggested.

'Green,' Elendina said. 'With your fair colouring, green would look great on you, Angeliki.' I nodded in agreement.

'How long will you stay?' Angeliki asked me politely.

'In Zakynthos? Maybe a month or two. I'll see.'

'Well, you could come and live here too. Like your sister. Come and sweeten this island with your beauty and your grace. You're all such beautiful girls. Your mother must be so proud of you.'

'Yes, but not just because we're beautiful, but because we're smart as well,' Elendina said, tapping her head.

After coffee we set off in the ute and did the rounds of the relations. We ate everywhere we went and there were tears from some of the older ones. It had been four years since my last visit. A cousin I remembered as a kid had grown into a young man, beyond recognition. A beloved uncle of my father's had died the previous spring and his widow cried as she reminisced about the first time I met him. I had walked out to the field where he was working and so absorbed was he that he didn't hear me approaching. I was right behind him before he noticed me. He dropped his spade when I told him who I was and the force of his embrace caused us both to fall to the ground.

We left the villages and headed for town, where my cousin Fioroula was expecting me. Fioroula was my age, but had always been years ahead of me. The first time I met her she was reading Lacan and verbalising her disagreement with the text as if talking to the author himself. She was shocked that I had never read de Beauvoir and had set about teaching me what she called the basics of life. She was now married to Stavros, a lawyer on the brink of a career in politics, Elendina informed me as we drove to the house.

'He's all right,' she said. 'A bit on the boring side, as these political types tend to be. But he means well.'

The door flew open before we reached it and Fioroula ran out like an excited puppy. She had cut her hair short and spiky and she was pregnant. Nobody had said anything.

'Isn't it great?' she said, touching her stomach.

Yes, it was great, but it was so unexpected I was speechless. She'd been married for a few years so it made sense, but she was not the skinny wild-child I remembered. She took us inside and we caught up on each other's lives: she still ran the manchester shop with her sister and was still politically active, though not a member of any party. I asked her about Stavros and his political candidature, but she seemed bored by the subject.

'Yes, he's running with that band of sell-outs that call themselves socialists – PASOK. He's on the Good Morning Zakynthos ticket,' she said.

The other contenders were the Morning Star coalition and the New Dawn group. They liked the metaphor of mornings, these very night-prone people. Then there were the communists and the odd independent.

'That's who I vote for,' Elendina said when Fiorula named one of the independents. 'An environmentalist. He won't win, but the others won't do anything to help this place.'

'That's what I like about you girls, you've got principles. A vote for the left might be more practical, mind you,' Fioroula said, raising her eyebrows at Elendina, 'but at least you vote according to your beliefs. Unlike these other idiots who are into "progress", which means, Let's vote for whoever allows us to fuck up this island as quickly as we can in our pursuit of money.'

'But surely Stavros –' I began, but she waved him away.

'Stavros believes in progress with government intervention. Everyone can make money, but within certain limits. What a vision! Let's put it this way, I'm not with him for his politics.'

We talked all through the afternoon and then escorted Fioroula to her shop when trade resumed for the evening. I always thought my cousin would go on to do other things. She had the brains and the front to do anything, and I was surprised that she was still selling bed linen and tablecloths after all her studies. Surprised, and disappointed for her. But this was Zakynthos, as she explained, and opportunities were not plentiful. We strolled along Alexandrou Roma Street. It being a Friday night, all the shops were open. A soprano was singing through the open window of an upstairs music school. I watched a dentist probing some poor bastard's mouth and heard talk of elections in doorways and corners, accompanied by coffee and cigarettes. The shopping strip had expanded not just along Alexandrou Roma Street, but along the two streets on either side of it as well. The shops were brimming with expensive goods and designer labels. Underwear shops had multiplied from one to at least six. It was a consumer's dream.

'Yes, now we have six shops from which to buy pretty

much the same thing,' Fioroula said. 'So, where are you girls off to tonight?'

Elendina looked at me and shrugged. 'Wherever Fiore wants to go.'

'Dionysis' place, probably,' I said. 'Yesterday.'

'I'd join you if it was the old Yesterday,' Fioroula said, kissing us goodbye, 'but the new place isn't my style. Techno is torture.'

Fioroula was right: Yesterday was no longer a laid-back place that played a variety of music. The decision to become a nightclub was financial, Dionysis told me as I took in the changes. He was a funny guy, Dionysis. Artistic and bohemian, but if there was a buck to be made he would make it.

I sat at the bar. That and the stools around it were the only things left untouched. I was reminiscing about the wild nights I'd had in this place when Elendina collapsed in a sweaty heap next to me. She'd been dancing for the best part of an hour. 'Who's that man looking at you?' she panted, motioning with her head towards the back of the club.

I turned and was taken aback to see Alex leaning against the wall, drink in one hand and cigarette in the other, looking intently at me. He was alone. Bettina had told me he would be in Zakynthos for Christmas, and here he was. Before Alex, I used to think that men who stripped you with their eyes were a myth. It was almost as if he knew everything about me there was to know.

I slid off the stool and went casually over to say hello, trying to pretend I was on my way to the toilet, but it was hard to get away with this kind of thing with Alex. Why don't we just get all this shit out of the way and fuck? was how I'd summarise the way he looked at me in response.

'What are you doing in Zakynthos?' I asked him as casually as possible.

'What are *you* doing?' he asked back.

'I came to spend Christmas with my family.'

'Is that your sister over there?' He motioned with his head in Elendina's direction.

'Yes, the youngest one.'

Elendina was next to us on cue, and once I'd taken care of the introductions announced that a few people were going out to eat. She invited Alex, who politely declined, and disappeared to fetch our coats.

'We'll see you around,' I said. 'Zakynthos is a small place.' I wanted to say he could call me but I couldn't remember Elendina's number.

'Who was that guy?' Elendina asked me on the road to Zantino's, where we were going to eat.

'Someone I met in Athens. Bettina knows him.'

'Very cool customer. Is he Greek?'

Here we go again, I thought wearily. 'He's a Pontian from Russia,' I snapped. 'Is that a problem?'

'I was just asking,' she said, 'because he has an accent.'

'What is this xenophobia everywhere?' I demanded.

'I didn't mean anything by it.'

'Sorry,' I said. 'Maybe I overreacted, but I'm getting fed up with some of these attitudes towards foreigners.'

'Well, Greece just used to be full of Greeks, but in the two years since I've been here it's changed a hell of a lot. There're people coming from everywhere.'

At Zantino's we sat facing the fireplace and Elendina and I shared a plate of spaghetti. Spaghetti at four in the morning! My body clock gets turned upside down in Greece. It's the only place where I frequently greet the dawn on my way home and go to sleep, or try to go to sleep, with the rooster's crow. We were expected for Christmas lunch at my grandmother's in nine hours and I thought it might be a good idea to go to bed soon. I was thinking about what I could do to have a better night's sleep than the previous one, when I looked up at the mirror hanging above the fireplace and saw the reflection of a man I had last seen in a dream. I spun around and saw that it was indeed Mihalis Xenitos. Striding towards me and smiling.

# CHAPTER EIGHT

When I came to Greece for the second time, I was no longer the starry-eyed nineteen-year-old with an open heart that Mihalis had first met. I had finished university, started work and got a relationship or two under my belt. We saw each other a few times but were not constant companions on that trip. Instead I embarked on a pathetic liaison with a married man that was supposed to be a secret. No-one said anything about it to me directly, except for Mihalis. He asked about it one afternoon, out of the blue. I lied, of course.

The problem with lying is that once you start you have to keep going. And you have to remember the lies you've told. I wasn't very practised in this, and I don't think Mihalis believed me. I sensed he respected me less too, but I didn't care. He believed in being honest, but in matters sexual it's different if you're a man. I'm sure if the shoe had been on the other foot, he would have told me the truth. A lot of clandestine sex went on in small communities and Mihalis found it distasteful, railing against the hypocrisy of it. He was open about sex in a relaxed, sixties kind of way. And he demanded the same from women. He challenged me and made me feel inadequate when I couldn't be that free about myself. But that kind of freedom is always much easier for men.

Despite his failings, I still wanted to spend time with Mihalis on that second trip; he was fun to be with. One day, we bumped into each other in town and he invited me to his place for lunch. He lived alone in a little run-down house in the town that he'd inherited from his grandfather. The kitchen was full of old furniture and there were cracks in the marble floor. Mihalis had made fish soup, and by the time we'd finished eating it was that dead hour of afternoon when everyone was asleep. He began to talk about the Spanish poet Lorca, having just read him for the first time in translation, and, as always in discussions of poetry and philosophy among Greeks, I felt myself floundering. When his brother visited with some friends for something to eat, Mihalis took me into his bedroom as there was not enough room at the table for everyone.

His bed was covered with an old red quilt. There were framed photographs of him as a boy with other members of his family, and a poster of the Fellini film *City of Women*. I sat on a chair next to his desk, which was piled with books and papers. There were more books on the bedside table. I liked his room; it had a warm feeling despite the fact that it was messy. He turned the heater on and produced an ee cummings poem in English – 'somewhere i have never travelled, gladly beyond' – which he asked me to explain to him. He had read it and made some sense of it, but he wanted my input. Pretty soon we had thrown ourselves into translating the whole thing.

We laboured over every word in order to capture the nuances. We had a big discussion about the word 'equals' in the line 'nothing which we are to perceive in this world equals/the power of your intense fragility'.

'It's not "equals" as in one plus one equals two,' I explained to Mihalis after he'd consulted the dictionary. 'It's more like nothing matches, nothing reaches.'

We were both excited and I saw a passion in him that reminded me of the old Mihalis. We finished the poem at two in the morning. He read it to himself over and over in Greek.

'Congratulations to both of us,' he said, pouring a brandy. 'We did a great job.' We clinked glasses; he smiled at me, flushed with happiness, and his gaze held me. I felt myself slipping into it and forced myself to look away.

'I want to go home,' I said quickly.

'Right away?' he asked in surprise.

'I don't want to sleep with you, Mihalis,' I blurted out to his baffled face.

Again this was a lie. I was enormously attracted to him, but I didn't trust him. More importantly, I didn't trust myself. If I slept with him, it might be too good to leave behind, and what if it meant nothing to him? I preferred my clandestine affair with a man I knew I was in no danger of falling for. I feared my feelings for Mihalis. I didn't want to be another one of his conquests. I didn't like the idea that he was frivolous in his sexual relations. And I wanted to show that he no longer fooled me; I was a worldly woman now, who knew his game.

'Don't worry,' he said, searching my face to determine the truth of my declaration. 'There's no danger of that.'

I hadn't expected him to be too friendly the next time we met, but when I ran into him at Yesterday he surprised me by asking me to dance. Actually it was more like a demand, but he was doing me a favour. Panayoti, my married lover, was there that night with his wife, and she wanted to kill me. I had come to regret this two-night stand with her husband because secret affairs are not possible in Zakynthos. Panayoti was paying me the sort of attention you usually see in teenage boys in the throes of their first crush, while his wife glared at me with a curse in her eye and gritted teeth. She looked like she wanted to tear me apart, limb by limb. When I'd slept with him I'd thought, Why not, I'm on holiday and to hell with the consequences. But this wasn't stiff-upper-lip country where people kept a neutral exterior over their seething rage. As I sat there feeling suffocated by my own stupidity, Mihalis came to the rescue. With a tight grip on my wrist, he led me around the dancefloor and defused a disaster in the making.

'Mihalis, can we leave?' I asked him after a few waltzes. I didn't see much point in hanging around feeling uncomfortable.

'Okay.' He shrugged indifferently. 'Did you have somewhere else in mind?'

I had going home in mind and he took me to my grandmother's house on his bike. She was away seeing doctors in Patras, so I invited him in. A few puffs of the joint he rolled exacerbated my misery. He asked me what was wrong.

'I feel like a dickhead,' I sighed, enunciating the word in English as I couldn't think of the Greek equivalent.

'What's that?'

'Dickhead, a stupid idiot. It literally means the head of a dick.'

'Really?' he asked, intrigued. He was always interested in my Australian colloquialisms. 'They use this word to describe an idiot,' he mused. 'So why do you feel like the head of a dick?'

'You know why. I lied to you about it when you asked me. It was a stupid thing to do.'

'Lying to me, or having sex with Panayoti? Wasn't he any good?'

I laughed for the first time that night.

'Don't beat yourself up about it,' Mihalis said. 'Just be smarter about who you pick for your bed partner next time. Life's too short for bad sex.' He winked at me conspiratorially.

I couldn't help laughing again.

'I'm glad you find the notion so hilarious,' he said with

deflated irony. He studied me for a minute, then asked in a serious tone, 'Don't you want me at all, Fiore?'

It was an impossible question to answer, and seeing me struggle he decided to launch into a confession of sorts. He spoke of the bad timing of our first meeting. He'd felt a deep attraction to me, but had been in a relationship at the time. I raised my eyebrows in disbelief. It would have been easy to believe him, but I had to keep myself wary. How did I know that he wasn't just feeding me a line? Bettina's words were ringing in my ears but I wanted to keep him talking. I was flattered.

'Despite your bolshevism, there's something very girly about you that disarms me,' he said.

'Really?' I flirted back.

He was lying on the couch, I was sitting cross-legged on the floor, and we talked about the things we'd done together on my first trip. Somehow we ended up in bed, but within a few minutes the warning bells were going off and I had regrets. But how do you get out of a situation like this?

'What about we just sleep together like friends?' I suggested lamely, knowing it sounded ridiculous.

He looked at me as if I were mad. 'I don't know about you, but I don't sleep with my friends.'

'I have,' I said, omitting that one of them had been Nick and another a friend who was too drunk to sit up, let alone get it up.

'Good for you.' There was no mistaking his sarcasm.

'These male friends, were they all right? I mean, do they have some kind of psychological problem?'

I protested that there were men in the world who didn't just think of every woman in sexual terms and didn't want to necessarily screw every woman they met.

'I don't know any men like that except homosexuals or liars. Besides, who told you I wanted to screw every woman I meet?' He was indignant and offended. 'I want to screw you. Make that past tense, actually,' he said, doing up his belt. And he was out of the house and out of my life for the next four years.

A few days later, I left Zakynthos. Dionysis was on the boat with me. He told me I had hurt Mihalis and I shrugged indifferently.

'I'm sure he'll get over it, Dionysis. So he didn't get a fuck. What am I supposed to do, cry for him?'

'That's not the point. I don't think you behaved correctly towards him.'

'Well, I don't think he behaves correctly towards women, full stop,' I said.

'What do you mean?'

'You know perfectly well what I mean.' I looked at him. 'But maybe you don't? It's all you Greek men ever think about. Screwing every woman you meet.' I was on my high horse.

'Not every woman. And anyway, what's wrong with that? Why should I deny or hide my desire for women?' He was irritated at the attack on his sex and his national identity.

'Because it's oppressive and demeaning to women,' I explained.

'I don't understand you, Fiore,' he said, shaking his head. 'Men find you attractive and desirable and you think it's demeaning? Oh, my Saint Dionysis. And oppressive? I don't force myself on any woman. And I'd like to think that most of the men I know are the same.'

'But you *view* women in this way – as sex objects. There to respond to your needs,' I insisted.

'So, because I desire a woman I see her as a sex object? Let me get this right. If I meet a woman and think she's attractive, I'm not supposed to let her know. If she's available and so am I, I'm supposed to fight my impulse to sleep with her so as not to oppress her. How do you ever get a fuck in Australia? If I played by your rules I'd die of no sex. Can I tell you something? This is exactly what all those sex-starved northern European women like about us, and that's why they descend on Greece in hordes every summer looking to get laid.'

'Jesus, Dionysis,' I said. 'And you call yourself a leftie.'

Dionysis was indignant. 'What's this got to do with my politics? I support equal rights for women one hundred per cent. I back women every time they're discriminated against. But your feminism is very culturally specific. It reminds me of the Americans. When I was studying over there, all the lefties were totally puritanical in their attitude to sex. They're so obsessed with it. You were a bad, sexist man if you desired a woman. Oh, I better go have a cold

142

shower!' He laughed. 'And as far as the rest of America is concerned,' he went on, 'it's more important for them to have a total bastard of a president who screws all of Latin America, as long as he's not screwing a woman other than his wife. Doesn't matter that he supports poverty and injustice on a grand scale, because he's faithful to his wife.'

He shook his head, then gave me a long look. 'What's your hang-up anyway? You're an attractive woman. Men are going to find you attractive and they're going to let you know. If you're not interested, that's your business, but you can't fault a man for liking you and letting you know about it. Mihalis didn't do anything wrong the other night. It's you who doesn't know what you're doing. You can't lead a horse to water and then not let it drink. It's not right.'

Later, back in Australia, I felt some niggling guilt about the whole episode with Mihalis. I found an original edition of a cummings anthology in a second-hand shop and sent it to him. Later still I started to dream about him. I had dreamt of him before, but this was different; it was happening on a regular basis. They were erotic dreams, but there was an indecipherable tension in them as well. They left me feeling uneasy and a touch anxious, without knowing why. I would carry a vague memory of a dream around with me all day and it would gnaw at me, as if something I was ignoring needed my attention. The dreams were not all the same, but they left me with that same feeling.

The first time it happened I woke up feeling displaced.

I was in bed with someone else I was seeing at the time, and was surprised to find him next to me. Where was Mihalis?

I had three of these dreams within a few weeks. Why was I dreaming of Mihalis all of a sudden? A man who had nothing to do with the here and now. With such alarming regularity. It must mean something, I thought, so I turned to the expert.

'Mum, I'm dreaming about a man,' I said, not wanting to be too specific.

'What sort of a man?'

'What do you mean, what sort of a man?'

'Is he tall, dark, blond, short? If you see a dark-haired man it means a true friend, someone you can trust. If he's blond it means indifference – so if he's blond forget about him, you're wasting your time. And if he's a redhead it means betrayal. Stay away from redheads.'

Too bad if you're Scottish.

'If he's tall it means protection,' my mother continued. 'If he's short it means jealousy, a fat one means happiness, and a skinny man means stinginess. Stay away from the skinny ones. Do you know this man?' she prodded.

I lied and said I didn't, because I wanted to escape the inevitable questioning that would follow.

'What does he look like then?'

'He's tall, dark and not fat, but not skinny either.'

'A true friend wants to protect you from something. Be careful. Are you in some kind of trouble?'

'No, Mum, I'm not.'

144

'Well, maybe you can't see that someone is looking out for you. Think about it.'

One night two years ago, I woke up after yet another dream about Mihalis. I looked at the clock; it was four in the morning. Unable to get back to sleep, I decided to ring Fioroula in Zakynthos. We chatted about each other and our families for several minutes before I ventured a question about Mihalis.

'Mihalis? Good, I think. Actually, he's been a bit down lately.'

'Really, why?' I asked.

'His sister has cancer.'

'Oh, that's terrible.' I had never met his sister, as she had married a man from Ithaca and lived there. But I knew she was more like a mother to him than a sister, as their mother had died when Mihalis was nine years old.

'She's just turned forty. It's tragic.'

'Do you have his number?' I asked, and once I'd hung up, without stopping to think about what I was doing or what I would say, I rang Mihalis.

'Mihalis,' I said as soon as he picked up the phone.

'Yes.' His voice remained flat, indifferent.

'It's Fiore, from Australia. How are you?' I said tentatively. This was the first time I had rung him from Melbourne.

'Fiore! My little Fiore.' His voice picked up and was full of surprise and delight.

'Look, I'm sure you think it's strange that I've rung you,' I began.

'Not at all.'

How could he say that? It's not as if I phoned him every day. 'It's just that I heard about your sister and I'm very sorry. It must be a terrible time for you.'

He let out a sigh and gave me some details. He was hopeful that the treatment would be successful. 'She has two children, you know. I can't bear to think of how it will affect them.' He was no doubt thinking of losing his own mother at a young age.

I mumbled something about giving my best wishes to her and to all of them and he thanked me. There was nothing much more to say, but I couldn't let it go at this. 'Mihalis,' I said eventually, 'I wanted you to know that I think of you from time to time and . . .' I paused, searching for the right words. I had no intention of telling him about the dreams. 'And I always think of the good times we had together. You've been a real inspiration to me.' This was four-in-the-morning talk, where I had no idea of what I was going to say until I said it.

There was a silence, then he said, 'Oh Fiore, you enslave me with your words.'

'I mean it,' I said.

'I mean it too,' he replied with emphasis.

'I'd better go,' I said at last. 'It's four in the morning here.'

'Do you remember that poem we translated together?' he asked suddenly.

'Yes, I do.' I felt stupidly sentimental.

'I got that book you sent me. I think of that night often. I think about those lines from the poem.'

There was another long pause, one that stretched ten thousand miles. When I finally hung the phone I went back to sleep with his voice in my ears. 'You enslave me with your words . . .'

Armed with my new worldliness, I'd believed I would be more than ready for Mihalis when next I saw him. And now here he was, coming towards me. He was in his motorbike gear and I had to admire how handsome he still was. He glanced in my direction, looked away, then looked back immediately, his mouth open in a question. He rushed to my side and then stood back to take a good long look.

'I had no idea you were coming,' he said warmly, planting a kiss on my cheek. 'You look wonderful. The best I've ever seen you.'

But I'd had an idea I would see him. The anticipation of it had been like a fine layer of excitement sitting under my skin. 'Oh,' I giggled, brushing the compliment aside with a wave of my hand. 'Thanks, Mihalis, but I don't feel it. The years have taken their toll.'

He studied me with mock disapproval. 'What are you talking about?' He looked around to see if anyone was within earshot, then leant forward to whisper in my ear. 'You're not thirty yet, are you?'

The warmth of his breath on my ear was unsettling. His wavy locks had gone and his hair was cut short, a few strands of grey just visible near his sideburns. It made him look more serious. His face had hardened, but it was a hardness that disappeared when he laughed, bringing his boyishness to the surface again. The dark circles around his eyes were still there and he had put on some weight. It suited him. Ignoring the flutterings in my body, I asked, 'How are you?'

'Well, of course you heard about my sister,' he said.

I hadn't. I hadn't even thought to ask, and suddenly I felt guilty at having spent the last minute admiring his physical beauty. I looked into his eyes and saw that she had died.

'Oh Mihalis, I'm sorry,' I said, touching his wrist. 'Life to you.'

Someone called his name and he turned. A group of people were waving to him

'I have to go. We'll see each other before the new year, won't we? I'll be going away for a while after that.'

'Yes, yes,' I blurted. 'Definitely. When all the Christmas stuff is over, we'll get together and have a really good catch-up. I want to hear all your news.' I stretched up to give him a kiss on the cheek, then watched him as he walked away. He turned and gave me a wave.

'Merry Christmas,' he called.

'That Mihalis Xenitos is such a nice guy,' Elendina said once we were home. 'I'll never forget the first summer I was here. He was so good about showing me around and taking me out.'

The possibility of Elendina and Mihalis entered my head. Not her too. All three sisters? A new take on Chekhov. 'I bet he was,' I said, thinking out loud.

Elendina looked at me askance. 'No, it wasn't anything like that. He knew I had the hots for Dionysis as soon as I laid eyes on him. Everyone knew. I wasn't very good at hiding it, despite all Nina's advice.'

She lit a cigarette and sat down as if settling in for another chat. I was struggling to keep my eyes open.

'But you know what? All that stuff Nina used to go on about is exactly how all the Greek chicks act over here. The first night I met Dionysis, he bought me a drink. Then I bought him a drink. You know, I thought it was fair enough – he'd shouted me. But Fioroula nearly had a heart attack. She grabbed my wrist and asked me what I was doing. And all the way home she was giving me this big lecture about how it wasn't the done thing to go around buying men drinks.' Elendina rolled her eyes. 'But those rules are going to shit,' she added with a sweeping gesture of her hand. 'I mean, with so much tourism, people change. All these English chicks come over here and openly chase men and the men think all their Christmases have come at once.' She started to laugh. 'You know Uncle Yannis's brother-in-law Thimio – do you remember him?'

I nodded.

'He would have to be the ugliest man in Zakynthos, right? They don't call him the warthog for nothing. He had a job over the summer in a bar where the English tourists go. There was this couple staying there and every night the man got drunk to the point of paralysis. He'd end up falling asleep on the couch, and one night the woman told Thimio she wanted to have sex with him. As Thimio said to me, what could he do, say no? It happens all the time. Now he carries himself around like he's the greatest stud that ever lived. And if Thimio can score, then everyone else has got it made. Even my father-in-law, who's fifty-something, got propositioned by one of the women staying in their hotel.'

'Doesn't it bother you?' I asked.

'I don't really think about it. I suppose some of the village boys, and the desperate older ones like Thimio, might go crazy in the summer but most of them grow out of it. To tell you the truth, I'm more concerned about Dionysis' controlling mother than some English tourist.'

The next day, I woke up past midday slightly disorientated. We were expected at my grandmother's at one o'clock. Grandmother Phaedra had left Australia eleven years before. 'I'm going to Greece to die,' she announced one day, sitting in the back yard admiring the apricot tree that bore such luscious fruit she thought it was blessed. 'I can't leave my bones here in this strange earth.' We all thought that would be a long way off in the future, but she saved her pension cheques, the future came and she was ready to go. Finally, there she was in front of that door of no return. We all stood around her sobbing and wailing, grief-stricken beyond consolation. In her little black dress, dwarfed by the rest of us who were begging her not to go, she started to have second thoughts. The torment showed on her face. But my father intervened. 'Come on,' he said. 'Don't upset your grandmother. She has a long trip ahead of her and needs to keep her spirits up.'

'My little partridges,' she said to us now. We went straight into the kitchen where more relatives were seated, waiting for us. The walls were lined with photographs of her son's wedding, our baptisms, Nina, the apricot tree, and one of my grandmother with the lemon tree. 'Take me next to the lemon tree,' she had instructed me for this photo. Greeks have a thing about lemon trees. We ate, drank, ate some more, took a rest and had sweets. There was talk about my parents, more gifts to be handed out, and then everyone settled into a boisterous discussion on the elections.

My grandmother suggested I might want to go for an early nap and showed me the room she always kept for us, little changed since the last time I was here. I surprised myself by sleeping for four hours, and when I woke, the house was quiet. Everyone had gone, including Elendina and Dionysis, since I was spending the night with my grandmother. She was lying on a divan reading a book: Jackie Collins in translation. She sprang up immediately to make me a cup of tea and we sat at the table, which had been cleared of all the food from lunch.

'Now,' she said, folding her hands together in front of her. 'We can talk. Tell me your news.'

She wanted to know about my life, about work and about my prospects in the way of men. When I told her there was nothing to report in that quarter she nodded knowingly.

'Yes, I hear it's becoming hard these days. Of course, in my day we had no choice in the matter. Everyone married. You know, I was quite happy to stay single, but I was nearly thirty and it just wasn't the done thing.'

'I don't want to be with someone just for the sake of it,' I told her. 'If I wanted that I could have it.'

'Absolutely not. I completely agree, but I would like to see you happy.'

'If it comes, it comes,' I said. 'And if it doesn't, I have other things in my life.'

'That's exactly what I say to Angeliki's daughter – you know, your sister's neighbour. She's an educated girl and can't meet anyone. I heard her complaining recently that Greek men have become like Germans and they don't chase women any more.'

'Really?'

'Well, it's probably true. They have all the sex they want now with no strings attached. Not to mention all those English women coming over here every summer and throwing themselves at the men. When you have Thimio the warthog parading himself around town like a bachelor, you know something can't be right.'

A man walked past the window and waved to my grandmother. She called out to him and told him to come in for something to eat. He indicated that he'd already eaten.

'Come and have a drink then,' she said and he nodded, making his way to the kitchen door.

'Who's that?' I asked her.

'An Albanian who did some jobs around the house for me after summer. He's gathering olives now for your Uncle Yannis.'

The man came in and smiled at me tentatively, shyly shaking my hand. My grandmother made us coffee and talked to him about the olives and the weather. I asked him where he was from and he named a place that meant nothing to me. How did he find Greece? I asked him, and how long had he been here, what was Albania like, did he have a family there? He answered in as few words as possible, with an accent that was probably not too different from mine when I spoke Greek. His downcast glances and guarded responses I put down to his lack of confidence in Greek.

But then my grandmother started to talk about him in the third person, as if he wasn't there, with an unmistakably patronising tone in her voice, and I saw his shyness in a different light. His cautious demeanour was the mark of a migrant. I had seen it many times before.

'Why do people dislike them so much?' I asked my grandmother after he'd left.

'Who people? Not me,' she said defensively. 'They're seen as uncultured and desperate, and in a sense they are. Albania is a poor and backward country. They're easy targets because they're trying to make a living in a foreign land. Some people here don't know what that means, or maybe they do and they think it's their turn to step on others in order to feel good. I've been in some terrible fights with people about this. You know what I say to them when they start carrying on about the Albanians?' Grandmother Phaedra was standing up now, with both hands on her chest. 'I say I'm an Albanian.' She flicked the tea towel in anger and began to wipe the table. 'If you want my opinion, I find them very respectful. There are two families in the village and I baptised one of their children.'

'And what about the Pontians?' I asked, thinking of Alex.

'We don't get too many of them in Zakynthos. A lot of them came to Greece last year and they're still coming, now that the Soviet Union's fallen apart. They lived in Kazakhstan, Christians in what's become a Muslim state.'

'Are they being persecuted?' I asked.

'That's not the point. You don't have to be persecuted to know you're not welcome. Besides, who would want to stay there? There's no work, no money, no food, and the Mafia runs everything.'

'So they're coming here?' I echoed my father's amazement that these people should look to Greece for salvation. The country lacked the services and infrastructure for its own population, let alone several hundred thousand immigrants.

'Eh, you're looking at it through Australian eyes,' my grandmother replied. 'You don't know what wretched lives they're leaving behind. None of us do.' She sighed. 'But I can imagine.'

# CHAPTER NINE

One last customer remained in Fioroula's shop, having difficulty deciding between two sets of bed linen.

'I'm closing now,' Fioroula said impatiently. She wanted to
eat a cake. Her pregnancy brought cravings for sweets. 'Why
don't you come back tomorrow? I have plenty of both.' She
showed the woman the door.

'Let's go,' she said to me, locking up. 'I've been hanging
out for a galaktoboureko all afternoon.'

We made our way to Niro's cake shop, where, Fioroula
insisted, they made the best galaktoboureka in Zakynthos. As
she ordered the cakes I saw Alex walk past on the opposite
side of the road. Telling Fioroula I'd be back in a minute, I
rushed out to catch up with him.

He rounded the corner and was about to go into a hotel
when I called out. He turned with a curious look on his face.

'Merry Christmas,' I said when I caught up with him, a

little out of breath. I reached up to kiss him on the cheek and he leant down awkwardly and kissed me back. 'How are you?' I asked.

'Fine.' He smiled. It occurred to me that he was probably in Zakynthos looking for work and I wondered how he had spent Christmas. I berated myself for not thinking of this earlier and inviting him to spend it with us.

'Is this where you're staying?' I asked, looking at the hotel, and he hesitated slightly before nodding. 'Let's meet up,' I suggested. 'Are you doing anything tomorrow night?'

'I'm not sure.' He thought for a few seconds. 'Give me your number and I'll call you.'

I tore some paper out of my address book and copied Elendina's number. 'There're some great places to go to here,' I said, giving him the paper. 'I'll tell my sister and we'll come and pick you up and take you out. Do you have any friends here?'

'Not really.' He seemed in a hurry. 'Okay, thanks. I'll call you.'

His tentative behaviour made more sense to me now. What I had initially assumed was arrogance was more likely a form of self-protection. He must have felt like a stranger in this place, and I wanted to show him I knew what that felt like.

I ran back to Niro's cake shop and found Fioroula eating my galaktoboureko. Her own plate was empty.

'Who did you see?' she asked.

'Someone I met in Athens.' I sat down opposite her.

'A Zakynthian?'

'No, no. He's a Pontian.'

'What's he doing here?'

'Probably looking for work,' I guessed. I didn't have a clue.

Fiorula looked doubtful. 'Doing what? Gathering olives?'

Just then, Stavros arrived, keen to see me and hear my news. Fioroula's husband was going grey and had put on weight, but strangely enough it suited him. I had already seen his face in a photo – showing him looking wistfully to the sky – plastered on a hundred walls and on a banner hung over Alexandrou Roma Street. We talked at length about my work and the state of politics in Australia. He nodded knowingly as I lamented the rise of the free market in the West.

'It's Thatcherism. That bitch left a terrible legacy, and everyone else is desperate to prove they can cut government spending just as much as she did. Employers now want to pay everyone less than they did last year, even though they're making more money. We have an example like that right here in Zakynthos.'

'The toy factory,' Fioroula interrupted. 'Up near the airport.'

'There's been unrest there for some time,' Stavros continued. 'The union is demanding a pay rise and better conditions. Some heating and things like that. Nothing excessive, in my opinion. But the owners won't give anything.

157

There's already been some action, and you know what they say? That if this doesn't stop they'll shut down here and open up in Bulgaria. The operating costs will be lower, labour costs will be halved, they'll have more profits. I've told the workers this and they don't believe it. Fifty families live off that place. They think the owners are just bluffing. Mind you, having that old-style communist Pavlos the redhead leading the workers doesn't help.'

Fioroula cut him off. 'Leave Pavlos alone. He's a good man. If only there were another five like him.'

'Fioroula, my love, Pavlos is a great man, but he's out of touch with what's happening in the world today. When that factory shuts down and the workers are left with no jobs, they'll be sorry they followed him.'

'What alternative does he have?' Fioroula cried. 'If they give in, the owners will know they'll be able to do whatever they like.'

'They do what they like anyway,' Stavros replied. 'Besides,' he went on wearily, 'the worst thing about all of this is that it's going to explode during my campaign. Just what I need.'

'Good to see you have your priorities worked out!' Fioroula snorted. 'These negotiations have been going on for months. I'm sure they thought they'd pull a strike just for the purpose of upsetting your election campaign. And even if they are using the election to bring some attention to their plight, bravo to them. I don't blame them at all.'

'My wife the revolutionary.' Stavros winked at me. 'Fioroula never lets anything like a husband get in the way of her principles.'

'You're lucky to have me around to remind you of them,' she boasted.

He kissed her and she told him to get lost.


When Alex hadn't called by ten the following night, I gave up waiting and made arrangements to meet Sophie at the Logos Bar. She was sitting with a bunch of guys she knew from the summer and they started arguing about who would buy me a drink. When the music became too loud to talk one of them asked if I wanted to dance. On the dancefloor he began paying me an assortment of compliments that continued after the dancing finished. He was twenty years old and trying very hard but I couldn't take him seriously. I sat listening, amused by the whole thing, when I felt someone behind me. I turned and saw Alex.

'I rang but you'd already left,' he said, accepting my offer of a seat. 'Your sister said you were coming here.'

He ordered a drink and we sat watching the dancing in silence, until the music died down and the boys began to tell jokes. One of them told a Pontian joke. Sophie laughed and I nudged her.

She looked at me with a frown and I gave her a dirty look. 'What?' she asked.

'Sophie,' I said to her in English, 'think about what you're laughing at,' and I motioned to Alex. She still didn't get it.

'I don't think those jokes are funny,' I said in Greek to everyone.

'Why?' the joketeller asked.

'Because there's an assumption that Pontians are dumb.'

'They are,' my admirer said, laughing.

'Shut up, you,' the joketeller said to him. 'It doesn't mean that at all. It's just a joke. We say Pontians, but it could be anyone.'

'Yes, the English tell the same jokes about the Irish,' someone put in.

'They do?'

'I didn't know the Irish were stupid,' said my admirer.

Alex, who had said nothing during all this, stood to go. I gathered my things and followed him out.

'Oh, you've hired a bike,' I said.

'Would you like a lift?'

I told him I was staying in Skoulikado. I knew how to get there, but he might get lost coming back.

He considered this for a moment. 'I'm sure I'll find my way,' he said and we set off.

When we reached the house I invited him in, but he declined. 'Next time, perhaps,' he said.

I felt a little disappointed that he resisted all my attempts to befriend him.

'Fiore,' he said and I looked up. It was the first time he'd used my name. 'Why did you say all those things to those boys back there?'

'About the jokes? Because it's what I believe. Those jokes are a form of racism and I feel I have to speak out.'

'Why?' he asked impatiently.

'Because if I don't, people will think it's all right.'

'What does it change if you speak out?'

'People might think differently about things.'

He laughed at this and I felt taken aback. 'You shouldn't put up with it either,' I told him.

His eyes widened. 'You expect me to pick a fight every time a Greek tells a Pontian joke? That's the way of the world. People don't like each other. And people of different ethnic groups don't like each other even more. We came here for this reason. Pontians couldn't stay in Kazakhstan because we weren't one of them. Believe me, a joke is the least of my problems. You should think before you talk. It could get you into trouble one day.'

But I had trouble of a different kind when I walked into the house. Elendina was waiting for me in an agitated state.

'Mum and Dad rang,' she said. I prepared myself for some disastrous piece of news. 'You didn't tell me you left your job. Are you staying in Greece? Why haven't you told me any of this? What's going on? Mum's really upset. She was crying on the phone. Said she knew something was going on.'

I dropped my handbag on the floor and fell into the arm-chair. I learnt from Elendina that my parents had rung

Bettina to wish her a merry Christmas and she had told them. They'd been on the phone to my grandmother as well, looking for me and asking questions. I didn't want to think about any of it, or talk about it or deal with my mother and father. I couldn't. I didn't know the answers to the questions they'd be asking. I said as much to Elendina, who was not particularly sympathetic.

'It's tough, but you better call Mum and Dad. I don't know what you're gonna tell them, but you have to talk to them,' she instructed.

'I will,' I sighed. I gritted my teeth, fuelled by anger towards Bettina. Why had she told them? Why couldn't she just leave me to deal with things in my own way? 'Tomorrow,' I promised.


A week after Epiphany my sister was throwing a party. The idea had come to her on the day of Epiphany itself, January 6, when we were gathered on the pier to witness the priest throwing a cross into the sea and men diving in after it. This ritual makes more sense in Australia, where it's the middle of summer. At the height of a Greek winter it makes you shudder to watch the divers' bodies touch the water.

Elendina said the party was in my honour, but I think that was just an excuse. Things went quiet in Zakynthos after the New Year. Nights were bathed in darkness as nightclubs closed and didn't open again until the Carnivale, six to eight weeks later. It was a time of hibernation, when people shut themselves in at night, kept warm and slept a lot in order to recover from the summer and prepare themselves for the next one.

Greeks from elsewhere often grumble about the winter shutdown that happens on the island. From one extreme to the other, they argue, while the locals apologise to me for this state of affairs, feeling a keen responsibility to be good hosts. 'You always come in the winter,' is their common complaint to me. Elendina, who found any excuse to throw parties, thought we needed something to lift us out of the winter doldrums.

But I wasn't having a bad time, even without the parties. I had developed a routine of going into town in the morning, where I'd have breakfast and read the Greek and English papers. I went for walks along the beach if the weather was good, visited my cousins, and made my relatives happy by accepting their invitations to lunch or dinner. I spent a lot more time with my grandmother on this trip. I was interested in getting to know her better as a woman, now that she was no longer the disciplinarian who had raised us, no longer someone I viewed as anachronistic and irrelevant. Apart from some uncomfortable conversations about my plans for the future, I passed my days in rhythm with her village of Volimes.

Volimes is a mountain village, the furthest there is from the town of Zakynthos, an hour's drive by car. Its isolation from other villages meant that the Volimiotes were tradition-ally a tribal bunch. In the summer, the villagers sell their wares at roadside stalls to people passing through. It's not a place that's popular with tourists as it's not on the beach, and its inhabitants have not been able to share in the big money of the tourist boom that has happened elsewhere on the island. The people still keep goats and farm their land.

Grandmother Phaedra was always in for a laugh or a good time. She would sit with her legs apart, slapping her knees as she recalled some funny story, and the ones that made her laugh the loudest were the bawdy ones. When she and her neighbour got together they laughed even harder, recounting tales from their youth in the village. The clandestine meetings with boys at the well, the dancing they did at the paniyiria – where the men held them so close they could feel their erections – and the various sexual adventures of the mostly married village folk. The strict rules that governed the tradi-tional way of life were obviously often broken, just like we transgressed them as teenagers. Was there anyone who really believed in them? I'd always thought it was the old women who were the keepers of the rules, but you'd be forgiven for thinking otherwise listening to my grandmother talk. Yet she could just as easily swing back to the traditional village line about the proper thing to do, depending on whose company she kept.

During my stay, she was visited by two election candidates who were soliciting votes. They came a few days apart, at a respectable enough time after the siesta, and stayed for an hour and a half. They sat with my grandmother at the table and drank coffee while I sat at a distance from them. This seemed to unnerve them a bit. They were curious about me, but had to stop our discussion getting too deep as I didn't have a vote. This didn't prevent one of them trying to get me on the books. I laughed at the suggestion, explaining that since I didn't live there I wasn't familiar with the issues. I later found out that they didn't live in the village either. They'd both been born and bred in the town, although their ancestry was in the village. By their way of thinking, not only could I have a vote, but I could also run as a candidate myself. Like most politicians, they talked at length about the failings of the opposition while never actually saying what they would do themselves, or what they stood for.

My grandmother was in an uncomfortable position since both candidates were relatives. It was difficult for the people of Volimes to go visiting during this time, as a visit to any house connected with either one of the candidates could be taken as a vote for them. But running into them in the village square or out on the street was a different thing altogether. There they could talk for hours without fear of misinterpretation.

The villagers were always keen to hear my impressions of Zakynthos and quick to point out that, with modern transport, Volimes was not as isolated as it once was. When I told them it saddened me to see that so many parts of the island had changed for the worse due to tourism, and that I was glad Volimes was still beautiful, I was met with disbelief – no young person who had any choice in the matter stayed in the village. I was certain some of the people found me a bit strange, but I preferred their slower pace of life and their old stone houses, most of which were unrenovated.

My grandmother's home was without modern comforts and it made her life hard. She complained about reliable electricity still being out of reach, trying to quell my romantic notions about village life. But was the answer to completely discard the old, replacing it with the lavish, ugly mansions that had proliferated over the rest of the island?

Elendina was curious about my desire to spend so much time in the village, but that was more to do with her own state of mind. She was wholly wrapped up in Dionysis. She would often break into a dreamy smile for no apparent reason and create opportunities to talk about him. She finished Angeliki's dress and set about making Dionysis a shirt, which she sewed and unpicked and sewed again in pursuit of perfection. I tried to talk to her about Bettina and my time in Athens, and my anger and disappointment at her telling our parents something I didn't want them to know. Elendina listened, made appropriate noises, but as soon as Dionysis walked into the room a delirium took hold of her. She would jump on him, make cooing noises like a baby, pinch and bite and kiss him. It was primal. I had never seen this side of her. It's amazing what sex brings out in people. Dionysis was not much better. His usual cynical demeanour disappeared in Elendina's presence and he smiled from ear to ear like the cat that got the cream.

My sister made a list of the people she wanted to invite to the party. She got to the end and realised she had left out Dionysis' parents. 'I'd better invite them,' she said with resignation.

'Hopefully they'll leave early,' I suggested.

'Hopefully his mother will get run over by a bus.' I looked at Elendina with mock disapproval. 'I can dream,' she said. 'Back to business. Is there anyone else you can think of? Oh, Mihalis! Though I heard Dionysis say he'd gone to Athens.'

But I wasn't thinking of Mihalis. I hadn't seen Alex since the night before New Year and told Elendina I wanted to invite him. I didn't know the name of his hotel, so the next day I went in person to see if I could catch him. I sat in the café near the foyer and waited. The desk clerk kept looking at me and after a while he approached me.

'Excuse me, aren't you one of the Foskolos girls?'

'Yes,' I said, struggling to place him.

'I thought so. I'm a friend of your cousins, I've met you before. A long time ago, at a dance at the Carnivale,' he added. 'You haven't changed much. Are you waiting for someone?'

I didn't really want this man knowing my business; it would be all over Zakynthos that I was sitting in the foyer of a hotel waiting for a man. But what could I say?

'Yes, actually,' I said at last. 'His name's Alex. He's staying here.'

He looked perplexed.

167

'He's a tall man with curly hair,' I said.

'Oh, I know the one. Is he a friend of yours?'

He was fishing for gossip. I got up to go. 'Well, it was nice seeing you again, but I'd better be going. He's obviously not in.'

'Would you like to leave a message? Fiore, isn't it?'

'Yes, Fiore,' I mumbled.

'He has your number?' he asked politely, meaning, How well does he know you?

I flashed a look at him. 'I'm not sure. I'll leave it just in case.' I hurried out, cursing my luck.


Elendina and I were preparing the food on the afternoon of the party when the phone rang. It was my mother. I wanted to run and hide. I had put off speaking to my parents. Instead I had rung Bettina to give her a piece of my mind – I left it for her on the answering machine. She hadn't returned my call and I hadn't returned my parents' call. We were all avoiding each other. Elendina came back into the kitchen with her hands on her hips, berating me.

'I thought you said you were going to call them. Get on the phone now,' she said, pointing to the sitting room.

When I picked up the phone the barrage came immediately, the general theme being what sort of daughter was I? I listened, and when I had to answered in monosyllables that gave my mother no satisfaction.

'What do you mean, you don't know?' she demanded.

'What *do* you know? I was relying on you to lead by example to those aimless sisters of yours, but instead you've joined them. Haven't you sown your wild oats by now? Why can't you settle down like normal people?'

Good question. Why didn't we? Perhaps our parents had something to do with it, but this wasn't the right time to expound the theory. Besides, who said I didn't want to settle down? I might not want to settle down into something of their choosing, but I didn't say this either. I knew what the response would be: Who chooses anything in life?

'I knew something was up,' my mother said. 'I saw it in a dream. A wild pig.'

I wondered why she always dreamt of such things: horses, snakes, ships, guns, wolves, wild pigs. I wouldn't know what a wild pig looked like to dream of it.

'It bit you,' she continued. 'It ran wildly after you, then bit you.'

'My God,' I laughed. 'Where did it bite me?'

'I can't remember,' she said, peeved that I wasn't taking it more seriously. 'It's not a good sign. They say if a woman is bitten by a wild pig it means she'll be used by a terrible man.'

'There aren't any terrible men using me, Mum. Don't worry.'

'What about your sisters? What about Dionysis? Is Elendina happy with him? How do you see the situation?'

'Mum, they're all over each other night and day.'

'I'm not interested in that. Is there a future in it?'

'I think he probably wants to marry her.' I didn't know this for a fact, but I had a feeling.

'What about her?'

'Maybe.'

'Maybe? What's maybe about it? How many years will it take her to be sure? Two or three? By then they'll be sick of each other and looking for someone else.'

My mother had a theory that we spent too much time in relationships getting to know men. She said it was only natural that we became bored after a while, then of course we didn't want to marry them. Nina agreed with her on this one. What woman would want to marry any man if she really knew him? she would insist. And men were natural wanderers who wanted to savour something new. We'd all stay single forever. Her advice was to strike while the iron was hot.

There was a long silence on the phone and I thought my mother had hung up.

'Mum?'

'I'm here,' she said, and there was silence again. 'I don't know what to say to you, Fiore,' she said at last. The authority in her voice had been replaced by vulnerability. 'I miss you all. I love you and I want you all close to me. We had a black Christmas without you. Here's your father.'

I thought I was going to get another earful from my father, but he was more interested in news of Zakynthos and his mother. He was heartened to hear she was in good health.

It preyed on him, this insistence of hers to live in Greece, far away from her only son whose job it was to look after her. He was pleased that Elendina was living in Zakynthos, where she could look out for her, and pleased that I was spending time with her.

'She brought you up, you know,' my father said, reminding me of our debt to her for the sacrifices she'd made. 'All right? Take care of your sisters and don't stay too long. Your mother's very upset at the thought of you staying in Greece. Get whatever it is out of your system and hurry back.'

He was trying to understand.

Later, I was in the bathroom applying my makeup when Elendina came in to tell me that Alex had rung and would try to make it to the party. The news threw me into disarray. I tried on several different outfits and was unhappy with all of them. I resorted to Elendina's wardrobe and found a royal-blue silk Chinese dress with a split up the side.

'Oh, that's good on you. I was going to wear it,' she said when she saw me looking at myself in the mirror.

'I want to look my best. I'm trying to impress someone.'

'I thought Mihalis was in Athens?'

'I may want to impress someone else besides Mihalis. There are other men in the world, you know.'

'Oh?' She raised her eyebrows. 'In that case, leave it on. It looks great.'

'Are you sure you don't mind?'

'No. I just hope it works. Then you can tell me all about it.'

Work it did. Alex looked me up and down with a lazy smile as if he wanted to eat me.

'Well, do I measure up?' I asked him as he stood on the threshold. I'd had a drink or two.

'Measure up for what?'

'Whatever it is you're measuring me up for,' I said, taking his arm and pulling him into the house. I introduced him to people but was worried he might feel out of place. He didn't dance, despite my attempts to get him to, and insisted he was happy to watch.

Fioroula, meanwhile, danced with such abandon I was worried she might go into labour. 'I've got four months to go,' she laughed.

Later I found Alex outside. 'You dance very well,' he said as I approached, but his tone was matter-of-fact.

'You've seen me dance before.' I tried to deflect his compliment, even though I thought it was overdue.

'Maybe I only paid proper attention tonight.'

This was not the first time I'd detected an impatient tone in him. It bordered on irritation, as if I should have understood the first time around and then was asking too much of him that he didn't want to explain. Yet there was no mistaking his attraction to me. He stood slightly elevated from me; we were on uneven ground. He took a few drags of the joint and handed it to me. It was strong.

'Well, you know what they say,' I said, very blasé. 'If you know how to dance, you know how to fuck.'

Where had that come from? I wondered, slightly shocked. Alex looked at me out of the corner of his eye and threw away the remainder of his cigarette. 'Is that what they say, is it?' He moved closer, until he stood over me, and I looked past him.

'Hey,' he said, demanding my attention.

I was too nervous to meet his eyes. He unlocked my folded arms, took me into his, muttered something about me not wearing a coat and began to slowly caress my face.

With the backs of his fingers he touched my cheeks, my eyes, my mouth. Like a blind man trying to feel what he can't see. I shivered, but not from the cold. Our bodies were a centimetre apart and I finally looked up into his eyes. Lifting my chin, he kissed me tentatively on the mouth. I leant forward into him, my arms around his neck, and we kissed until I heard someone calling my name. He knew how to kiss.

'I have to go,' I said, pulling abruptly away. I recognised Sophie's voice and was already halfway back to the house, Alex dawdling behind me, when I saw her.

'What are you doing out here? Were you smoking a joint? Why didn't you invite me out?' Sophie was looking at me with suspicion.

Alex went past me into the house and Sophie was relentless in her pursuit of information. 'What happened?' she insisted.

'Nothing, Sophie, we were just talking. Come on, let's go back inside.' I avoided her eyes but my shaky voice gave me away.

'You're both acting very strange. And your lipstick is all around your mouth,' Sophie said dryly.

There was movement in the house as people left and others arrived.

'Where have you been?' asked Elendina, annoyed. 'People have been asking after you.'

'I was just talking to Alex,' I said, and headed for the kitchen to wash some dishes and to be on my own. My mind was racing and my heart wasn't far behind.

When Alex left not long afterwards I walked him out in silence. He mounted the bike and mock-saluted me.

'I want to see you again,' I said.

He leant over and kissed the side of my neck. Another shiver ran through me.

'So come and see me,' he said, always the cocky one.

Why this response? What was wrong with 'Yes, I'd love to see you too'? How long was he going to keep playing the cool customer with me?

I waited two days, hoping to hear from him, before I decided to be assertive and seek him out myself. I turned up at the hotel and this time he was there. Words about why I had come tumbled out of my mouth, but he pulled me into his arms as soon as he shut the door. We stood still, saying nothing. I undid his shirt, explored his chest with my hands and mouth. He pressed me against the door and kissed me until we slid to the floor.

# CHAPTER TEN

There's nothing like good sex to make you want to buy new underwear. Suddenly everything I had was insufficient for any future encounters with Alex. So I went shopping. I tried on a dark brown, see-through lace bra. I'd never worn brown underwear before. There was a sepia-like quality to it when I had it on, as if I were posing in an old photograph. I bought it immediately, along with a crimson slip and matching knickers.

As I was leaving the lingerie store, Dionysis emerged from the Captain's newsagency. The Captain was a cantankerous troubadour who satirised the events of every summer in song. He observed everything with the eye of a hawk and had a stinging wit. The last summer I was there, a local girl from a wealthy family who was a terrible snob and generally disliked, got a glass object stuck in her bum during some sort of sexual activity. The doctors in Zakynthos didn't have the instruments or the skill to extricate it and she was sent to

Patra. The story had done the rounds before she was aboard the ferry, and sure enough the Captain's song spelt out anything we might have missed. In a place like this nothing, not even your sexual peccadilloes, can be kept secret. I'd felt sorry for the girl and made a point of avoiding the Captain. He'd even bestowed that nickname on himself, a sarcastic reference to a failed career in the merchant navy.

'Fiore,' Dionysis said. 'Come in and have a coffee with us.'

Before I could think of an excuse I heard the Captain's staccato voice from inside the shop. I wanted to run for cover.

'Is that who I think it is?' he asked. 'Bring her here and let's have a look at her.'

Dionysis went off to get the coffees and I walked reluctantly into the shop. The Captain and a priest turned towards me.

'Where have you been?' the Captain asked. 'No-one's seen you since you got here. I've been asking everyone, Where is our little Fiore? The little jewel. Let me have a look at you. Not a day has passed on your face.'

I smiled politely. This was all leading somewhere. The Captain was not into flattery.

I nodded hello to the priest, who was seated at the counter. There were always a few chairs in the shops so people could drop in and have a yarn.

'What's happened? Your old friends aren't good enough for you any more?' the Captain continued, leaning on the counter. 'You've obviously found some more worthwhile personalities.'

Jesus, I thought, it only happened yesterday and the whole island knows already. I switched to safer ground. 'Who do you think will win the election?' I asked. 'Do you think Stavros has a chance?'

'Definitely,' the Captain said. 'It's between him and the other PASOK candidate.'

'You mean there are two? How can that be? I thought each political party had only one candidate.'

'One was elected by the party machine, the other was the preferred candidate of the Zakynthos branch – that's your cousin's husband,' the Captain explained.

'I hope Stavros wins then,' I said.

'Because the people want him as opposed to the one imposed by the party hierarchy?' the priest asked. No-one had introduced us, and since when did the wild boys of Zakynthos hang out with priests? 'The irony is that the party's choice is a better man. No offence to your cousin, but just because the masses elect someone, doesn't mean they know what they're doing. Democracy has its flaws.'

'Well, what do you suggest as an alternative?' the Captain said aggressively. 'A benign dictatorship?' When the priest didn't respond, he asked me, 'What about your sister? Who's she voting for?'

'An environmentalist,' I told him. Stavros had seen to it that both my sisters were enrolled to vote in the town – the council where he had nominated – to try to secure himself two more votes. Although neither of them lived in the town,

177

they were eligible to vote there because it was my mother's birthplace. They could have voted in Volimes, but that would be of no use to Stavros.

'Hmm.' The Captain raised his eyebrows at the family treachery of Elendina not voting for her cousin's husband.

'And the other one, that troublesome one? Is she coming to vote?'

I had no idea if Bettina was coming or not.

'An honourable vote, the environmental vote, but a wasted one,' the priest put in. 'Unfortunately.'

'Why unfortunately?' I asked him.

'Because a lot of people have become very rich very quickly out of the tourism thing. Environmentally, this place cannot sustain the onslaught that happens here every summer. It's destroying the island, but that's a secondary consideration to making money.'

Dionysis came back with the coffees. 'PASOK reckon they're going to get serious about illegal immigration,' he said, perusing the headlines.

'Well, I hope they have the good sense to leave it until the olive season's over. Can't get anyone else to do the work,' the Captain said.

'Especially at the wages you're paying,' the priest commented.

'And you call yourself a socialist,' I added.

A fiery discussion ensued about illegal immigrants, with the Captain insisting that he had nothing against them personally, but that the country couldn't be overrun by hordes.

'But you don't mind the hordes staying for the olive season,' I said. 'How humanitarian of you. Whatever happened to your politics anyway?' I was addressing all of them, assuming they spoke with a common voice, although I didn't know the priest at all. But I didn't care; I was becoming increasingly uncomfortable with the language that was being used every time somebody mentioned immigrants.

'What's the matter with you?' The Captain looked aggrieved. 'I employ these people and pay them. They were starving in their country and they came here begging for work. If they're illegal immigrants, what can I do? That's the law.'

'You don't understand,' I said. It was a weak response, but I felt frustrated that they didn't see this as a basic human-rights issue. That they weren't revolutionaries ready to storm the barricades any more was one thing, but a meek acceptance of racist policies was another.

'What don't I understand?' he protested.

'What they're going through. It's not enough for you to pay them for the work they do. You should care about them as people. They should have rights in this country, the same as you. Your indifference is nothing but a form of racism.'

'Racism! Us?' The Captain put both hands on his chest. 'I'll tell you something, my girl. Our tolerance towards foreigners has been historically documented. Don't you know what happened here during the war? No Jew went to Dachau or Mauthausen from Zakynthos. They were *all* saved.' He looked at me in disgust. 'You should know what you're talking about before you open your mouth.'

It was the priest who came to my rescue. 'She has a point,' he said, before turning to address me directly. 'It's true there's a lot of intolerance towards other races coming to live in what has been up to now a fairly homogenous society. There's been a certain amount of acceptance of immigrants in your country, but that's taken a long time and we're right at the beginning. Besides, we are a small country, without the wealth of a place like Australia. You invited people to come for economic reasons, you needed them to work. But I doubt you'd be that welcoming to hundreds of thousands of people crossing your borders if you didn't need them. Even when that does happen to Australia – and it will, eventually, because of the way the world's going – we Greeks will always have a much bigger problem than you. Australia is so far away and much harder to get to.'

I wanted to say that I wasn't making comparisons, nor defending Australia, but the Captain was quick off the mark again.

'All of a sudden we're bad,' he said. He had been leaning over the counter and looking into my shopping. Now he changed his tone and winked slyly at the others. 'I wonder who's turning your head. A Pontian, perhaps?'

I picked up my bags quickly. 'I'm going,' I said, heading for the door. 'I'll see you all later.'

'Pleased to have made your acquaintance,' I heard the

priest say on my way out. Where had my manners gone? I should have turned back and responded, but I was too angry.

I saw Alex one more time and then he disappeared. We had arranged to meet at a café in town several days after our night together. I was nervous and excited, my head full of possibilities. I thought of things I would say to make him laugh, and what he would say back. I thought of eating with him, going places, getting to know each other. I thought of knocking down the fortress he kept between himself and the world, so that he'd allow me in. I wore my new underwear. But he was an hour late and by the time he arrived I was no longer nervous, but impatient and irritated.

'I was held up,' he said, seeing my arms folded across my chest. I fumed. 'Settle down,' he chuckled. 'An hour's not that long. We're not English. Would you like a coffee?'

'No, thank you, I've had two already.' I looked away from him. Across the road a shop was being transformed into the headquarters for Stavros' campaign. The Captain was there, directing one of the workers. He saw me and smiled, and nodded at Alex. Just what I needed – to provide more gossip fodder for the Captain.

'Where have you been anyway?' I demanded. I wasn't prepared to be distracted from my justifiable anger.

'I had things to do,' he said casually. 'You know how it is.'

What things? I wondered. Why was he always so evasive?

'So, you want a coffee?' he repeated.

I relented and we finally slipped into conversation, but he kept fiddling with his little packet of sugar, until finally it split, the grains scattering on the table. He swept them up and threw them into the ashtray.

'Right,' he said. 'I better go.'

'Just like that? After I waited so long?'

He looked uncomfortable. 'I have to meet some people. I'm sorry, it just came up.'

Some people. Obviously he didn't want me to know about whatever it was he was doing. The thought occurred to me that he was seeing someone else, but I didn't want to show my paranoia by asking. I hesitated. 'Well, do you want to meet for dinner later?'

'I'm sorry, I can't.' He paid for the coffees, pulled on his jacket, and I walked with him to the door. We stood outside for a few seconds.

'Which way are you going?' he asked, rubbing his hands in the cold.

I wasn't going anywhere in particular but I motioned towards the beach.

'All right. I'm going that way.' He pointed in the opposite direction.

'Maybe we'll catch up soon,' I said feebly.

'Sure.' He turned and walked quickly up Alexandrou Roma Street.

A familiar feeling of disappointment surged within me. So much for the underwear.

Stavros was having a fundraising party at Markos' taverna. After his death, Markos' widow had continued the business and people flocked there to support her and remember him. In season, out of season, it was always full. My uncles had lifted their ban on the place. In death, Markos had been forgiven. After all, they had nothing against his wife. Her father and her two brothers did the singing now and anyone could join in their performance of traditional Zakynthian serenades.

The rain was pouring and it was biting cold. Dionysis, Elendina and I arrived to find Sophie huddled by the wood heater, teeth chattering. No wonder – she was wearing a black dress with lace sleeves and a lace section on her midriff. It was far too glamorous for an occasion like this, but she was interested in one of the musicians and wanted him to notice her. I'm certain even the table napkins noticed Sophie that night. Elendina looked modest next to her in a white velvet dress with black buttons and a bow that she had whipped up for herself the preceding day. Other women looked at her with envy and she had many queries about getting one made for themselves. Fioroula looked stunning in a maternity outfit also made by Elendina, and it drew its fair share of attention. 'Dressed by Elendina,' she said to everyone who asked.

The place filled up quickly, and once the singing started

the temperature went through the roof. Elendina nearly fainted. There goes that testosterone, I thought, and said as much to Dionysis.

'It's the spirit of Markos. He had that effect. I think every woman who saw him sing must have wanted to fuck him. Men used to bring their wives here if they wanted to get them worked up for a night of sex.' Dionysis was pouring the red wine as if it were water and both Elendina and I were feeling the effects of it. Dionysis joined in the singing at one point, but he had a terrible voice. Watching him, I found myself wondering what he knew about my mother. Everyone knew everyone else's business on the island, but this was a previous generation and my mother was long gone and out of sight.

When I returned to Australia after my first trip, I felt obliged to tell my mother about Markos' death. I would have wanted to know in her place. I thought of saying something casually, without revealing that I knew about her connection to him. Since she'd never once mentioned him in all the stories she told about Zakynthos and her youth, it was obviously something intensely private for her. If she didn't want me to know, I didn't want to intrude. But she surprised me by asking about him straight out. I was telling her how several people – total strangers – had come up to me in the street in Zakynthos to say that I was the image of her. A less beautiful image of her, I added, and she laughed.

'Was one of them Markos Kallinikos?'

I had been struggling with how to do it for a week and she

184

had done it for me. I nodded and told her what happened, but she already knew. Xenophon had phoned her. She began to cry. I sat on the edge of her bed, watching her, thinking I should comfort her but not knowing how. I was out of my depth.

'The bastard,' she sobbed. 'He's not worth a single tear.'

I should have left it at that, but I did something I would come to regret. I told Bettina. I was dumbfounded by her response.

'The hypocritical bitch,' she said, pacing her room. 'All this time she's been so strict with us, saying that good girls don't have boyfriends, and now this!' She ranted against the unfairness of it, being told one thing while our mother had done another. 'That's it,' she said. 'I'm not putting up with this bullshit any longer. From now on, I'll do exactly what I want and they can both go jump.'

I could see her point. I was nearly twenty and Bettina was eighteen. We were getting fed up with the arguments about coming and going as we pleased. We were at university; we had friends who lived on their own, who were responsible for themselves. But it was my trip to Greece that changed me. If my parents believed they were raising us according to the Greek way, they were deluded. They were either having us on, or Greece had changed. Either one, it didn't matter; I just didn't buy it any longer. But Bettina needed more leverage. When she decided to move out, the war began. She threatened our mother.

'If you stand in my way, I'll tell Dad everything about your Markos,' she said in a voice dripping with determination and menace. My mother fell to pieces. I wanted to grab Bettina and throw her across the room. I hated her at that moment. Defeated, my mother looked at me as if to say, You too?

Years later, I concluded that my father must have already known about Markos and my mother. How could he not have known? He was in Zakynthos while it was going on. He owned a nightclub. My mother's brothers worked for him. My mother went there with them. Markos went there. But my father was a man of honour; he had a man's way of staying silent, of not searching in every crevice to unearth the detail of things. He was definitely a minority in a house with five women who wanted to replay and ponder and analyse.

Bettina believed she had got her way about leaving home due to Mariza's fear of my father finding out. But to my way of thinking, my mother's shock and distress was caused not only by the realisation that her power over her children was no longer absolute, but by the fact that it was taken from her in such a brutal manner. Had her relationship with her daughters come to this?

I was jolted back to the present by the singing getting louder as more and more people joined in. From the other side of the room the Captain waved to me, before crossing to speak.

'Alone, are we?' He was full of curiosity, and full of

186

implication about Alex. I didn't want another argument and was trying to think of an excuse to get away when a voice interrupted.

'What I would give to be the subject of your pleasurable thoughts. Blessed is he who is.'

I turned to see Mihalis standing behind me, a glass of wine in his hand. I laughed spontaneously and took his hand. 'Mihalis, you're back!' I offered him the seat next to mine, which had been vacated by Sophie who had gone to flirt with the accordion player. Eager to avoid further conversation with the Captain, I asked, 'How long have you been back?'

'Why? Have you been missing me?' He winked at the Captain.

'The talks at the toy factory have broken down,' the Captain said to Mihalis. 'The workers are meeting tomorrow to make their decision, but it looks as if they'll strike. There's a march afterwards in the square.'

'We should show our support.' Mihalis sipped his wine and scanned the room.

'What time is it? I'd like to come,' I offered.

'That *will* be a treat for us,' said the Captain. 'Being graced by your company.'

I ignored this remark but it only provoked him further.

'What's wrong with us Zakynthian men anyway,' he said, throwing his hands up in a dramatic gesture. 'Aren't we good enough for you? A whole island of Zakynthians and you go for a Pontian. Listen here to me, girl, and let me tell you a few things about Pontians you obviously don't know. You being from Australia, you're not well informed.'

I glared at him. 'Look, I'm not interested, all right? So save it for someone else.' To my relief he walked away.

'I used to think the Captain was funny, but he's not so funny when you're the object of his acid tongue,' I said to Mihalis.

'Come on, Fiore, it's not as if you're the only one. He's the same with everyone. He found your weak spot and you rose to the bait.'

I was wondering what exactly my weak spot was when Fioroula approached us, glass of wine in hand and singing along with the band. 'Here's to you and your health, my beautiful cousin,' she said, slapping me on the back. Turning to Mihalis, she added, 'Thanks for coming. Let's hope Stavros doesn't get elected and sell out. Although it's very probable. Everyone else does.'

'Come now, Fioroula. What about working for change from within?' Mihalis teased.

She looked at him askance and said, 'I'll see you at the march tomorrow. I have to go and play the political wife.'

Mihalis swivelled in his seat to face me. 'Now, tell me what's been keeping you so busy.'

'Nothing much.' I toyed with my glass. I knew where he was headed and I didn't want to talk to him about Alex.

'Oh, like that is it? Wasn't it any good again?' An arched eyebrow completed his cheeky expression, which forced a chuckle from me. 'Where is he, by the way?'

'Look,' I said defensively, 'he's just someone I met and it didn't work out. That's all there is to it. It happens, you know.'

Mihalis leaned back in his chair. 'Yes, I do know. That's what we're all doing. Stumbling our way through the minefields in search of love. Trying to meet the right person.'

'But is there a right person, Mihalis? There's no perfect match. It's hard to make a relationship work.'

'Really? I don't know about that. I think it's difficult to meet the right person, but once you've met them I can't see why it should be difficult to be with them.'

'So after all these women you've been with, you haven't met the right person?'

'There you go again about all these women I've been with. Why do you attack me in this way? Would you think better of me if I was a monk? What about all the men you've been with?'

'That's different,' I said.

'Why is it different?' he demanded.

'Because it is. You know it is. I wasn't just using them for sex.' I was full of indignation at him putting my experiences on a par with his.

'No, that's right, you fell madly in love with Panayoti and you slept with him because you were looking for a deep and meaningful relationship.'

I put my fingers to my mouth to quieten him down. He laughed and placed his hand on my shoulder. 'Are you trying to keep it from everyone else, or from yourself?'

189

I shook my head. 'I was young and reckless. It was a silly thing to do and completely out of character for me.'

'Ah, it's all right for you to make mistakes attributed to the folly of youth, but the rest of us are tainted by our transgressions for the rest of our lives.'

The singers, who had been moving from table to table with every song, reached the table next to ours, making it impossible for us to speak. But I wasn't finished with Mihalis, and I was frustrated that I couldn't get my point across. Frustrated that he had the notion I was single and alone by choice; that he knew nothing of the pain I went through whenever a relationship ended, nothing of the feelings of failure I had to overcome as I prepared myself, yet again, for the next round. Love was not a sport for me.

It didn't occur to me that he might have been trying to tell me the same thing.

# CHAPTER ELEVEN

Suddenly I became anxious about time. Nearly two months had passed and I was still in Zakynthos. I toyed with the idea of going somewhere else. Perhaps Thessaloniki to visit a cousin who lived there. But the Carnivale was about to start and Zakynthos is a good place to be for the Carnivale.

Elendina organised a sewing bee to make costumes for the ball and enlisted the assistance of Sophie, who could also sew. Sophie arrived armed with materials, costumes that needed altering, and a sewing machine that belonged to her aunt.

'It's an antique from before the war, probably, but I'll manage. Hey,' she said, turning to me as if remembering something, 'you didn't tell us anything about knowing a rock star.'

'What?' I asked in a fog.

'I rang Bettina yesterday and she told me this guy, the lead singer from the Sub Urbans, rang there looking for you. He saw your parents in the city and told them he was

191

going to be playing in Greece. Apparently Nick Cave's doing some concerts in Athens and they're supporting him. And your mother gave him Bettina's number and encouraged him to call.'

I was dumbfounded. 'You're kidding?'

'I'm not. Bettina's rapt. She'll get to meet Nick Cave.'

I took matters into my own hands and rang Bettina. We hadn't spoken since I left Athens. I was still fuming over her spilling the beans to our parents about my leaving my job, but I put that aside for the moment in order to find out what was going on with Bruce.

'Hey, village girl,' she said. 'Where've you been? I expected you back ages ago.'

'I've been here. Hanging out. What's going on with Bruce? Sophie tells me he rang you.'

'Yes. You're a sneaky thing. How come you didn't say anything about him? Anyway, this is fantastic. The band'll be here in a few weeks and I get a job out of it. I'm going to be working with Nick Cave!'

'A job? Doing what?'

'Well, Bruce and I got talking on the phone and he happened to mention that there were problems with the tour because the cook quit. The promoter's girlfriend had the job, but they split up and she pulled out. They were going to hire someone different every place they played in, but I said I'd do it. I told them I'd had experience and he spoke to the promoter, who rang me. And we organised it.'

I was speechless. This was a different Bettina to the one I'd left in Athens. She told me they were flying her out to Prague, then Budapest, then back to Greece. I was stunned by this turn of events.

After exhausting that topic, she asked how I was.

'Kicking back in Zakynthos, as the T-shirt says. I saw Alex a few times.'

'Who?'

'Alex, your friend,' I reminded her.

'Oh, *Alex*. He's not really a friend of mine. He's Stelios' friend.'

'And how's he?' I asked.

'I don't know. I haven't seen him for ages.'

This was good news. 'How come?'

'I don't know. He hasn't called. Or maybe he has and I wasn't here. Maybe he's in love. Who knows?'

There was a pause and I heard Bettina taking a puff from a cigarette. 'Well, I've got things to do, babe. If you want to come to Athens while I'm away, grab the keys off Antonia.'

'I'll probably stay here for the Carnivale,' I told her.

'Fine. I'll be back before then. I'll only be away nine days.'

'Bettina,' I said, just before she hung up, 'take care.' What could I say? Beware of Bruce? She didn't need that kind of advice. I did.

When I came out of the bedroom, Sophie was pinning a mermaid costume on Elendina. They were as stunned as I was when I told them Bettina's news.

'You've got to hand it to her,' Sophie said, speaking through the pins in her mouth. 'She always finds her feet. Didn't I tell you in Athens not to worry about her? There, it's done.' She took a step back to observe her work.

'The bottom's too narrow,' Elendina complained. 'I can't walk.'

'You're not supposed to walk. You're a mermaid.'

'Well, how the hell am I going to get around? In a wheelchair?'

'Come over here and stop carrying on,' Sophie ordered, and Elendina teetered towards her like a woman with bound feet.

Sophie took the pins out and put them in again. 'Is that better?' Elendina nodded. 'Go and look in the mirror.'

'The top part doesn't go,' she said when she came back.

'No, it doesn't,' Sophie agreed. 'But I know something that will. I saw it yesterday at the fabric shop behind the cathedral. I'll go and pick it up. I told Fioroula I'd bring her up here as well, so I may as well go now.'

I was preoccupied with Bettina's news. What had Bruce told her? I wondered. What had he told my parents? What possessed them to give him Bettina's phone number? But then again, I'd told them he was just a friend and they knew nothing about the rest. Elendina asked me what was wrong and I was taken unawares that she'd noticed something was up. She listened to the whole tale and had some cold, hard words of advice.

'You shouldn't put up with any bullshit at your age,' she said, shaking her head. 'You, who could quite easily march up to the prime minister himself and tell him what you think, yet you let these losers stuff you up. It doesn't make sense. They're not worth it. You shouldn't be chasing any man. Why don't you try making it with someone you actually like, rather than just falling flat on your face with anyone who crosses your path?'

There aren't a lot of men who cross my path, I wanted to say. How do you find someone you like? Where do you look? And you can be prescriptive about who and what you want, but the chemistry still has to be there. Some women, once they're attached, forget the dramas associated with being on the market. It's so much easier then to retain the moral high ground. You forget how you compromise yourself, give someone the benefit of the doubt and allow yourself to be open to possibilities. The irrational creeps in and you're surprised to find yourself doing things you'd caution your friends not to.

Elendina brought two glasses in from the kitchen, opened a bottle of wine and poured it. She put an Alkisti Protopsalti record on and danced around the house. After two glasses of wine I was up with her, dancing to a song about wishing the other person would burn in flames and drinking fire from your tears. It was a good revenge song. A poetic way of saying, Fuck you. Elendina always knew the power of the song. Whenever we had parties and no-one was dancing, she put on 'I Will Survive'. Every woman there would be up and throwing herself into it before the first bar was over.

We danced to another few songs, until Sophie returned with Fioroula and my grandmother.

'The party's started early,' Fioroula said, putting down her things and joining us for a dance. My grandmother sat watching us with delight.

'Bravo,' she shouted when we finished. 'I love to see you enjoying yourselves. Do it all while you're young, while you still can. Ah, you don't know how lucky you are to be living in these times.'

We danced until Fioroula became breathless and then set to work on the costumes.

I felt better indeed.


Sophie went to the ball as the merry widow. Elendina decided against the mermaid costume and went as a clown, and I was a can-can girl, with a mask that covered half my face. The ball was held at the Casino, which was not a gambling place, but a building that was used as a cultural centre. It was called the Casino after the gentlemen's club of old, which was destroyed in the 1953 earthquake. The buildings that fell to the ground during that quake may have left Zakynthos bereft of its Venetian grandeur, but the cultural practices of the old empire were still intact, the Carnivale being one of them. It was this two weeks of the year, coming out of the gloomy winter months, when Zakynthians donned their masks and costumes and went out partying.

There were parties everywhere but the big balls, like the one at the Casino, were the best.

A sea of colour confronted me as soon as I walked in. So many beautiful, inventive and colourful costumes overwhelming the senses. Not everyone was wearing masks, and I saw one of my uncles dressed as a sailor. Another had come as a sheik with four brides. I didn't recognise Fioroula and my other cousins, dressed as harlequin dolls, until they came and spoke to me. Fioroula's costume was made in such a way as to disguise her tummy. She was busy dancing with what looked like one of the Three Musketeers.

There were plenty of stories about confusion of identity and trickery at these events: men being fooled into thinking they were pursuing a young woman when it was an older woman in disguise, others dancing all night with someone they assumed to be the object of their desire, only to be rewarded with a complete stanger. That's the Carnivale.

My first offer of a dance came from a Casanova. I had no idea who he was, but he sure knew how to dance. He moved me swiftly and sweepingly across the expanse of the dance-floor for two waltzes and a polka. He had Mihalis' build but I knew Mihalis would make himself known to me. Every few minutes I would laughingly cross paths with my sister and Sophie, whose partners were an Ace of Spades and a pirate.

'Fioroula, I need a drink,' I said when Casanova released me. The man was in training for the marathon.

I had one drink. Only one. And I became, as they say,

legless. The last thing I remember was the room swirling around me. In fact I was swirling around it, dancing with one of the Three Musketeers, who had a very long nose. The dance had just started when I felt myself folding into his arms. I remember thinking I knew the voice that was sounding concerned and frantic at the same time, and realised as I went under that he was not a musketeer at all, but Cyrano de Bergerac.

'That's why you've got such a big nose,' was the last thing I said.

I had drunk a bomb. I didn't know it at the time, but everyone told me afterwards.

'You drank a bomb,' Elendina declared.

'Yes, it was definitely a bomb. They totally knock you out. It happened to me once in Paros,' said Sophie.

'What's a bomb?' I asked, thinking it might be a cocktail.

'A bomb, you know,' said Sophie. 'They sell you some type of cheap alcohol, made God knows where, in who knows what conditions. No-name brand. You think you're buying a Johnnie Walker, but it's filled with this other, cheaper stuff.'

'Cheap and sometimes nasty,' added Elendina.

When I came to, I felt very cold. It took me a minute to realise I was in the back of a car, covered by somebody's coat. It was hard to move and I felt groggy. When I finally pulled myself up, I felt sick. I opened the door and threw up. The cold wind hit my face and I was fully awake. I heard noises. People were shouting and there was commotion on the other side of the car. In the faint light I saw costumed people standing in a line, confronted by a truck with its high beam on. The cops were there as well, standing by having a chat, and someone with a microphone. What on earth was going on? I got out of the car, pulling the coat on, and walked unsteadily over to where the action was.

The first person I made out from a distance was Sophie, then I saw Fioroula and my other cousins. The people standing in line had linked their arms, and a few of them had broken into song. Many still had their masks on. I'd made it as far as the truck when I heard Mihalis arguing with a policeman.

'Cyrano,' I chuckled almost to myself, but he heard me.

'Fiore! You live,' he said.

'Mihalis, where are we? What's going on?' I was still in a daze.

He grabbed me by the arm. 'Come here. We're at the toy factory. That's the picket line.'

'Who are you?' the policeman wanted to know.

'She's from Australia,' Mihalis began.

'Australia!'

'She's Phaedra Foskolos' granddaughter.'

'Caesar's daughter?' The policeman was incredulous. 'Another one? Don't tell me you're living here now too. Caesar was such a sensible man. How could he have produced three daughters with such crazy ideas?'

'You know my father?' I asked him.

'Yes, I know your father. He was my brother's best friend.

Which one are you?' he asked, stepping on the butt of his cigarette.

'I'm the oldest.'

'Well, since you're the oldest, you should have more sense. Take your sisters and get out of this mental asylum we call Greece. Ah, I should have emigrated years ago, when your father offered to sponsor me. Look at this situation, my girl, and tell me what I'm supposed to do.' He waved his hand in the direction of the picket line.

That night, while all of Zakynthos partied, word had got out that the owner of the factory was planning to lock the workers out and bring in scab labour to do their jobs. This was a shock to everyone. Stavros' mother, who'd arrived from Athens early that evening, told her son that she'd noticed a group of foreigners travelling together on the boat. She overheard snippets of their conversation, but could only decipher 'Romiri' and 'factory' from their tongue. The factory was in Romiri. She wondered who they were and why they would be talking about it. The dispute wasn't major news in Athens. She thought they looked suspicious.

Stavros didn't know what to do. The last thing he needed with the election looming was industrial strife. On the one hand, his party, which also held the seat of Zakynthos in the national parliament, encouraged companies to set their businesses up in regional areas with all sorts of government subsidies. He knew the owners of the toy factory. He doubted they were PASOK supporters, but he couldn't be seen to be too close to the workers, whose demands were regarded as excessive. If they had to comply with them, the owners maintained, they would shut the factory down. It employed fifty people – a substantial business in a place where there was no other industry to speak of. But nor could Stavros publicly take a position against the workers. It wasn't just a matter of losing fifty votes, there were all their family members' votes as well.

Fioroula did not share his dilemma. She was very clear where her loyalties lay, and sent the word to the agitator, Pavlos the redhead. Pavlos, dressed as a gladiator, was about to go out with his wife. He took a detour to Romiri and when he got there the place was in darkness, as was usual for that time of night. He went to check inside but his key wouldn't turn in the lock. The locks had been changed.

He had to let everyone know. But all his workmates were out, so he and his wife started doing the rounds of the nightclubs and taverns. It wasn't an easy job finding people, since almost everyone was in disguise, and he didn't want to make announcements in case the perpetrators were among the revellers.

Pavlos was already at the Casino when I passed out. He'd found Fioroula and told her that he and the others were going straight to the factory to set up a picket line. They feared the company might send in scabs the next morning, possibly even before that. Fioroula set about gathering people to join them as soon as possible.

Mihalis was the first person she found because he'd taken

off his mask. He was struggling to carry me out, with the help of Elendina.

'There's a fair bit of stress involved in going out with your sister,' he said to Elendina. 'You spend half the night worrying she might pass out. It's not the first time I've been in this situation with her.'

'Tell me about it. We'll be sitting around smoking a joint and Fiore will be holding court with some hilarious story one minute, go off to the kitchen to make custard and the next thing you hear is *thud* and you run in to find her passed out on the kitchen floor. Drugs just don't mix with her.'

I heard this exchange as I briefly returned to consciousness, but I felt too numb to speak and I didn't have the energy to open my eyes. Then I was out to it again.

By now I had a throbbing headache from the freezing night air. 'How long are we going to spend here?' I complained. 'I want to go home.'

'What do you mean? This has just started. We can't leave now.' Sophie said this as if she were still at the ball, not a scene of industrial unrest. Vasili, her accordion-playing lover, was there, the only one not in fancy dress.

Elendina wasn't interested in leaving either. 'This is fun,' she said. 'I haven't done this since those peace marches we used to go on in the eighties, where they burned effigies of Reagan and the Russian guy.'

'You used to burn effigies of Gorbachev?' asked Pavlos in disbelief.

'I think it was Brezhnev,' I volunteered.

'Brezhnev? Why?' He asked.

'Well, it wasn't just the Americans who were developing nuclear weapons,' I said.

'What do you mean? It was the Americans who dropped the atomic bomb. They did it to show the rest of the world they could destroy us, to submit us into the slavery of capitalism. What were the Russians supposed to do? Turn their bums around and say, Screw us? They had to defend themselves.'

'Yes, you're right,' I sighed, having no desire to continue the argument at this hour, and in my precarious state of health.

'Burning effigies of Gorbachev,' he said again, shaking his head. 'That's the strangest thing I've ever heard. Very politically naive, you Australians.'

All of a sudden a cheer went up. I turned and saw that the truck was leaving. As it reversed and headed out to the main road, people on the picket line started throwing stones at it and calling out obscenities.

'Dirty Albanians, coming here to take our jobs. Get out of here!' they yelled.

Pavlos claimed it as their first victory. He grabbed the megaphone and made a speech, even though we were all within earshot and could hear him perfectly well without it, and Sophie's boyfriend started to play 'Good Morning, Sun' on his accordion.

Mihalis finally came to the rescue and offered to take me home. We were halfway there when we saw the truck up ahead.

'I wonder where they're going?' he said. 'Poor devils.'

I looked at him in surprise. 'Do you feel sorry for them?'

'Yes, I do. The company is using them. They don't care about them any more than they care about the workers they're trying to replace. And these Albanians, a lot of them are desperate for work. God knows what's brought them here.' He paused while he overtook the truck. 'God knows what's brought them here,' he repeated when we were safely past, 'but I think I know *who* brought them here.' He pulled over to the side of the road and looked at me with meaning. 'Did you know about any of this?'

'Know what? What are you talking about?'

Mihalis adjusted the rear-view mirror to the passenger's side until I had a clear view of the truck. Its powerful headlights bounced off our car and illuminated the cabin. There in the driver's seat, a cigarette hanging on his lips, was Alex.

I got out of the car and stood waving at him in the middle of the road, then stepped to one side, waiting for the truck to stop. But it kept going. I called out after Alex. He didn't even turn his head to look at me.

# CHAPTER TWELVE

I was ordered not to show my face in public. Elendina told me there were conspiracy theories flying left, right and centre. People were talking – and they were talking about me. Saying I'd been swanning around Zakynthos on the arm of a strike-breaker, and no wonder I was getting hot under the collar when someone told an innocent joke, and wasn't I ashamed to be working against my own people, and it was Caesar's daughter, of all people, who had been going around question-ing everyone else's socialist principles. Fioroula wasn't talking to me, my relatives stopped ringing, my grandmother gave me a huge lecture and hung up in my ear.

'But I had nothing to do with it, I had no idea what he was doing here,' I protested to the only people who listened: Elendina and Dionysis. They didn't have much choice in the matter as I was staying in their house.

Elendina was furious with me. 'I have to live here,' she

said, waving her finger at me. 'Anything you do incriminates me. To think we invited him to a party in this house!'

Dionysis observed me with his arms crossed, wondering how it was that I'd suspected nothing. I tried to defend myself, saying I thought he was here looking for work. Gathering olives, like the Albanians.

'People who come here looking for work – to gather olives, as you say – don't stay in fancy hotels,' Dionysis said.

'Fiore,' Elendina said, exasperated, 'how could you think such a thing? Have you seen the people who come to work in the fields? They don't look like Alex. He looked like he was in the money.'

'He was in the money, all right,' Dionysis said. 'I'm sure the company spared no expense getting scabs in to break the union.'

'I had no idea,' I insisted. 'Honestly. If I'd known such a thing, I'd have told him what I thought and had nothing more to do with him. You have to believe me. I only saw him a few times, anyway. It's not as if we were particularly close.'

'You're a stupid idiot for not having your wits about you,' Elendina said, spitting on the ground.

I yearned for some leniency but none was forthcoming. If some people weren't talking to me, others were telling me to my face. A few days after dropping me home in silence on the night of the ball, Mihalis appeared at the door to have it out.

'How come you weren't suspicious? Didn't you think to ask him what he was doing in Zakynthos in the first place?'

'Lots of people come here – they don't need a reason.' I was sick of having to defend myself. All of a sudden everything was my fault.

'I thought there was something shifty about him,' he said.

'All right, Mihalis, we can all be clever with hindsight,' I retorted.

'What did you see in the guy anyway?'

I ignored this. What I saw in him was lust, but I was in no mood to get into a discussion about that with Mihalis.

'Go on. I'm curious,' he said. This wasn't just about the strike. Mihalis was putting on a show of jealousy that might have been real or might have been an act.

'I don't owe you any explanations,' I said matter-of-factly.

'No, but I thought we were talking as friends.'

'Friends of mine would never assume that I was a part of something like this. And they would be more sympathetic, not coming to stick the boot in.'

'Oh, would they? Are these the same friends who sleep with you but don't want to have sex with you?' he asked, and it made me laugh despite myself. 'It seems I lack a number of prerequisites to be a friend of yours.'

It was one of the few laughs I had in that stressful time. I felt humiliated. In Zakynthos, of all places, people thought I was a union buster's girlfriend. On the one hand I thought the whole situation was ridiculous because I was completely innocent, but on the other I wanted to hide away from everyone until it all died down. This was a slim hope, since,

Carnivale aside, the strike was the most exciting thing happening in Zakynthos. I felt trapped. I spent several days and nights sitting in my pyjamas moping, smoking and drinking coffee. I ate only at the insistence of Elendina, who had never seen me take so little interest in food. Reports came in from the picket line. There had been violence. A young man related to the husband of Dionysis' sister had been in a fight and broken his nose. The police had arrested two Albanians who claimed they were acting in self-defence. I listened to it all and wanted both to hear and not to hear about Alex's involvement.

One afternoon in the middle of all this, Fioroula arrived on the doorstep with a suitcase. Expecting a tongue-lashing, I was surprised when she threw her arms around me and consoled me for my misfortune.

'You've got nothing to feel bad about. You weren't to know,' she said. 'I'm sorry about the way I reacted. I've calmed down now and I know you had nothing to do with it.'

'I should have known better,' I said.

'We all know better after the fact.'

'Fioroula, he was a guy I thought I identified with. I don't know why, I thought I could read his hurt and wanted to reach out to him. But he didn't want to have anything to do with me. If he hadn't cut me off, I would have continued seeing him.'

'That's why he cut you off. He didn't want to have anything to do with you because he knew you'd be caught up in it.'

'Perhaps he had some honour after all,' I said, trying to justify my attraction to a man who was now an ogre.

'Don't you start defending him. If I ever set eyes on him again, I'll send him to hell and back. He deserves to hang from the highest belltower in Zakynthos.' Fiorula opened up a bag and produced a bottle of ouzo. She held it up for me to see and asked, by pointing to it, if I wanted some. I nodded. She found two little glasses and poured me a big dash, and herself just a nip.

'Got to be careful,' she said, indicating her stomach. 'Let's put some music on. It's time to dance.' The next minute Kazantzidis, the original 'revenge' crooner, was blaring through the speakers. At Fioroula's insistence we were both up dancing

'Let's go to a doghouse,' she said. 'Let the drink soak up our grief and smash everything.'

A doghouse. My least desirable destination sounded like a good idea. Then again, dancing wasn't on top of the list until Fioroula showed up either. I fell onto the couch for a break and collided with her suitcase.

'Fioroula, where are you going?'

'Nowhere. I'm coming to stay here for a few days.'

'Here?'

'Stavros and I had a fight,' she said, and I turned the music down.

'What happened?' Here she'd been consoling me all this time when she had her own dramas going on.

'He hasn't said or done *anything* to support the workers since the strike started. The election's on Sunday and I told him he could stick his election. Unless he comes out and gives his support to the workers, I told him I would have to rethink our marriage.'

'Are you serious?'

'Of course I'm serious. So snap out of your misery and help me with this campaign. What good are we to the revolution if we're crying over a lost love?'

'Are you telling me you've left Stavros?' I asked in disbelief.

'No, but he thinks I have and that's exactly what I want. He has to wake up to himself, and the only way that will happen is if I take some drastic action. He's like a spoilt little boy. He has his mother and me and his father all looking after him, and on top of it all he's not doing the right thing by his own people. I'm going to put his two feet in one shoe.'

I was unsure about the effectiveness of Fioroula's plan. Stavros and Fioroula lived on top of his mother, in the manner of many Greek families, and I imagined that his mother would just take over where Fioroula left off. I'd once attempted to explain to Dionysis and Mihalis the economics of life in Australia. I told them most people saved for a deposit to buy a house, then took out a bank loan that took years to pay off. They looked confused.

'Why do you go through all of that? Why don't you just build on top of your mother's?'

I tried to explain the notion of independence and distance

from your family, but it was no use. Living on top of each other, a family's dynamics were heightened by constant interaction, involvement in the children's affairs – even when the latter were adults – and, inevitably, arguments. I saw it as a lack of choice due to financial dependency, but they saw the Australian option as financial slavery to a bank.

Grandmother Phaedra came down two days later from the village, ostensibly to visit the picket line, but she dropped in to see us. She too had started to thaw in relation to me.

'Next time beware of foreigners,' she warned. 'It's a bit of a mess. The workers have a point, but on the other hand, that factory provides a lot of families with an income. Maybe they should have tried another tactic. It will be a shame if they have to shut it down.'

Dionysis agreed with her, and a huge discussion about the issue erupted in the house over dinner. Fioroula and Elendina maintained that the strike was the right and only tactic in the face of the company's intransigence. Dionysis and my grandmother held that the workers might have the moral upper hand, but taking this course of action would drive the company out. Striking might be the right thing to do, but was it the smart thing to do?

I sat listening in a half-haze and Sophie was painting her nails. Occasionally the phone would ring for Fioroula, but she kept telling her husband she was not going back. When three hours had passed without any more phone calls, we thought he'd finally given up. Until we heard the singing outside.

Stavros had arrived with Sophie's accordion-player, and two cousins with good voices to serenade his wife back home. We all looked out the window and saw him singing his earnest little heart out. But instead of a love song, he was belting out an old Dalaras number about a strike.

'What sort of a song is that to be singing when you want to woo a woman, Stavros?' laughed my grandmother, leaning out the window. 'You're under a balcony here, not at a protest march.'

'You can stay out there and sing all night, but I'm not coming back until you do the right thing, Stavros,' Fioroula said, loud and clear.

'Fioroula, be reasonable. What do you mean, the right thing? It's not that I don't support the workers. It's just that, well, once I win the election then I'll be in a position to do something about it. Let's concentrate on winning first, then I'll do whatever I can, I promise you.'

'That old social-democratic line. Let's concentrate on winning first, then we'll change the world. Who are you kidding?'

By now neighbours were coming out of their houses to see what all the commotion was about.

'She's got a point there, Stavros,' said Vasili, who had stopped playing. 'You socialists have won a lot of elections and we're not exactly living in socialism.'

'I thought I brought you along for support,' Stavros said, annoyed.

'I do support you, but your wife's right.'

'Anyone else want to have a go at me? Seems I can't do anything right.' Stavros ran his fingers through his hair in exasperation.

'What do you want from us now, sympathy? We're not giving any, so go home and get it from your mother.' Fioroula slammed the window shut.

'Fioroula,' he pleaded to the house, and the accordion struck up another tune.

'For God's sake, shut up,' he said to Vasili.

Inside the house, Fioroula was being pressured to let him in.

'He can't be expected to stand out there all night,' said Dionysis, taking the man's side. 'At least let him in and you can talk in here. The whole village is there by now.'

'Good. Let everybody know where Fioroula Andreola stands on this issue. I will not shame my family and betray my conscience and my class. If Stavros wants to do so, he can live with the consequences.'

Dionysis and my grandmother thought she was judging her husband unfairly.

'Well, I for one haven't heard him say anything against the workers,' my grandmother said, but this failed to shift Fioroula.

'Yes, I'm aware that he's been a very effective fence-sitter. Am I supposed to be impressed?'

It was Sophie's intervention that finally persuaded Fioroula to let Stavros in. She could see Vasili outside, rubbing his hands together trying to keep warm, and announced she'd had enough of this nonsense and wasn't going to let him freeze to death.

In they all marched, greeting us furtively with downcast glances. Stavros' cousins were handsome, beefy village boys with good manners. They politely accepted Dionysis' offer of a brandy, while being ever so mindful of the delicacy of their situation. Sophie was all over Vasili, causing my grandmother to shoot her some disapproving glances and motioning to her to behave herself. Stavros and Fioroula made up. They disappeared into the bedroom, and in less than an hour they returned reconciled. I don't know what agreement was reached, but Stavros promised to make a public announcement of support the following night, at a fundraiser for the striking workers.

During my exile from the social life of Zakynthos, I became restless. I had been in limbo for a long time, living each day with nothing much to do. Initially it was a relief to be free of the pressure and constant rush of work. I needed a big rest and I'd had it. Now I was conscious of the fact that everyone around me had a routine of sorts, a rhythm and purpose to their day, and I began to feel at a loose end. I'd left Australia with no definite plans, open to all possibilities. It was time to consider those possibilities.

I started to think about going home. I was missing it. I was missing people who knew me well, with whom I didn't have to make an effort. I was missing the familiarity and predictability of my old life. There was a safety in it that I'd taken for granted. But as soon as the problem of what I was going to do about work entered my mind, I pushed it away, and every time the notion of staying in Greece presented itself, this was the obstacle. I liked the idea of living in Greece, but actually making the move seemed like a huge step that I wasn't prepared to take. I didn't want to just throw myself into the complete unknown; I needed to plan and think and organise, and I needed to do this from my home base. If I seriously wanted to live in Greece and do it properly, I knew I would have to go home first.

With this thought in mind I rang Australia to check out the lie of the land. I went into town and rang Jane first and a recorded message told me the number had been disconnected. Next I rang Nick. He sounded groggy. I checked my watch – it was eight in the morning in Melbourne. I imagined him sitting on his bar stool in his trendy kitchen – painted bright yellow and purple, a combination that actually worked – having breakfast and reading the paper.

'It's Saturday,' he said. I apologised and offered to call back later.

'I'm awake now,' he yawned. 'How are you, lovey?'

I gave him a rundown of my misadventure and he made sympathetic noises.

'Poor thing. Go to Athens and throw yourself into a wild affair. The villages are the pits, if you ask me. And make sure he's not a Pontian.' Nick told me that Jane had moved house and was living on her own, that he was still at the centre and that Victoria had replaced me. So much for keeping my job open. Nick detected my disappointment.

'Well, no-one's heard from you. Besides, you don't want the job.' He told me to keep my perspective, take it easy, and reminded me I was on holiday. 'When *are* you coming back, by the way?'

I told him I didn't know. That I was putting it off, but feeling bored with nothing to do.

'I think I might come back and work towards moving here for good,' I said.

'That's what you said last time.' There was a pause. 'Lovey, try and have some fun and you can think about it all when you return. You'll be back here in no time, kicking yourself that you spent all this time in Zakynthos moping. You have nothing to be ashamed of. You did nothing wrong. Go out and have a good time!'

I left the post office feeling better. The sun was out, the sea was calm and there was little wind. It was cold and sunny. My favourite Zakynthian day. Nick was right. I was going to walk down the street, hold my head up high and look people in the eye. Stuff them. I wasn't a murderer, for Christ's sake. I straightened my posture, turned the corner to enter Piazza San Marco, and ran straight into Bruce.

He was sitting on a bench with his legs stretched out in front of him and his face slightly raised towards the sky, as if sunbathing.

'Bruce!' I gasped, without thinking. Avoiding him might have been an option, but this wasn't St Kilda, this was Zakynthos. This was my place. What was he doing lounging there, his body casting a shadow across the square? His presence required an explanation.

He turned lazily towards me and pulled his sunglasses to the edge of his nose, as if to see me more clearly. 'Fiore,' he said. 'I thought it might be you.'

'What are you doing here?' I demanded.

'I, ah . . .' He searched for the right words. 'What a way to greet an old friend,' he said with mock offence.

I tried again. 'Aren't you supposed to be in Prague?'

'That's finished. We're playing in Athens next week and, ah, we're having a break. Looks like we might do a gig. Something to do with a strike or something.'

The Sub Urbans were playing at the fundraiser? It was inconceivable. Who had organised such a thing? Before I could ask, he told me.

'Yeah, Bettina reckons we should do it. Hard woman to say no to,' he chuckled, shaking his head as if recalling a private joke.

'Bettina's here?' I asked. Typical of my sister not to let anyone know she was coming.

'We arrived on the boat this arvo.'

There was silence between us and that old awkward feeling returned.

'Right,' I said after all this had registered with me. Not

interested in exchanging any more pleasantries with him, I tightened the scarf around my neck and said goodbye.

'Fiore,' he said. 'Hang on.' A look of minor discomfort came over his face. 'No hard feelings, mate.'

Was he asking me or telling me? In any case, he was months too late and I was beyond caring.

Back at the barn in Skoulikado, I found Elendina in bed. It was after six in the evening, or what the Greeks call afternoon. I let her sleep. She'd been up all night making costumes for people for the last event of the Carnivale. I got on the phone, searching for Bettina. Sophie wasn't home. I woke her aunt, who said she hadn't seen her in two days and thought she was at our house. She sounded cranky. I hung up and made no more calls. This wasn't a good time to ring people. They might be sleeping.

I decided to lie down. I picked a book off the shelf, a translation of a French writer I didn't know, read three pages and fell asleep. It was a deep sleep and I could have slept all night, except I began to hear movement around me: doors shutting, people talking, lights going on and off. I forced myself to wake up. The room was in darkness. I stumbled out of bed, out into the cold and into the bright light of the kitchen. A cheer went up.

'You're awake,' said Elendina, who was dressed in white velvet with a high white wig on. She was Marie Antoinette. So was Sophie, except she was in blue. Dionysis was Louis the XVI, or perhaps the Scarlet Pimpernel. Whatever, they were

218

both on the same side during that revolution. I sat down in awe. The costumes were exquisite. Elendrina had done a marvellous job.

'You look superb,' I said breathlessly, looking from one to the other. 'How come you're dressed already?'

'Fiore, it's nearly ten o'clock. You've been asleep for hours,' Elendina said.

'Are you leaving soon?' I asked them.

'In about twenty minutes.' Elendina said this without conviction, meaning it could be forty minutes.

'Can you wait for me? I've decided I want to come.'

'Yeah?' My sister was full of curiosity. 'You sure?'

I nodded and stretched into a yawn. 'I'm sick of hiding.'

'Good on you,' Sophie said. 'Now, get off your arse and move it.'

I asked Dionysis to make me a coffee while I shuffled off to the back of the house where the various costumes were hung. Then I remembered Bettina and returned to the kitchen.

'Bettina's here!' I announced to them all.

But they already knew. She had called Elendina that afternoon when I was out, and Sophie had seen her in town.

'She'll be at the fundraiser tonight,' Sophie said. 'I think she went to see your grandmother.'

I expected more enthusiasm from them, particularly Elendina. This would be the first time in ages that all three of us were together and I looked forward to it with the excitement of a child at Christmas.

I took out some costumes. I was looking at the mermaid and wondering if I could get away with such a brazen outfit when I heard a tap on the door. Then a man's voice. In the doorway stood the Devil, holding a cup of coffee. I let out a scream.

'I didn't realise it was so effective,' Mihalis said.

'Oh, it's you,' I said, feeling vaguely foolish. I took the coffee and gave him the dress. He was in black leotards and leggings and had red horns, a pike and a big red cape. His face was painted beyond recognition. Once I'd had a good look, I laughed. He held up the mermaid costume, looked at me, then back at the costume.

'Hmm,' he said. 'You want to make some waves?'

I wasn't sure, but now that he mentioned it, why not? I had a few points to score. Bruce would be there and I wanted to look as fabulous as possible to spite him. Furthermore, this was my first public appearance since my fall from grace in Zakynthian society and my comeback was not going to be humble. But I must have still looked doubtful.

'Come on, wear it,' Mihalis said. 'Let me tempt you. After all, I'm the guy who invented temptation that only saints have been able to withstand. And you, my lady, are no saint.'

I decided to wear it.

Mihalis sat cross-legged on the floor and pulled some gear out to roll a joint. 'By the way,' he said changing the subject, 'I have news. I'm leaving for Athens. A teaching position has become available.'

This *was* news. 'I had no idea you were planning such a thing.'

'Well, how would you know? It hasn't been in the newspapers and it's not as if we've had much of an opportunity to talk about what's new.' He paused. 'It's time to get out of Zakynthos. Besides, my brother-in-law has moved there for various reasons and I want to be near my nephews. I've been thinking about it for a while.'

'I'm leaving too,' I said. I delivered this as the thought came to my mind. My phone conversation with Nick had convinced me it was time to move on. 'In a few days, a week at the most.'

'It couldn't be before then,' Mihalis pointed out. 'A lot of people have come to vote, and for Carnivale, so you'd be hard pressed getting a ticket on Monday or Tuesday.'

I finished the coffee and he finished rolling the joint. He took a drag, observing me through squinting eyes. 'I've hardly seen you this time around,' he said, passing me the joint. 'Each time you come, I see less and less of you, thanks to your shenanigans with various *malakes*. Last time it was Panayoti, this time the Pontian.'

I heaved a sigh. 'Mihalis, thanks for reminding me just when I was beginning to feel better.'

'You need reminding. What's the matter with you anyway? You don't seem the type of woman who wants to be a victim, who keeps falling for bastards.' His voice had grown serious.

And you included, I felt like saying. Instead I put on a

formal voice, as if quoting from a psychology textbook. 'I think there's a soft, sensitive layer underneath their tough veneer that only I am going to be able to bring out, and hopefully I'll reform them.'

'Sounds like quite a job. Don't you help enough people in your work without devoting your love life to it as well?'

'We all want to be Eva Marie Saint to a Marlon Brando.'

He frowned momentarily, perplexed at my reference, then nodded in comprehension. 'Hollywood's got a lot to answer for. Romanticising inarticulate social outcasts, making them desirable to an otherwise sensible woman like yourself.'

I shrugged. 'Our desires don't develop in a vacuum. Now, could you leave me for a minute so I can get changed?'

I put on the mermaid outfit and came into the kitchen, where everyone was waiting impatiently for me. Dionysis and Mihalis whistled in unison. I threw on my coat to howls of disappointment.

'Now you've ruined it completely,' Mihalis said. 'What's the point of wearing it if you're going to cover it up with a coat?'

'Don't worry,' Elendina said to Mihalis. 'I'll make sure she takes it off when we get there.'

The fundraiser was held in a hall of a village I'd never been to. The place was packed when we arrived. I scanned the room for Bettina, and eventually spotted her in ancient Greek dress, but she could have easily passed for the Statue of

Liberty. She was surrounded by people. Pavlos the redhead was patting her on the back and the union organiser from Patras was standing beside her with his hands in his pockets, smiling at her.

'The best Foskolos girl,' I heard Pavlos say in a loud voice. Elendina rushed forward and fell into her embrace. They hadn't seen each other in months.

Right next to Bettina stood Bruce, who was surrounded by what looked like the Zakynthos chapter of the Sub Urbans fan club. About twenty student-looking types were attempting to communicate with him in faltering English. Some of the fans had turned their attention to Bettina. She was the cool local girl who had brought Bruce Stewart to Zakynthos. Legends are made of such things. I had not gone forward to greet them, I was frozen where I stood. For Bruce was not simply standing next to Bettina, he was holding her hand and his fingers were intertwined with hers. They were an item.

I fled to the toilet. I thought I was going to be sick. The bastard. So this was what he'd meant by 'no hard feelings'. It wasn't 'no hard feelings that I stuffed you around and I was a bit of an arsehole'. It was 'no hard feelings I'm screwing your sister'. He obviously hadn't had the guts to tell Bettina about me and he didn't have the guts to tell me about her. I took deep breaths and told myself to calm down. My thoughts went to my poor sister. How was I going to tell her that he was not only a worthless coward, but one who had screwed me first? This required tact. Thoughts were ticking over in my brain with phenomenal speed and came to a screeching halt when the image of Bruce's fingers intertwined with Bettina's flashed before my eyes. There was more affection in that gesture than I'd felt in all my encounters with him. It occurred to me that there might be something serious between them. Just because he was a cad with me, it didn't mean he was a universal cad. Perhaps he had changed. It was possible. If that was the case and this was the beginning of something big, it wouldn't be right for me to throw a spanner in the works. The first thing to do was find Elendina and instruct her to say nothing.

I was unlocking the toilet door when I heard Bettina calling my name. I came out of the cubicle to find her in front of me.

'Fiore. What are you doing?'

'Nothing, nothing, I just felt a bit sick,' I said, trying to appear normal.

'Are you upset?' She looked at me.

'No, why should I be upset?' I turned my back to her, looking in the mirror to check my face.

'About me and Bruce.'

She knew!

'You're not upset about it, are you? He told me it was nothing between the two of you.'

Words failed me. These things happen, I told myself, but twice? Weren't there enough men in the world for her? Was that why it was necessary for her to take up with my old flames? And just to rub salt in the wound, they were old flames who'd rejected me. I began to cry. They were tears of rage. I imagined the two of them in their intimate moments, making a joke at my expense. Why did she want to hurt me so much? Had I been such an ogre of a sister? I tossed the issue this way and that, struggling to find evidence of my evil. No, it wasn't there. A grave injustice had been done to me, and it wasn't the first time. I dredged up everything else Bettina had done in the past, the major hurts and the minor ones, and I let her have it.

'Fiore,' she interrupted, not knowing she was better off saying nothing. 'You're feeling shit at the moment because of all this business with Alex, but don't take it out on me.'

I fronted her and she took a step back. 'This has nothing to do with Alex,' I said loudly, poking my finger into her chest. 'This has everything to do with your penchant for sticking the boot into me.'

'What are you talking about?' Bettina was keeping her voice even. 'If you think I did this on purpose to get at you, you're crazy. This has nothing to do with you.'

'Of course it has something to do with me. Don't insult me,' I yelled.

'Calm down and –'

'I will *not* calm down.' But what if she was telling the truth? Perhaps she hadn't set out to get at me, but that made it even worse. Could anyone be that insensitive? 'Didn't you stop to think that it might not be appropriate?' I went on.

'That I might mind? I would. I *do*. The last thing I'd want to do is get involved with one of your exes, let alone bring him to Zakynthos to flaunt him in your face! Things don't just happen in life, Bettina. We can set limits. You think life is one big party and hang the consequences. Well, we all have to live with ourselves when the party's over.'

'Are you in love with Bruce or something?'

'No, I'm not,' I snapped. 'This is not about Bruce. This is about you and me.'

'Why are you so angry?'

'Because. First Mihalis, then Bruce.'

'Mihalis?' she cut me off. 'There was never anything between Mihalis and you.'

No, there wasn't, and she'd made sure there never would be. Mihalis was always an incomplete sentence for me. I'd once liked to imagine how things could have been, but Bettina had finished the sentence in a way that had never figured in my daydreams. Back then I'd convinced myself that she'd done me a favour, but the truth was, I was still angry and jealous.

I gave my sister a slap that had been years in the making and she reeled backward, falling against the wall. I ran out of the toilet as fast as my costume would allow me, away from the party, and tried to find my way through the village. I looked back once when I heard someone calling me. The Devil was after me but he couldn't see me. He was looking in the wrong direction and I didn't correct him. My heart was

226

racing. I looked at my hand as if it were a stranger's. It was the first time I had ever hit one of my sisters. It was the first time I had ever hit anyone and I felt good and bad. There had been a few situations in my life when I'd thought I should have hit someone and regretted I hadn't.

I was well away when I stopped to get my bearings. I wanted to walk into town but wasn't sure how far it was. I was in no hurry to reach any destination or speak to anyone. I couldn't recall another time in my life when so many things had converged to make me feel so miserable. I walked and walked in the darkness, close to the road so that I wouldn't get lost. I had taken off my shoes and ripped the seam of my costume from the knees down. The signposts weren't visible, and when it started to rain I began to wonder if I was heading in the right direction.

A car drove past and slowed down, and then I heard my name. I didn't recognise the voice.

'It's me, Dimitri,' a man called through his rolled-down window.

I didn't know any Dimitri. I moved closer to the car to get a better look.

'We met in the Captain's shop,' he said, and I saw it was the priest.

'Oh, hello,' I said distractedly. 'Is this the right way to town?'

'No, it's the way to Lithakia.' He looked at me, full of curiosity. I must have been a sight in my torn costume and no

227

shoes. 'It's a long walk to town from here,' he went on, 'and you're drenched. Get in the car, I'll give you a lift.'

Despite my anti-social mood, I did as he said; I was cold, wet, tired and lost. He asked me where I wanted to go. I didn't want to go to Elendina's because my sisters would come looking for me and I couldn't face another confrontation. I didn't want to have to explain my behaviour to anyone. Not just yet.

'We're a minute from my house,' Dimitri said when I hesitated. 'Come and have a brandy with me. I definitely need one. I've just been called out to perform the last rites to a dying man, someone I didn't have a lot of time for while he was alive. It's one of the downsides of the job.' When he saw that I needed more convincing he said, 'Come on. Actually, I wanted to see you again to ask about your father. I didn't know who you were that day I saw you in the Captain's shop.'

'You know my father?'

'I knew him more than he knew me, let's put it that way. He's nearly ten years older than me but I used to hang around him all the time, the way kids do.'

My father had never had much time for priests. According to him, they were reactionaries who had supported the military junta in the sixties and early seventies, and they'd opposed nearly everything the socialists stood for. He had successfully passed his wariness of the clergy down to his children. Still, the offer of a warm room and a brandy was tempting.

Dimitri's wife and children were asleep, so he directed me to a formal sitting room where we wouldn't disturb them. We had two brandies before he put some music on I hadn't heard before. Soft, ethereal and with a low, mournful voice.

'Layos,' he said. 'Do you know him?' I shook my head.

'A great Zakynthian who left us too early.'

Father Dimitri was a good-looking man. He had golden hair and a matching beard with flecks of red in it, red cheeks on alabaster skin, and dark brown eyes. I learnt that he was an outspoken defender of natural habitats and he lobbied vigorously for better planning and conservation laws to limit the development frenzy. He was often a lone voice in this area and one that was considered eccentric.

He put some more wood in the stove and began telling me stories of my father's exploits in the village as a young man, some of which I already knew. But others were completely new to me, including one about a motorbike ride where the brakes failed and the whole village watched as my father tried to save his own life. Funny how parents are reluctant to reveal the risk-taking activities of their youth to their children.

'He was a big loss to the village,' Father Dimitri sighed. 'Too many good people left in those years following the war. Too many.' He shook his head.

'My father thinks it's amazing that so many people are coming here now for the same reasons he left to go to Australia.'

He nodded. 'So do you still think we're a bunch of rednecks?' he joked, referring to the encounter in the Captain's shop.

'No, not all of you. But I feel for the Albanians. I relate to them. They have it hard enough as it is, without all the racist attitudes. But things will change. It's inevitable that immigrants will influence and alter a place.'

'In the meantime they need our support.'

'Yes,' I said. 'But soon enough they'll be doing it themselves. Getting assertive and demanding their rights.'

I was enjoying this exchange. It was one of those interactions in a time of emotional turmoil that carries you away somewhere for a while and makes you forget about your problems. When you return you might be looking at yourself with a different eye. It's happened to me before with taxi drivers, in those hours between night and morning. For some reason you come away from them feeling not quite as dark as you did. This time it was a priest, an Orthodox priest at that. I'd read about progressive priests in South America, in South Africa, even in Australia. But not Greek priests.

I recalled Nick telling me once about a priest he'd seen in Melbourne. He had gone at the insistence of his parents, who thought the priest might be able to talk Nick out of being gay. They'd met for lunch and had an interesting intellectual discussion. At one point the priest said something about Greek culture being the foundation of Western civilisation. Nick asked the priest if he thought Western civilisation was anything to be proud of, at which point the priest gave him his phone number and told him to call him any time.

'Imagine if I got together with him,' Nick said. 'Now, that might make my parents happy.'

I told Father Dimitri the story and he laughed heartily.

When the sky was lightening I knew I would have to start moving, but I didn't know where to go. I didn't want to face my sisters, the rock stars, my grandmother, my cousins, anyone. I really wanted to be alone, but there was nowhere for me to be alone in Zakynthos. I longed for the anonymity of my house in Melbourne, where I could get into the bath, have a decent cup of tea, put the answering machine on and shut out the world – and my family in particular.

Father Dimitri was dropping hints at the lateness of the hour. He had a service that morning and a baptism before lunch.

I want to stay here, was what I wanted to say, but I felt too embarrassed to suggest it. 'Take me to a hotel,' I said finally. 'In town.'

He dropped me off at a hotel that had seen better days. 'If the door's locked, ring the bell,' he said, looking at his watch. 'The porter often falls asleep at the desk. Who can blame him at this hour?'

I got out of the car and went around to the driver's side. I wanted to thank him for a lovely night, to tell him how awful I'd been feeling before he came along. I put my hand out to shake his and he took it and put his other hand over the top of it, smiling at me.

'I don't know what happened tonight and why you were walking into town in that state. I don't meant to be nosy, but I heard about that business with you and the strikebreaker

231

and it will be all right. It will pass. I'm glad we had a chance to get to know each other.'

'Me too,' I said warmly. 'Thanks for everything. I'll tell my dad I saw you.'

He raised a clenched fist in solidarity with my troubles and then, after doing one of the worst U-turns I've ever seen, drove the wrong way down a one-way street and out of my view.

I hadn't known there were such priests in the world. Zakynthos surprises you.

# CHAPTER THIRTEEN

I woke up in my hotel room to someone knocking at the door. I looked at the clock – it was after seven at night. I had slept for almost thirteen hours. I had missed the whole day. The Carnivale was finished, the election was over and I'd slept through it all.

The knocking developed a voice. Someone was calling my name. Out of the haze of sleep, I recognised Mihalis. I dragged myself out of bed and opened the door. He was all dressed up in a suit but he didn't look too pleased.

'I've spent half the night looking for you, thinking you'd fallen into some ditch and broken your head.'

I crawled back into bed and pulled the covers over myself.

'Fuck it, Fiore. If you wanted to leave, why didn't you tell me? You just disappear without a word to anyone.'

I pulled the covers away and sat up. 'Jesus, what happened to putting a call through to the room before letting someone in?'

'What do you think this is, the Ritz?' He sat on the edge of the bed and looked serious. I wasn't in the mood for a drawn-out explanation of what had happened, but I didn't want Mihalis in a bad mood with me. I had enough enemies at the moment.

'I'm sorry, Mihalis. I didn't stop to think you might have been worried. I got into a fight with Bettina and I just ran away. I was too upset to stay there with all those people. Everyone was having such a good time . . .'

'What upset you so much?'

I sighed. 'It's a long story.'

'Well, get moving and tell me.'

It seemed I had no choice. 'That guy Bruce,' I said slowly.

'The singer?'

'We saw each other in Australia for a little while. He treated me fairly shabbily. He'd come over and have sex and then I wouldn't hear from him; he didn't return my calls, he stood me up, then he'd reappear making excuses. It's my fault. I should have just told him to fuck off, but I didn't. Now he's over here and involved with Bettina. It's the last thing I expected.'

'Were you in love with him?' There was concern in his voice.

'No. Just desperate.'

'Oh, Saint Dionysis,' Mihalis chuckled, looking at me in disbelief. 'What are the really desperate ones supposed to do?'

I went through the whole story for him, censoring my

anger at Bettina and putting the blame on Bruce. I was ashamed of my sister's behaviour and I didn't want Mihalis to know. It was private stuff. I called Bruce an unethical pig. Someone I was quite happy to avoid but whose presence in Zakynthos on my sister's arm made that a tad difficult.

Mihalis took it all in. Finally he asked me the obvious question. 'Does your sister know?'

I was evasive. 'Know what?'

'That you were involved with him. That he's an unethical pig,' he said, quoting me.

I said no, maybe, I didn't know.

Mihalis tapped his foot on the floor. He knew what was going on.

'All right, yes, she knows,' I conceded at last. 'I'm angry at her too, and not just for this. For everything. Including you. Yes, that's right. Did she *have* to sleep with the man I fell in love with? And did you have to with her? Why are you looking at me like that? As if you didn't know how I felt about you.' I heard my voice as if from far away. It was loud and accusing. 'Anyway, I don't care any more,' I asserted calmly, wanting this to be the case. 'It's just that this episode's brought it all back.'

The minute I stopped speaking I was surprised by my outburst and regretted it immediately. Why should he care about any of this? There had never been anything between us except desire; it was unreasonable for me to carry on like a betrayed lover.

'Look, forget it,' I added before he could respond. 'You didn't owe me anything. I have no right to be angry. Don't pay any attention to me.'

Mihalis gave me a searching look. 'Which is it to be, Fiore? Do you care or not? Are you angry or not?' He looked confused. It was a good time to go to the toilet.

I caught a glimpse of myself in the bathroom mirror and saw to my horror that my hair was stuck up on one side and my makeup was smudged all over my face. I looked hilarious. A fine state to be in while pouring out my innermost feelings. I looked wasted and realised I hadn't eaten since lunchtime Saturday. It was now Sunday night. For the first time since I'd set foot in this country I was hungry.

I took a deep breath and began to wash my face. When I sensed the floor beneath me move I thought I was feeling faint, but the floor was actually moving. I had felt tremors in Zakynthos before, but this was stronger and it wasn't stopping. An earthquake! I ran screaming out of the bathroom into Mihalis' arms. Without releasing me, he walked me to the door, opened it, and we stood in the doorway until it was over.

'Fuck,' I said at last, still trembling.

Mihalis breathed a sigh of relief. 'Thank God it was just a small one.' He looked down at me. 'So it takes an earthquake for you to come into my arms?'

Slowly I moved out of his embrace, more uncertain than ever. 'If that was a small quake, I'd hate to experience a large one. Is it over?'

'Who knows?' He shrugged. 'Sometimes the second one can be more powerful than the first.'

'Jesus, I'm surprised you're not all nervous wrecks.'

'Who says we're not?' He stroked my hair. 'Do you want to sit down?'

I shook my head.

'Fiore, about what you were saying before, it's not a matter of having the right to be angry. Emotions aren't rational.'

'No, but I don't like being irrational.'

'Like it or dislike it, that's how we are. Don't fight it all the time. Come on.' He put his arm around my shoulders. 'Let's get something to eat.'

We stopped at Sophie's aunt's to fetch some clothes for me to wear, keeping explanations to a minimum, then set off to a tavern of Mihalis' choosing in Kiliomeno. The aromas from the kitchen brought back my appetite, and after I'd eaten to my heart's content the gods brought back the earthquake. This time I just managed to get myself off my seat when it stopped. In those ten seconds I noticed everyone halt in an expectant pose before going back to normal. I wondered at the way these people coped with it all.

'They don't happen all the time,' Mihalis assured me. 'Last year we didn't have any.' He poured some wine and filled me in on what I had missed at the fundraiser. A lot of money had been raised. The band was a success, but Bruce had drunk a lot and was unable to stand by the end of the night. He had to be carried to the car. I asked whether the scabs had surfaced again and learnt that Pavlos had sought the help of the local Albanians in Zakynthos. He asked them to approach some of the strike-breakers and get a feel for what was going on. They discovered that none of the unfortunates brought over from Athens had known they were coming to break a strike. Some of them wanted to go back to Athens but had no money and were frightened of recriminations from the company and its henchmen. The union had come up with some money to enable a few of them to return.

'That's a good tactic,' I said. The political landscape was not as bleak as I thought. 'Shows a lot of forward thinking.'

'Ah well.' Mihalis sat back in his chair. 'The Communist Party legacy isn't all bad. The old "workers of the world unite" philosophy still holds sway with a few diehards. Pavlos is a decent man but not everyone thinks like him. He's worried it might get ugly, that some idiots might want to take it out on the local Albanians, just because they're in the mood for a fight.'

The tavern began to fill up. Two teenage students of Mihalis' arrived with an older man. The teenagers looked delighted to see him and began talking excitedly about the concert the night before.

'The Sub Urbans in Zakynthos! It's surreal,' one of them said.

Surreal indeed.

'And that dude Bruce Stewart, too cool,' the other put in. 'We hear he has a preference for Zakynthian girls.'

'Yeah, he's going out with one of the Foskolos sisters. She's a nice-looking woman,' said the first.

They chatted on about other things, then made their way to their table.

'They like you a lot,' I said when they'd gone.

Mihalis smiled and said he couldn't really tell sometimes whether his students genuinely liked him or were just being polite.

'No, they think a lot of you, it's obvious,' I reiterated. 'Do you like your job?'

'It's a job. You know, some days are good, some days are bad. Sometimes I'm inspired, sometimes I'm bored. It's a job.' He shrugged.

A group of old men sat down at the adjacent table. 'Kiliomeniates,' Mihalis said. 'They have the look of mountain men.'

A few drinks later, a guitar appeared and the men began to sing a song about leaving your hair loose so that it blows in the wild wind. Their soft voices tentatively filled the room. Another group came in, including Dionysis with a couple whom Mihalis knew. Dionysis raised his eyebrows at the sight of me but Mihalis asked them to join us. Elendina was still recovering from the night before. The woman in Dionysis' group was called Danae and I liked her immediately. She was a lawyer and her story was very familiar to me.

I told her I worked in a community legal centre and she was intrigued. 'I know it sounds impressive,' I said, 'but the practice doesn't match the rhetoric. We're grossly under-funded and we can't provide the service we should.'

'If I lived in a big city,' Danae said, 'that's the work I'd like to do, but in a place like this you're very limited. Still, you can't have everything in life. You make choices and do the best you can.' She told me her husband wanted to live in Zakynthos in order to raise a family. 'I think it's great,' she said, 'that you chose to work in this area of law.'

Everyone murmured in agreement.

'I don't know to what extent I made the choice,' I said, describing how I'd more or less fallen into it.

Danae wasn't convinced. 'You didn't choose to represent rich people,' she said. 'And you have more choice than most people. You're educated.'

A discussion on the pros and cons of the adversarial legal system ensued. In Greece, when questioned about law and politics, I am often reminded of Australia's similarities to England. Greeks have a strong impression that Australia is a hot England with unusual animals. Dionysis began to express his antipathy for English systems and English culture, and somehow we arrived at the topic of the offerings of ancient Greek civilisation to the rest of the world. These discussions always centred on the superiority of that civilisation, a position Dionysis took wholeheartedly.

'I don't know what use it is to constantly assert the superi-ority of one culture over another, or one cultural heritage over another,' I said to him.

'There's no need to assert it. It's a fact,' Dionysis replied grandly.

'It's that "fact" that gave Europeans the justification to oppress and kill indigenous people in the countries they colonised.' I said. 'It was that assumption that led to many of the terrible things that happened to the Aborigines in Australia –'

He cut me off. 'Who cares about the Aborigines? In the scheme of things, what have they offered the world?'

Danae and Mihalis told him to shut up and stop being a racial chauvinist.

'I don't understand what brand of left you identify with if you really think like that,' I said.

'It's the KKE way of thinking,' Mihalis explained, referring to the Moscow-aligned Greek Communist Party. 'They didn't think left, they just wore red.' I was beginning to see Mihalis' political disillusionment in a different light.

'This isn't an issue of left versus right,' Dionysis persisted. 'It's about the progress of mankind.' This was Dionysis as I remembered him. No other opinion mattered but his, and he delivered it with pomp and ceremony. 'Some cultures are more advanced than others and it's inevitable that the primitive ones will be overrun. If you haven't advanced beyond the spear, you don't stand much chance of survival against civilisations that are in the industrial age.'

Again he was howled down by Mihalis, Danae and her husband, who up until this point had remained silent. 'Your tacit acceptance of the notion of progress is a political issue in itself,' the latter said, and I was relieved. I had been struggling with my Greek to say just that.

But Dionysis would not be moved. 'The thing is, we're unique, we Greeks,' he said, with an arrogance so staggering it was comical. 'We enlightened the world. Everything that followed – all those great cultural, artistic and intellectual movements of the West – it's all down to us.'

'Who's we Greeks, Dionysis?' I asked. 'What connection do we have with the ancient Greeks to claim such lineage? With four hundred years of Turkish rule, we are ethnically and culturally a mix of so many people. How can we claim continuity?'

He looked at me aghast. 'What is this nonsense! Of course we can claim that lineage. We are Greeks living on the land of our ancestors, who were the ancient Greeks. That's who were here. Not the Babylonians, not the Persians or the Aborigines.'

Danae too looked at me with concern. 'We may have had other influences over time,' she argued, 'but of course we are descendants of the ancient Greeks. You can see it clearly in our folklore, in our language. We speak Greek, and modern Greek is a derivative of ancient Greek. And many cultural practices have their roots in ancient times.'

Dionysis was deeply offended and had more to say on the topic, casting doubt over my education on matters historical. I thought it better not say any more because we were headed for another blue, and since he was practically my brother-in-law it didn't seem like a wise thing to do. There was an uncomfortable silence at the table until another set of patrons arrived, bringing news of the election. A big cheer went up when it was announced that Stavros had won. Everyone started to talk at once. People were congratulating me on account of him being married to my cousin. A carafe of wine was delivered to every table by the proprietors in honour of the victor. Stavros was from Kiliomeno, the local boy made good. The singing at our neighbouring table resumed at a more boisterous level, with some of us joining in. Dionysis' booming voice took over 'Sleep Entangled You'. He sang completely off key but with a lot of gusto. Late into the night, when the mountain men looked like they had exhausted their repertoire, I asked Mihalis to sing. He refused, despite my pleas, saying he didn't really sing any more.

Sitting with Mihalis in the company of others, with songs going on around us, threw me back to the time I first met him and the feelings he'd stirred in me. Feelings that made no sense, that I had difficulty explaining and which therefore annoyed me. Here was a man I only saw on and off, with whom I didn't really have a past and with whom there was no conceivable future. I wanted to regard him as a friend. Oh yes, I could easily have imagined him as a lover, but I fought it; there was too much risk involved. It was all right for Mihalis to say I shouldn't fight my irrationality, but I had to be rational about this.

'So how long are you staying?' Danae asked, forcing me to take my eyes off Mihalis. 'I would very much like to see you again.'

'I'm leaving soon,' I said. 'As soon as I can get a ticket.' I'd had enough of drifting, I'd decided. My lack of direction was getting on my nerves. Until some direction came to me, I could at least fill my days usefully.

'I'm sorry to hear that. If you can manage to come over one night before you go, I'd like that very much.'

I was touched. Obviously I hadn't been completely written off by all the islanders.

On leaving the tavern we saw utility trucks with hand-drawn signs and people hanging out windows, waving flags, singing, shouting and cheering. Stavros' victory had brought on one hell of a party. I was feeling better. I had had a good night in good company. The world was not as bad as I thought.

Mihalis suggested we drive to Bohali to take in the view. We sat in the car with the windows wound down while he smoked a cigarette.

'I had a really good time tonight, Mihalis,' I told him. 'Thanks for taking me out. You're a good friend.'

He found this amusing. 'A good friend? What is this with you and friends? Do you eat all your friends with your eyes the way you were eating me tonight? And are these the same friends you sleep with without having sex? The friends who give you sympathy when what you need is a kick up the arse?'

I just shook my head and smiled at him.

'So,' he said, looking at me cheekily, 'do I have to forget everything you said in your outburst in the hotel? Even the bit about you falling in love with me?'

'What do you want from me now, Mihalis? Compliments? It was a long time ago. I thought you were pretty hot. I was in awe of you, but I didn't really know you. It happens when you're young and naive.'

'And now you're old and bitter?' He chuckled.

'No, but there were things I couldn't see. Your womanising, for example.'

'Fiore, that's enough of that. We're either talking seriously or we're playing games.'

'Well, it's true.'

I felt his hand grip my arm. 'Stop that nonsense.' His voice was firm. 'Because I slept with Bettina one night does not mean that I sleep with women indiscriminately. And who are you to take this holier-than-thou position?'

'Don't take it personally,' I said matter-of-factly.

He grew flustered. 'You're talking about me, how else should I take it?'

'Because it's not just you. A lot of the men are like that here. They chase women.'

'A lot of us here? What do you mean? Don't men chase women in Australia?'

'Not the way they do here,' I said. I was beginning to hate these conversations.

'So it's our method you disapprove of?'

'No,' I said, feeling frustrated that he didn't take my meaning. 'It's the tourism thing. It's a way of life for you every summer. I'm sure you don't think there's anything

245

wrong with it; it's the way Zakynthos has changed. It's all, Let's make heaps of money and let's chase women. Look at my cousin Achilleas, he's married with children and every summer he's still on the prowl for any English or German girl looking for a good time. He wasn't like that when I first met him.'

Mihalis laughed again and said I didn't know what I was talking about; that Achilleas had been like that his whole life, and that maybe the other qualities I'd seen in him had dissipated, or weren't there in the first place. 'You really think I'm a womaniser like your cousin?' he asked.

'Another version of the same thing,' I joked, but I knew it was the wrong thing to say as soon as the words came out of my mouth. 'What I'm trying to say is that all that put me off. I . . .' I swallowed. 'I wanted something big with you and I was frightened because it wouldn't work out for so many reasons and I'd get hurt.' My heart was beating uncomfortably with the admission of my weakness, and I wanted some reassurance from him, some sympathy. Instead Mihalis unleashed a tirade of words that poured over me in the confines of his little car like an avalanche.

'Let me tell you something, Fiore, if I've got things you don't like, well, welcome to the real world. You want the fairy-tale? Go find it somewhere else. I'm not interested in fairytales.' He shook his head in disappointment. 'I never stopped thinking about you after I met you. I remember the Captain saying that the funny thing about you was you had the personality of a village girl but with an education. I liked that about you: it was a charming and disarming combination. The second time you came, you were walking around with your nose stuck in the air every time you saw me, as if I carried a foul stench around with me. You tell me you want to go to bed with me and then you kick me out. Then,' his voice went up a few decibels again, 'you tell Dionysis that the only reason I was upset was because I didn't get a fuck.' His voice caught. His face was red and his mouth tight.

I recoiled. His anger was real and I became afraid. He looked at me as if searching for something. I couldn't think of what to say and looked down at my feet.

Mihalis lit another cigarette and smoked it slowly. I wanted to touch him, to say sorry, but I was frightened of his reaction. He stubbed the cigarette out and put the key in the ignition. 'Maybe because I'm getting older, maybe because of my sister's death, maybe a combination of both, but I'm not interested in wasting my time on silly games any more. I think we've said enough,' he mumbled finally, poison in his voice.

We could hear the noise of the election revelry down below. Two people passed us on a scooter, yelling excitedly.

'Shut up, *malaka*,' one said to the other. 'We're disturbing the lovers.'

# CHAPTER FOURTEEN

Zakynthos was abnormally quiet the next morning, except for a strong wind. I went for a long walk, starting at the Piazza San Marco. I watched the wind sweep the torn posters and leaflets from one end of the piazza to the other. The streamers would catch on a ramp, then fall again with the lull. As I headed to the beach, several shopkeepers were opening up. A few taxi drivers gathered to talk about the election result and children argued about which game to play. It was cold and sunny, but the savage wind rendered walking difficult. I persisted – I had nothing else to do and I like Zakynthos when it's quiet and cold.

At the dock I stood and watched the ferry leaving. The Zakynthians who had come to vote were going back home, and that's where I would be heading in the next few days. The Ionian Sea would carry me away from here with the mess of my doings behind me, as it did each time I left. I did things in Zakynthos that didn't come home with me; things I could leave and not think about again. There were no signposts in Melbourne to remind me of them. It was easy, over time, to remember and imagine things differently; easy to put my own slant on events and change the narrative to suit myself. There was never anyone around to challenge me.

Mihalis was furious with me. I had assumed his attitude towards me was a playful one, that he never took me seriously. So I had done the same. I had dismissed his feelings four years ago because I refused to believe I had hurt him. But I was wrong. I could see that he'd been hurt by my words the previous night. My opinion mattered to him. People you don't care about can't hurt you in that way. I, who had been so protective of my own feelings, was always ready to ride roughshod over his. I felt bad, but what could I do about it now? I thought about the way we'd parted, and disillusionment consumed me. His anger had quickly subsided into a decisive indifference. No more silly games, he'd said. He didn't even look at me to say goodbye when he dropped me off at the hotel. He had come to end of his tether with me.

I watched the waves and the boat disappear into the distance and knew that I couldn't leave things like this. I would never be able to think of Zakynthos again without feeling the sting of Mihalis' words, and sorrow that anger had been the last thing between us. As I stepped over rubbish and cursed everyone for making this beautiful place so ugly and dirty,

I resolved not to let that happen. I didn't want silly games either. From now on I was going to play a straight bat with him. It did occur to me, though, that my resolve might be a little too late. Mihalis had looked like he'd made some resolutions of his own.

By the time I'd reached the Espresso café in town, there were more people in the streets. As I took a sip of my caffelatte Elendina floated past me, her lean body wrapped in her purple cape. I ran out into the street and called after her. She turned and let out a cry of surprise and relief. She talked quickly about how she knew everything and how terrible I must be feeling.

'What are you doing now?' she asked, flustered.

'I'm having a coffee.'

'Could you finish it quickly and come down to the council with me? I want to talk to you but I have to pay this water bill. It's the last day to pay and there'll be a queue.'

I gulped the remainder of my coffee and hurried with Elendina down to the council office, where people were milling around in queues waiting to be served. There were about ten people in front of us and the line wasn't moving.

'I've been so worried about you, but Dionysis told me he saw you last night with Mihalis. Thank God you're okay. You are okay, aren't you?' Elendina was still gabbling. I assured her I was fine.

'I had a huge fight with Bettina myself,' she said. 'Of all the men in the world, does she need to go out with your ex? No offence, Fiore,' she said, lowering her voice, 'but what did you see in him in the first place? And what does Bettina, for that matter? He's a dickhead.'

She filled me in on Bruce's bad behaviour, how he'd been drinking nonstop since his arrival. At a club the previous night he'd apparently invited a girl to come and sit at the table with everyone. When he found out her name was Piyi he giggled incessantly and proceeded to call her Piggy.

'She didn't understand what he was going on about,' Elendina told me, 'but I felt like I was at Yarraville Primary again, listening to some kid making fun of a wog name. Bettina wasn't impressed either but she pretended to ignore him.' I knew Elendina was trying to make me feel better, but I didn't really want to hear about it.

We reached the head of the queue, only to be told by the clerk that we'd come to the wrong counter. 'Over there is where you pay the water,' he said, pointing at another queue.

'Great,' Elendina snorted, and motioned for me to follow her to the end of the new queue. 'As I was saying, he was making a complete dickhead of himself until one of the other guys in the band told him to shut up.'

Before she could go on, I interrupted and told her I was planning to leave. Disappointment masked her face.

'But I thought you were staying a while,' she said, confused.

The clerk called the next person and it was our turn. I nudged Elendina and she turned and marched towards the

251

window. She handed the bill to the woman, who looked at it strangely.

'What's that?' she asked.

'The Greek constitution, what do you think it is? The water bill.'

'This isn't where you pay the water bill. Over there,' she said, indicating the first queue.

Elendina stamped her foot. 'I already waited in that queue,' she said, 'and he sent me here. Now you're sending me back there. Maybe I should just send *you* all somewhere instead!' Her voice was rising.

'Spiro,' said the woman to the clerk of the first queue. 'Isn't that where you pay the water bill?'

He looked up and nodded.

'Then why did you send this girl here?'

'*I* sent her to you?' He pointed at his chest to stress the ludicrousness of the suggestion.

Elendina snatched the bill from the woman and marched back to the first queue, muttering profanities under her breath. I followed at her heels.

'You'll have to see Bettina before you go,' Elendina said to me. 'You can't leave it like that. She's upset as well, you know.' When I didn't respond, she said, 'I'll be there too. It'll make it easier for you.'

I was doubtful. Elendina had great belief in putting aside differences and pretending we were all one big happy family, but her previous attempts at reconciliation hadn't proved too successful. 'We'll see,' I said tentatively. 'I might spend one more night in the hotel. I hope you don't mind?' She shook her head and patted me on the back.

'Next!' the clerk called and Elendina moved forward.

'Finally,' she sighed.

I said goodbye and told her I'd call her. Suddenly I felt tired. The sleepless night was catching up with me and I needed a nap.

But I was distracted by the English cemetery as I walked along the sea back towards my hotel. I was intrigued. There had been a short period in Zakynthos' history when it belonged to the British Empire, whose dead were buried separately. A university lecturer of mine had once told me his great-grandmother was buried there; I remembered this because Zakynthos doesn't ring a bell for too many Australians. 'When you're next there,' he had said to me, 'if you happen to pass by you might want to light a candle for me.' I had been too busy on my previous trips to even think of such a thing, but now here it was in front of me and I was in a mood for tying up loose ends.

I walked up some stairs, unsure where I was going and looking around for someone to ask. Turning a corner, I found someone: Stelios! He was with two other men, sitting with his profile to me, but I knew it was him from his stone-washed leather jacket and that unmistakable voice of his. They hadn't noticed me and I quickly stepped back out of view.

Three out-of-towners gathered in an unused English

cemetery in Zakynthos at the hour of the day when not a soul stirred could only mean they wanted to meet in secret. It was hard to hear what was being said, but Stelios' voice rose every now and then with sharp words.

'I did what I was asked,' he said. 'If things have gone astray, it's nothing to do with me.'

The others, who had their backs to me, kept their voices low and I could make out only occasional words.

'It's all too political now,' Stelios went on. 'Fuck it, I don't want the rest of the money. I'm not taking any chances with my boy. Every man and his dog here owns a gun. This isn't Athens, sort it out yourselves.'

There was more talk, then suddenly they rose and I saw that one of them was Alex. He put his arms up in a stretch and turned his torso in my direction. I wheeled around and ran as fast as I could.

Back at my hotel I rang Fioroula, but there was no answer. I waited an hour and tried again, but still no-one picked up the phone. Impatience had taken a strong hold on me. It was not simply what I had seen, I was also keen to redeem myself, since there were still people very much in doubt about my innocence in this affair. I walked to my cousin's house and found it empty. I looked at my watch – nearly three. The shops wouldn't reopen till five-thirty. I couldn't wait. On a whim I decided to go to Mihalis' house and kill two birds with one stone. Tell him the news and . . . I would think of what to say about the rest when I saw him.

Mihalis lived on the edge of town. He took a while to come to the door, and when he did his hair was all messed up.

'What now?' he said, half asleep and obviously not over-joyed at the sight of me.

I quickly explained, adding that I'd tried Fioroula before intruding on him. With some reluctance he invited me in.

I looked around the front room. The red curtains were still there, the old Persian rugs on the marble floor, the kitchen was still in a dilapidated state. The place hadn't changed since the ee cummings night. I thought of Petros' comment that Mihalis chose to live this way, when all he had to do was marry one of the growing number of girls with good dowries, some of whom had looks as well. Mihalis sat down and combed his fingers through his hair. He pointed to a chair for me.

'Where was this?' he asked again, still waking up.

'The English cemetery.'

'And what business did you have there?'

'I was walking past and decided to go and light a candle for someone I know.'

'You were walking past? What business did you have in that end of town.'

I stood up angrily. When I'd been thinking of people who still doubted me, I hadn't reckoned on Mihalis being one of them. 'I didn't come here to be put through the third degree, I'm telling you the truth.' I glared at him.

Mihalis considered me for a moment, then rang Pavlos and a long conversation took place. There was a great deal of speculation about why the men would have been meeting in the cemetery. Was there a possibility that another local was involved in this, someone besides the company, who didn't want to be seen with them? They threw around some names, possible motives.

As they talked, my eye caught a framed photo on the bookcase. It was of me, Fioroula, her boyfriend at the time and Mihalis, taken the night of the Carnivale ball on my first trip. I picked it up to take a closer look. My hair was still long then, and I was wearing a black fitted dress and a pair of expensive stockings that I'd bought in Melbourne. The saleswoman had told me they were the brand Sophia Loren wore and I'd bought them on the spot. I must have really wanted to impress him. In the photo Mihalis was sitting next to me and we were both smiling. His arm rested on the back of my chair, his hand just touching my shoulder. The expression on my face was pure joy.

'This whole dispute has become a farce.' Mihalis' voice brought me back to the present. He was off the phone. 'It's not as black and white as it's presented. The workers are now saying they'd prefer the place to be shut down rather than see their jobs go to anyone else. You know, most of them have property and business interests. It won't take long before every Zakynthian will be a boss. There's development everywhere and people are making a buck. I support the workers in principle, but let's see how far these principles get us. There're all those villagers coming down onto the picket line with their guns as if they're going to a wedding. But what can I do? You have to defend your principles. Pavlos is really having a hard time keeping this together.' He scratched his head, his mind in transit, and said he had to make some more calls.

By the way, about last night, I wanted to say, but now was clearly not the right time.

# CHAPTER FIFTEEN

I booked my ticket for Athens and I was headed home. I had three days left on the island and I had things to do. See my grandmother and other relatives, sort things out with Bettina, and deal with Mihalis. The last two were the hardest and I put them off. I decided to go to the mountains, but first I had to pick up some clothes from Elendina's. The one person I had no desire to see was there.

'God, Fiore,' Bettina said with her mouth open, not sure which way to go.

I went straight to the bedroom and packed my bag. She was standing in the kitchen when I was on my way out.

'By the way,' I said, speaking to her for the first time since our punch-up. 'Stelios is here.'

'Stelios! You're kidding?' She looked shocked and worried.

'What, don't tell me you're surprised,' I said. 'I find it hard to believe you didn't know what he was involved in.'

'Funny, that's what everyone is saying about you,' Bettina said acidly.

I slammed the door so hard the handle fell off.

Grandmother Phaedra let out shrieks of delight when she saw me. She hastily wiped the backs of her wet hands on her apron before reaching out to embrace me and planting twenty kisses on my cheek. I looked in the sink and saw the half-peeled potatoes and wondered who she was expecting for dinner.

'You,' she answered. 'Who else?'

'But how did you know I was coming?'

'The bus driver rang his wife to ask her if there was anything she needed from town before he left and he told her you were on the bus. Then she told me.'

I wondered how anyone could commit a murder in Zakynthos and get away with it.

She didn't take her eyes off me during dinner and whenever she opened her mouth to say anything she started crying. 'Your life is all I have to look forward to,' she said, 'and it pains me so much that you're going again, and that I will only know you through words on sheets of paper.'

'At least Elendina's here and Bettina's not too far away,' I said, trying to give comfort.

She wiped her nose and sat up. 'True, but I love you all the same, and until my last breath I only want to know your happiness.'

259

I shifted in my seat, feeling uncomfortable with this show of emotion. I felt sorry too, but what could I do? I asked her the question.

'Nothing. What can you do? That's our life. Whoever thought my only son would be so far away from me in my old age?' She began to sob again.

'Grandma, come back to Australia. Come back with me now.' I knew she wasn't going to go anywhere, but it was something to say, a weak offering of a solution to the pain of all this geographical separation. She was simply acknowledging what was there, while I was trying to fix it.

'What for, my child? All this moving around at my age. I'm on my last legs and I don't want to die over there. Forget it. Leave me in my peace here.'

'That's what you said years ago, and look at you. You look so healthy,' I said encouragingly. She was in fact ageing and had slowed down considerably.

'It's the mountain air and my blood. We have strong genes in my family. Nobody thinks I'm nearly eighty. Anyone who meets me thinks I'm in my late sixties.' She smoothed her hair back with pride.

I helped her clear the table and then she made me sit down with a list of people to whom I had to give her regards. There was a bag of gifts for a select few.

'Tullamarinis. Don't forget Tullamarinis,' she said, referring to two brothers who were called Tullamarinis because they lived in the suburb of Tullamarine, and because they needed to be differentiated from cousins who had the same name.

I wasn't paying attention. She had no idea that I never saw these people. Since moving out of my parents' house I no longer accompanied them to dances, weddings, or anywhere else they were invited by other Zakynthians. It was unlikely these people would cross my path.

'Which Tullamarinis?' I asked absently.

'There's only one! His brother's here now. He came back years ago.'

'Did he? Which one?'

'Jimmie. It was five years ago. Where's your mind? You should know these things. They're relatives of ours. Look, he even gave me something for you to pass on to his brother.' She looked through a bag and pulled out something big and rectangular wrapped in newspaper and tied with string. 'And these,' she said, handing me three blocks of mandolato, a locally made almond nougat, 'are for him as well.'

God, where was I going to put all of this stuff? This happened every time I left. I'd be loaded up with all sorts of things for people in Australia. When I was returning from my second trip to Greece a distant relative was on the same flight as me. She had made a rushed visit to her father on his deathbed, but she didn't make it.

'His eyes shut forever and he never saw me again,' she relayed to me in tears somewhere between Athens and Singapore. When we were going through Customs in

Melbourne her bags were inspected and something in a plastic container was being scrutinised.

'What's that?' one of the customs officers asked her.

'Oh, this very special dish from my island,' she told him. 'My brotherlaw go hunting and kill birds fresh from mountain and my sisterlaw cook for my husband.' She stopped for a minute, turned to me and asked in Greek, 'How do you say quail in English?' But it wasn't necessary. The officer was already telling her she couldn't bring it in. She was horrified at this suggestion and tried to argue with him, involving me as an interpreter, but he would not be swayed.

'Okay, I can't bring in, then I eat here. Now.' And she sat down and ate it.

'There's a book for Nina,' my grandmother said, handing me a novel. 'Tell her it's a good read. There's also an ashtray for her. Does she still smoke? Good old Nina.' She pulled herself up and put her hands on her hips, looking into the distance.

'I remember those days we'd sit under that apricot tree and she'd tell me about her life. All those riches, all gone,' she said, shaking her head.

The phone interrupted her reminiscing. It was Elendina, ringing to say they were all heading out and did I want to go with them? I told her I was staying put for the night, but promised that the following night I'd be hers.

'Why don't we have a party?' she suggested.

'Are you sure?'

'Absolutely. It's been ages since we had a party.'

I put the phone down and remembered that the last one had been just over a month ago.

'Now,' my grandmother said with a dramatic change of mood, 'let's sing.'

She sat upright on her chair with one leg stretched out in front of her and her hand on her thigh. She looked ready for action.

'How many hearts have you withered, how many have suffered while you laughed?' she sang, her voice booming through the room. She finished that song and started another, telling me to join in. I knew the song. I sang and she went into harmony, causing me to lose track of the melody. Once again I had followed the other's voice instead of my own, and the song was ruined. I wasn't a very good Zakynthian when it came to singing.

'Try and hold on,' she said, stopping, and we started again. I concentrated hard on maintaining the melody and not being distracted by my grandmother's voice. And suddenly I had it. I could clearly hear her voice and our two voices together, but for the first time I still managed to hold my own.

My grandmother refused to say goodbye the next morning. 'I'll come and see you at the ferry,' she said, hugging me close to her and kissing me on the face. I wanted to tell her not to bother going all the way into town, but I knew it would be useless. She lived for these things: departures, arrivals. They were the events in her life – in all our lives, really – and there was no way she wouldn't be there.

I spent the morning doing the rounds of the relatives again. It was emotionally exhausting. There were more tears this time, as the great-aunts and uncles knew, better than I did, that they might not be alive next time I came. Amid the embraces and kisses and crying, there were yet more gifts for people in Melbourne.

I had arranged to be at Elendina's house in the early afternoon, but it was empty when I arrived. There was a note on the table saying they were on the picket line. 'Come if you want' was scribbled quickly as an afterthought, but I decided to stay and make some phone calls.

'Fioroula,' I said.

'Hey, little cousin, how are you?'

'I thought you might be on the picket line.'

She filled me in on the details. The rest of the scabs had been found and approached. They didn't like the situation and were wary of the gangsters from Athens who had brought them here. 'We told them we'd look after them,' Fioroula said. 'I don't know if they believe us.'

I told her I was leaving and invited her to the party.

'You too? Mihalis Xenitos is going as well. He's got a job in Athens. Do me a favour, Fiore? Ask Liam to come to the party.'

Liam was the drummer in the Sub Urbans. 'I don't know . . .' I said hesitantly.

'Come on,' she pleaded. 'He has a boyish innocence about him that I find irresistible.'

What was she up to, a married woman and all?

'I'm in no state for anything other than watching,' Fioroula said, as if she could read my mind. 'But at least I can do that.'

After agreeing reluctantly I hung up, then looked at the phone for a good minute before dialling Mihalis' number. I wanted to suggest seeing him that night. I wanted to apologise, I wanted to tell him he was important to me, that I'd been an idiot. When I finally dialled, the phone had almost rung out before I heard his voice. He sounded groggy – I must have woken him up again. Not a good start.

'Mihalis, it's me. Fiore. Sorry, did I wake you? I'll call again later. Go back to bed.'

'No, it's all right. I'm awake now.'

There was a pause while I searched for a way to begin.

'What is it?' he asked with impatience in his voice.

'Well, I'm leaving and I was wondering if I could see you tonight?'

'I can't tonight. My students have organised a farewell for me.'

'Oh. What about tomorrow?'

'I'm not sure if I can. I'll try.'

'There's a party at Elendina's house.'

'Fine. I'll see you then,' he said and hung up.

The party at Elendina's house was not the backdrop I had in mind for my exchange with Mihalis, but beggars can't be choosers.

On the afternoon of the party, Dionysis was in the armchair trying to read *The Independent* that I'd bought that morning. He scratched his head and pulled a face. 'My English is worse than I thought,' he said.

I was reading a book and Bettina was helping Elendina cook while talking to someone on the phone. It was the calm before the storm. Dionysis threw his coat on and told us he'd see us later. We three sisters were left alone, me in one corner, Bettina in the other, and Elendina in the middle.

'All's quiet on the Romiri front,' Bettina said after putting the phone down. 'No-one's been to the picket line and no-one's seen Stelios or Alex.'

I found this hard to believe on an island where everybody knew what you were up to. I wondered where Bruce was and what was going on in that quarter, but I didn't want to ask.

'Well, here we are,' Elendina said, sitting down after putting the food in the oven. She smiled at us both in turn. 'When was the last time we were together like this, hey?'

'Before Bettina left for Greece,' I said.

I could see Elendina casting her mind back, her eyebrows knitting at the memory of that night. 'Yes, well,' she said. 'Hasn't so much happened to all of us since then?'

I nodded. Bettina remained silent.

'If you'd told me then that I was going to be living here too, I would have said you were crazy,' Elendina went on, lighting a cigarette. 'Are you all right?' she asked an increasingly glum-looking Bettina.

'No,' she answered.

'What's the matter?'

'I'm angry with *her*.' She pointed at me and finally turned to speak to me directly. 'Are you going to hold what happened with Bruce against me forever? What do you care anyway? You dumped him. It was over between you. It's not as if I stole him from you. You're exaggerating the whole thing. The same goes for Mihalis. Nothing happened between the two of you and then you're all upset because we had sex. I can't help it if he wasn't attracted to you. What am I supposed to do, say no to men because they don't want you?' Bettina was on a roll.

'Bettina, stop right now,' Elendina demanded. 'Or I'll never speak to you again!' But I was already up on my feet, giving as good as I got, telling Bettina everything I'd withheld over the years. That she was insensitive and uncaring and that I'd had enough of it.

'You always hit below the belt,' I said, reminding her of the time she'd blackmailed our mother. Elendina was shocked. Bettina left the room in tears, slamming the door behind her, but before we could take a breather she was back with a force as strong as a cyclone.

Recriminations went back and forth. All sorts of stuff was dredged up from the past. Bettina accused me of living my life as a lie; of preserving my image as the perfect daughter while forcing her to do the dirty work, the results of which I was happy to reap.

Elendina was shouting at both of us to stop. 'The whole fucking village can hear you.'

'Who cares?' Bettina said. 'They can't understand what we're saying anyway.'

The slanging match continued and the yelling escalated. Again Elendina called for us to stop but we ignored her. Suddenly Bettina and I were covered in water. Cold water. It shocked us into silence and I turned to find Elendina with a large empty saucepan in her hands. Before any of us could speak there was a knock on the door and Angeliki was in the house, looking anxious and concerned.

'I just came to see if everything is all right,' she said, glancing from me to Bettina to Elendina until comprehension appeared in her eyes.

'Everything's fine,' Elendina said, making her way to the door. 'We're having a difference of opinion, that's all.' She led her neighbour gently out of the house.

I was drenched, my hair and clothes soaked through. Bettina's teeth were chattering. We set about drying ourselves and changing clothes. I propped myself in front of the kerosene heater with my head thrown forward to dry my hair. Elendina mopped up the excess water, but a large area of the rug was wet. Bettina returned in dry clothes and sat down to put on fresh makeup. Elendina's diversion had worked. We had both calmed down.

'Now,' Elendina said in a low, even voice that sounded like it was on the edge of exploding. 'I've had enough of the both of you. I'm sick to death of these fights. You.' She pointed at Bettina. 'If you want to be free and do whatever you like without any consideration for anyone, especially your own family, then don't expect us to be there for you. What are you doing, testing us or something all the time?' Before Bettina could answer, Elendina turned her attention to me. 'And you – you have a real attitude problem towards Bettina. You've been shitty with her for a long time and you're just looking for a reason to write her off so you can say, See, I was right all along. And what if I say to you, Yes, you're right – do you win a prize or something?'

I looked down at my feet but she hadn't finished. 'You both fight to win, like there's some special reward you're desperate to get. What is it?' She threw her hands up and looked from me to Bettina. 'I mean, here we are, together for the first time in years, and instead of us behaving like a normal family it's World War III. Well, I've had enough. I'm leaving you to it and you can tear each other's hair out for all I care.' She picked up her bag and threw on her cape. 'I'll be back around nine, when the guests are expected,' she said. 'And before you kill each other, can you put the potatoes in the oven?'

Bettina and I sat in silence until the phone rang. We looked at each other expectantly, neither of us rising to answer it. I was prepared to let it ring, being in no mood to talk to anyone, and Bettina was obviously of the same mind. I dried my hair some more and when I finally sat up Bettina was smiling at me.

'What?' I asked.

'I'm just thinking about Elendina throwing that water at us. It must have looked pretty funny.'

I had to agree.

'The last time that happened to me, I was eight,' Bettina went on. 'Grandma Phaedra threw a bucket on me in bed one morning, remember? So I would wake up and go to bloody Greek school.'

I remembered all right. The bed had taken several days to dry out, and in the meantime Bettina had had to sleep top to toe in my bed, where she kicked me all night.

There was silence between us again. I let it sit for once, just to see where it might take us. Bettina's earlier words were still ringing in my ears, feeding my hurt, but I thought of what Elendina had had to say as well. I liked to think of myself as the reasonable one, but Elendina was right. I had been judgemental of Bettina. I cringed at the memory of the times I had cut her off, dismissive of her concerns, always the lawyer. I would hit out at her with rational argument, feeling very much superior about how right I was. God, what an unbearable, exasperating pain in the arse I could be.

'Bruce has gone,' Bettina said, breaking the silence. 'I sent him packing. He's a dickhead of the first order.'

'I know,' I mumbled. 'And I was thinking there might be a serious love affair waiting for me.'

She looked at me and laughed. 'We were sucked in big time!'

I didn't find it quite so comical, but I knew laughter was Bettina's attempt at building a bridge with me. Her way of apologising without actually apologising.

'You're all right, Fiore. I just wish you'd get off my case.'

I sighed. 'It's only because I think you have brains and potential and I don't think you do the best with them. If I didn't love you, I wouldn't hassle you at all.'

'What if I don't want to do anything with my potential? You never think of that because you're so busy telling me what I should do. If you'd just ask me, any of you, I'd tell you I never wanted a professional career. You all want me to get a proper job so you can breathe a sigh of relief that I'm on the right track. Well, it ain't gonna happen. I'm going to stay on the wrong track. It's not a phase I'm going through.'

I shook my head. I wanted to disagree with her, to say that all I wanted was her happiness, but she had other territory to cover. Our parents were the root of the problem, Bettina claimed. Too busy working, they had never given us enough attention and we had grown up without them really knowing us. This source of grief was one I had heard before from Bettina, and one I did not share. It was all true enough, but what use was it to keep on about it? Our parents had done the best they could under difficult circumstances.

But this was a rational view of the world, Bettina argued, and we were emotional beings. 'I can't talk to them about anything deep.'

I interrupted her. 'But what if they're not capable of the kind of relationship you're demanding?'

'Well, that's very sad. Doesn't that make you sad?'

'No,' I said impatiently. 'It does not. That's the way it is. In fact, I think all these demands for a "proper" relationship with our parents is so middle class. Who defines this so-called proper relationship that we've supposedly missed out on?'

My attitude angered Bettina even more. She saw it as dismissing the legitimacy of her feelings and burst into tears. 'See, this is what I mean,' she sobbed. 'What's important to me is just bullshit to you.'

I put my head in my hands.

Bettina eventually stopped crying, took some deep breaths and blew her nose. Keeping her voice steady she said, 'I'm going to play by *my* rules now. It's time for some honesty in this family and if you can't deal with it, that's your problem.'

I realised there was no point arguing with her, attempting to get her to see the truth. In families there are lots of truths. Bettina saw, experienced and felt things differently to me. Rather than listen, I had been too busy trying to correct her. We had been brought up in the same family, yet clearly things that had been major upsets for Bettina were like water off a duck's back to me.

But there was something else. She accused me now of never confiding in her, never telling her what was really important to me. 'I'm always trying to second-guess where you're coming from,' she said.

I was about to defend myself. Why does it matter that I don't confide in you? I wanted to say. I don't have these expectations of you. But I realised that she was talking about her pain, about feeling hurt and pushed out by me. When Bettina used Mihalis as an example of my not revealing my true feelings, I flinched. She swore black and blue that had she known, she would have steered well clear of him.

I believed her because I had to. I had no choice. She was not a friend I could discard in order to find a new one. Even if she lived ten thousand miles away and I never saw her again, I would carry her around with me forever. I thought of Nina mourning her sister who'd died in Greece thirty years after they'd last seen each other. She was in our kitchen crying like a baby, with my mother and my grandmother on either side of her, consoling her.

'I didn't like sleeping alone in my room,' she'd sobbed, 'and everyone made fun of me about it, except my sister. I'd climb into bed with her and she'd always comfort me. Always.'

This was the sister that Nina carried within her. Perhaps this was what troubled Bettina's heart? That the image she carried of me was an authoritarian, unforgiving one. But could we rewrite such things? I saw too much as being set in stone – maybe I had to learn to bend a little, let myself be more flexible. One thing I was certain of – things weren't going to stay the same for our family from now on, whether because of me conceding my failings, or Bettina's remorse, or because Bettina's new approach in dealing with our parents was going to break open the floodgates. Once again Bettina would lead the way, and it was sure to be a bumpy ride. That's the price agents of change pay. The rest of us follow, often reluctantly, on a smoother road.

Cocooned as we were in the warmth of the room and by the weight of emotion in us, we were startled by a knock on the door. I looked at the time and remembered the potatoes and Bettina reluctantly answered the door. It was Liam. I could hear the surprise in her voice as she invited him in.

'What's he doing here?' she asked me in Greek.

'Fioroula asked me to invite him,' I explained, and Bettina gave me a sly look that I shrugged away. 'She can only look.'

We were grateful for Dionysis who arrived a few minutes later. We left him to entertain Liam while we got on with the cooking, which was way behind schedule. Fearing Elendina's wrath, we rushed to get as much done as possible. I returned to set the table and found them talking about saints.

'Ah,' Dionysis said, obviously without a clue what Liam was saying. 'What's he saying to me about the Catholics?' he asked me in Greek. 'And where did this water on the carpet come from?'

I clarified one issue and evaded the other.

Elendina arrived minutes before the guests. Sophie had just taken the first puff of a joint when Father Dimitri walked in. She nearly choked at the sight of him.

'What's he doing here?' she said to me in a whisper. 'Oh my God, imagine what my parents would say.'

'I invited him, Sophie. Stop carrying on.'

The joint was passed around awkwardly in an attempt to keep it away from Father Dimitri. Everyone was talking about the strike. A rumour was doing the rounds that the company intended to close down the factory in Zakynthos anyway, so this strike was just speeding up the process.

My heart sank with every half-hour that passed and the growing realisation that Mihalis would not come. Oblivious to my pangs, people ate and drank heartily and dancing followed soon afterwards. Fioroula was the first one up, joined by the others. Everyone except Liam and Father Dimitri, who were deep in discussion about the split of the Church into East and West, and how the Pope of the time could have sent help to save the Byzantine Empire from going under. Four hundred years of Islam could have been avoided if it hadn't been for the Catholics, Father Dimitri claimed, and Liam was learning something about his church that he didn't know.

We all drank to each other's health and good fortune, with an emphasis on mine since I was departing. 'To Fiore – may she have a good trip and may it not be too long before we see her again,' Dionysis said and we all clinked glasses. Vasili went outside and fired a few shots from his gun.

'What's he doing?' I asked.

'Oh, you know, just for the hell of it,' Sophie said, completely delighted.

Around midnight, Mihalis arrived with Stavros and a great cheer went up from everyone but me. I was emotionally exhausted from watching the clock and agonising over the reason for his not coming.

'Welcome, Mayor,' Dionysis said, bowing in exaggerated deference.

Stavros gave him a curt sideways glance, then greeted everybody else. I congratulated him on his victory and he proceeded to tell me how surprised he was to have done so well in booths where he thought he had no hope.

Fioroula cut him off. 'Stavros, let the girl alone. She's leaving tomorrow. What does she care whether the booth at Akrotiri voted three to one for you?'

I laughed and offered Stavros and Mihalis something to eat, but they weren't hungry. 'I found him eating with the Captain at Mallias' restaurant,' Stavros said, gesturing towards Mihalis, 'and I ended up joining them. That's why we're late. He wasn't going to come and I had to talk him into it.'

I looked at Mihalis, who was talking to Father Dimitri. I felt rejected, but who could blame him for his indifference?

Fioroula cut across my thoughts. 'You were thinking of leaving us without saying goodbye?' she scolded him.

There was curiosity about Mihalis' departure, and people began plying him with questions.

'I want to be closer to my nephews,' he said in his own defence. 'Besides, sometimes I feel I'm missing out on so much here.'

'Like what?' Sophie asked.

'Like everything,' Bettina said. 'Wasn't it Marx who commented on the idiocy of rural life?'

Those who considered themselves Marxists shifted uncomfortably.

'Marx was a man defined by his time and place. Not everything he said stands up to scrutiny,' Father Dimitri said.

'I miss the cinema and the theatre,' Mihalis said. The closure of the cultural centre in Zakynthos meant there was nowhere to see movies any more.

Dionysis took this as a criticism of himself, since he had been a main player in the cultural centre before abandoning it for his business pursuits. 'It's up to everyone to keep the cultural centre going,' he asserted.

'Perhaps, but we've all deserted it,' Mihalis said.

'Well, then we reap what we sow.'

'We've had this out before, Dionysis,' Mihalis said, clearly not interested in doing so again. 'I'm not blaming you. That's what's happened. Everyone's interested in other things now and I can't do it on my own. That's that.'

Father Dimitri said the issue was a lack of interest from the community as a whole. 'Say you all died, what would happen then? Who would take over from you?'

'Correct,' Fioroula said. 'But that's our error. We didn't involve other, younger people in what we were doing. We controlled everything like good little Stalinists. We showed bad leadership.'

'There you go, attacking Stalin again,' Dionysis said, and pretty soon they were in full flight, shouting out their differences. If it hadn't been for Stalin, Dionysis maintained, we'd all be citizens of the Third Reich.

Liam looked at Fioroula with a mixture of awe and fear. 'What's going on? Why is she so angry?' he asked Sophie, who was never very good at grasping the essence of a political discussion.

'They're arguing about Russia,' she said offhandedly. 'You know, about whether Stalin was a good bloke or not.'

'What?' Liam said in disbelief.

Father Dimitri leant across the table towards Liam. 'It's our version of *The Big Chill*,' he said.

'There's much more emphasis on making money now,' I put in. 'It's noticeable everywhere.'

'That's because there's money to be made,' Father Dimitri said. 'Before the tourist trade, who was going to become rich farming their little plot of land?'

'Excuse me, but I don't see the problem here,' said Vasili. 'There's been a huge improvement in the standard of living. My uncles all drive BMWs now. Twenty years ago, they could hardly afford a tractor, let alone a car.'

'But at what cost to our way of life?' Fioroula wanted to know.

'If our way of life was poverty, then who gives a fuck if it changes?' Vasili declared.

'There's still poverty,' Father Dimitri said. 'Maybe those

278

who were poor no longer are, but others have become the new poor in their place. But things do change when the focus of a place is on making money. If you see the possibility of making a lot of money and you put all your energy into that, what kind of spiritual life do we have?'

'Fuck it,' Dionysis said, banging his fist on the table. 'Being from Zakynthos used to mean something. Great art and theatre and writing came out of this island. And I can't see it anywhere any more. Now we're left only with the name.'

I reflected on my own feelings of disappointment in the changes I had seen in Zakynthos. Fioroula was right in that there were fewer and fewer younger people interested in pursuing the kinds of things that impassioned us. I'd thought my parents were trapped in an image of Greece that was outdated and frozen in time, but what I hadn't realised was that the same thing had happened to me. I wanted the Zakynthos of my first trip. That's what I'd expected to find, and I was disappointed and disoriented to see that it wasn't there any more.

'Well, let's do something then,' Fioroula said, her cheeks red from the wine and the temper of the discussion. 'I'm not going to sit around complaining about it. We,' she included us all in a sweep of her hand, 'we are part of this place and we can work towards preserving it. We can't just say that's the way it is and let it go.'

Mihalis let out a sigh. 'It's the turn of others now,' he said. 'We've had ours, maybe someone else can do a better job.'

'Surely this is something you could address,' I said to Stavros, who had been curiously silent during the discussion. All eyes turned to him.

'Of course,' said Dionysis, 'now that we have our own man in the job.' I couldn't tell if he was being sarcastic or not.

'Yes, absolutely,' Stavros said. 'But we have to look at what people want, and reopening the cultural centre isn't a priority for most of them.'

'You can't just do what people want,' Mihalis argued. 'Most people want to make money. It's up to you to show leadership and do things that are valuable for people, if they don't know it.'

'That's right.' Fioroula was up on her feet. 'What do we have politics for if we can't apply them? Just to believe? And that goes for everyone, not just Stavros. If we don't get together and work towards the things that matter, then who is going to do it? This is where we live, this is where our politics matter. I've heard enough talk from you boys to last me a lifetime. Put your balls on the line and show me some action.'

Dionysis, Stavros and Mihalis immediately began defending themselves, all three talking at once.

'She takes no prisoners, your cousin,' Father Dimitri said to me as the discussion raged.

It wasn't that long ago that I'd bemoaned what I considered to be the limitations of Fioroula's life. The limitations of being a woman in a rural community with restricted opportunities. But there was nothing to bemoan in her. She was a feminist with a capital F; a walking, breathing example of one with guts and determination who acted on what she believed in. That was what I thought I did, but she seemed to have so much more fun. If there was something to be done, she didn't sit around to see who would do what, she just did it. Rather than wait for opportunities to come her way, she made them. Even in little Zakynthos. And when she acted, she took people with her and inspired them, while others were still wavering, ever conscious of doing it right or wrong, or wondering whether they should be doing it at all. The way she lived her life shook to the core my Western liberal notions of feminism, with its emphasis on careerism and work. Just as she had shown me one road to feminism when I was nineteen, she now showed me another. People like Victoria did not own the patent on how to be strong, independent women, and I finally felt I had the courage to let her know that.

Father Dimitri was the first to leave, just after two, and Stavros went with him. 'I want you to know how happy I am to have made your acquaintance,' Father Dimitri said seriously, shaking my hand. 'Give my regards to your father, and please tell him that there are many of us here who would very much like to see him again.' I stored this information away with all the other messages I had to pass on to my stored, and thanked him again for his brandy and wise ear the other night.

Stavros apologised for leaving early. 'I don't have my wife's stamina, despite her pregnancy. Besides, I've been up since six this morning, or yesterday morning actually.'

I waved goodbye to them as they drove off in Father Dimitri's revved-up vehicle. For an environmentalist, he drove a car more suited to a seventies rock star. Loud and big.

'What's wrong?' Mihalis asked when I went back inside. 'You look forlorn.'

'Father Dimitri is such a nice man,' I said. 'This is the hard thing about going. Meeting good people that you have to leave behind.'

'Don't start crying about it now,' he said, only half joking.

'I'm not going to cry.' I went to the kitchen to make some tea. I filled a saucepan with water and put it on to boil.

'It's not unlike you,' he said, following me. 'I'll never forget your last night in Zakynthos the first time you were here.'

'Oh?' I said vaguely, thinking now would be a good time to say everything I wanted to say. 'Mihalis,' I began, but was interrupted by Elendina calling out for us to join the game of charades.

Loud laughter was coming from the sitting room as I took in the tea. My sisters and I loved charades, and Sophie and Liam were right into it, teaching the Greeks, who had some trouble following it. On his turn, Liam acted out the title of a song. He lay on the floor with his legs open, grimacing and moaning. Nobody could guess. It was 'Born To Be Wild'.

We three sisters were in our element. We loved games of any sort, and from a young age we'd round up any takers in the neighbourhood to join us. When it was Bettina's turn she got down on all fours and imitated some kind of wild animal.

She looked so comical and I saw the little Bettina in her again.

Mihalis found some disco and soon we were all up dancing to Barry White.

'This is one of the best nights I've ever had,' Liam said, by now quite drunk. 'But do you Greeks ever stop dancing? I'm exhausted just watching you.'

Some time after four in the morning, Mihalis declared he had things to do the next day. He offered Liam a lift to town and then he was at the door, throwing a scarf around his neck.

'You may as well take me with you,' Fioroula said, gathering her things.

'Goodbye, Fiore.' Mihalis was already out of the house. I had to be quick. He was disappearing before my eyes.

'I'm coming too,' I blurted out. 'Wait, I'll get a coat.'

'Where to?' he asked, his whole body poised in a question.

'Bohali,' I said. It's amazing what the mind can do under pressure. 'I want to see Bohali one last time.'

His body relaxed. 'That's a good idea,' he said and my heart raced with excitement. All we had to do was drop the others off and the world was at my feet. When I got to the car, Fioroula was sitting in the front and I sat in the back with Liam. I jumped out at Fioroula's house to walk her to the door.

'What are you up to with Mihalis?' she asked, holding me close to her. Fioroula didn't miss much.

'We exchanged some heated words and I want five minutes alone with him to apologise,' I said.

'Talking's not what's needed here,' she said. 'If you ask me there's been too much talk and not enough of anything else. What you need to do is fuck him, and what better place than Bohali? Sex with a view.' She winked at me as if we had reached some sort of deal, and I laughed, tears running helplessly down my cheeks. We embraced, both of us crying by now, apologising for not spending more time together and making promises for the next trip.

I staggered back to the car, still crying. I sat in the front and blew my nose. Before I had come to my senses we had almost reached Bohali, with Liam in the back. A threesome was not what I had in mind.

'Where are we going?' I asked.

Mihalis looked at me as if I were an imbecile. 'To Bohali. Isn't that where you wanted to go?'

'Yes,' I said, but not with Liam. 'I thought we were dropping him off at his hotel.' I tried to sound as indifferent as possible.

A weary exasperation marked his face as he ignored me and addressed Liam in English. 'Here we are.' There was a whistle of wonderment from the back seat as Liam took in the view.

'That's awesome,' he said and got out of the car. He walked to the ramp and looked down at the twinkling lights on the edge of the sea. Mihalis and I watched from the car in silence. Now is the time to say something, I told myself, before Liam gets back to the car, but when I turned to Mihalis I saw, in the faint light of dawn, that his eyes were wet. He sighed quietly and said, 'Fuck Zakynthos.' I reached across the tight confines of the car and kissed him once on both eyes. As I pulled back, my elbow hit the horn. Liam, thinking it was meant for him, turned, waved and walked back to the car.

We dropped Liam off and in no time at all were back in front of Elendina's house. The mood for saying anything of consequence had passed. We talked vaguely about meeting in Athens and I scribbled Bettina's number on a piece of paper I found in the glovebox.

'It's very late,' Mihalis said. 'And I have a lot to do tomorrow.' It was unlike him to be worried about mundane things. He drove down the hill and out of sight, leaving me with the taste of salt from his tears in my mouth. I had no faith that I would see him again.

I dreamt I was leaving against my will. I was hoping for some catastrophe – a storm or an earthquake – that would prevent the boat from sailing. It did happen, with terrible consequences. There was an earthquake and everyone blamed me. 'Why didn't you just say you didn't want to go, instead of causing this disaster? As if we haven't had enough earthquakes without you causing one,' they said. I woke with the feeling that I had done something wrong, and it kept returning to me all day, like a question that needed answering.

This wasn't the first time I'd had dreams about not wanting to leave Greece. My impending departure always made me feel uneasy in my last few days there. Leaving destroyed my fantasies of staying.

When I got up and caught my reflection in the mirror, I noted how exhausted I looked. I told myself I'd get some sleep in Athens. Who was I kidding? Sleep in Athens is a contradiction.

There were hundreds of people milling around at the dock next morning. My sisters debated what to do. Should we go for a coffee? Should we just go for a walk? Bettina wasn't coming back with me, but was staying in Zakynthos for a while.

'I need the fresh air of Volimes,' she said, agreeing with our grandmother, who was telling her how thin she looked.

'This new fashion of looking like you've been through the famine is not to my liking at all,' Grandma Phaedra remarked.

Then Sophie found us. It was hard to miss her in her white fur coat and red high-heels. She was wearing the dress she'd bought in Athens. It was even tighter now that she'd been fattened up with her aunt's winter cooking. She'd insisted on coming to farewell me, despite my protests that it wasn't necessary. She too was staying in Zakynthos, with some vague idea about using her marketing skills in the tourism businesses.

'I've got nothing to lose,' she said. 'And now that I've found Vasili I'm in no hurry to rush back to Athens.' She broke into giggles.

Grandma Phaedra stood looking at me from head to toe, just as she had when I arrived. She clutched onto me and burst into tears. 'Oh my child,' she sobbed. 'God knows if I shall ever lay eyes on you again.'

I was crying by now, and Bettina, Sophie and Elendina were teary as well. 'You'll see me again,' I assured her. 'I'll be back. I always come back. Elendina will get married and we'll all come over for the wedding.'

Then everyone started talking at once. '*Are* you getting married? Give my love to Mum and Dad. And Nina. Give the keys to Antonia when you leave. Don't forget to ring Fotis and Mario. Take care. I don't know when, we'll see. Have a good trip.' We hugged and kissed and promised to write and ring.

I made my way to the top of the ferry and looked down at my sisters and Sophie and my grandmother waving at me, and I cried some more. I was still crying as the ferry pulled away. I sat watching the sea, feeling sad and heavy about everything I was leaving behind in Zakynthos. Again.

# CHAPTER SIXTEEN

The bus terminal in Athens was a nightmare. Several buses from various destinations had arrived within minutes of each other and there were long queues for taxis. I ended up sharing one with a policeman from Corfu.

'Are you from Australia?' the driver asked.

'How can you tell?' But I knew it must be because of the seatbelt.

'You put your seatbelt on as soon as you got in. I lived in Australia for fourteen years. Are you from Melbourne?'

He was delighted to hear that I was and keen to tell me about his time in Australia, most of which had been spent running a café in Gundagai. I told him I knew about the place but had never been there, and he proceeded to tell the story of the dog on the tuckerbox for the policeman's benefit.

'A man was out in the bush with a herd of cattle, maybe bulls, I can't remember. Near a creek, five miles away from

Gundagai, the yoke broke. To top it all off, the dog had a shit on the container where they had their food. On the tucker-box,' he said, enunciating the last word in English. He laughed. 'So they made a statue of it.'

I couldn't remember hearing this particular version. 'They have a statue of a dog having a shit?' the policeman asked, incredulous.

'No, it's just a dog sitting on the box. But people come from all over to see it,' the driver said, with some obvious hometown pride.

'Are you serious?' The policeman was still coming to terms with the idea. 'Don't they have any poets to make statues of?'

'Of course they're not serious. That's the point of it. It's their ability to laugh in the blackest hour. This is a story from the last century. Imagine, they're five miles from the town,' the driver said, stopping to do a quick conversion to kilometres, 'stuck in the middle of nowhere, and their food gets ruined by the dog. Instead of killing the dog and pulling their hair out, they laugh.'

'Laugh at what?' The policeman was still puzzled.

'The situation they're in.' The driver could see the policeman wasn't getting it. 'You have to know Australians to appreciate it.'

The policeman looked at me as if searching for a sign that might help him understand the eccentricity of Australians. I shrugged and looked out the window. We were approaching Bettina's street. The driver stopped right

289

outside the apartment, double-parking in the middle of the street, and took my suitcases out of the boot.

'Goodbye,' he said. 'And give my regards to Australia. You never know, one day I might be back for a visit.'


Athens was having a mild winter and I spent my days walking everywhere in the sun and stopping when I wanted to eat. And eat I did. I always gorged myself on my last days in Greece, eating everything I couldn't get in Melbourne. I went shopping and bought shoes and a dress. I visited an elderly aunt in Piraeus, went to the museum, and got a lot of exercise by walking to the Acropolis three times because it was shut the first two – once due to a strike and the second for reasons unknown. I went with Fotis and Mario to a Maria Farantouri concert that made the hairs on my arms stand up, her powerful voice accompanied softly by the audience. I tried to sleep. I read the papers and sat in Bettina's apartment on sunny afternoons with the shutters open. I spent hours listening to music in shops and bought lots of CDs. The relative anonymity of Athens was a welcome change after Zakynthos. But even though it was a big city, people still engaged with you in a way I found disarming.

I felt at home in Athens. The pace of life invigorated me and it was easier to imagine living here than in Zakynthos, even when the difficulty presented by the simplest of tasks infuriated me. Like getting my hair cut. An assistant washed my hair and told me that someone would be along to cut it in a few minutes. I waited for nearly half an hour with wet hair while several women who'd come in after me were seen to first. Finally I went up to the desk, where the receptionist was surprised to see me. It appeared that the cutter booked for me was nowhere to be found.

Through all of this, I waited for Mihalis to call. I knew he was coming on the weekend, but the weekend came and went. Monday passed and still he hadn't called. On Tuesday morning, the phone woke me from a dream I didn't want to leave. Disoriented to find myself out of Mihalis' naked body and in Bettina's apartment, I had a brief conversation with someone looking for Bettina with an offer of a job. I scribbled the details and went back to bed in the hope of returning to my dream. But the dream was gone.

The following day, I went to the airline office in Syntagma to book my flight home. The possibility that Mihalis would not contact me had now become a probability, and there was no point hanging around Athens for a call that might never happen.

'There are no flights on Saturday,' said the attendant coolly, before ignoring me to answer the phone.

'What about the following Monday?' I asked when she'd finally hung up.

She tapped again on her computer. 'No, there's nothing available then either.'

'Next Thursday or Friday?' I ventured. But there were no

291

seats for the next three weeks. 'Why are they all booked? It seems very strange,' I said, thinking aloud.

'How do you expect me to know? People travel. That's why we're in business.' She blinked at me expectantly.

'What about this Friday?' I asked, hoping nothing would come up.

'Yes, we have seats for Friday.'

'The day after tomorrow?' I asked, staring ahead, my mind in the land of indecision.

She pulled a mirror out of her handbag, checked her hair, glanced at her watch, inspected her nails, then looked at me. 'What would you like to do?' she said impatiently.

I didn't really want to leave on Friday, but I gave in and she tapped on the keyboard, stapled something to my ticket and handed it back to me.

'You fly out at midnight. Be at the airport an hour before departure.'

I put my ticket into my bag and turned to leave.

'Sometimes we have cancellations,' she said as an after-thought. 'Try calling last thing tomorrow, there might be something available for the following Monday.'

I thanked her and stumbled out of the office into the Athenian sun.

I rang Elendina and sister number two answered the phone, asking me what I'd been doing during my Athenian sojourn.

'I'm leaving on Friday,' I said, 'and by the way, you wouldn't happen to know if Mihalis has left Zakynthos?'

'I think so. You heard he got beaten up?'

My heart leapt out of me. Bettina filled me in. One of the workers had been talking about setting fire to the factory and was criticising Pavlos the Redhaired's tactics. It came to blows, Mihalis intervened and got a few bruises and some very sore ribs. It was the straw that broke the camel's back – the company finally called a meeting with the union.

'The bosses heard the news of the fight and the talk about burning down the place, so they called Pavlos, who suddenly appeared very reasonable to them. Now they want to talk. They haven't got a choice. Nearly all the scabs have gone, including the thugs from Athens, better known to us as Stelios and Alex. I still can't believe that Stelios was involved in this. He's not very bright, you know.'

I told her that being bright wasn't necessarily a prerequisite in that line of work.

'You were right to be suspicious of him,' she said. But before she could give me any more accolades about my foresight, I reminded her that it was me who had pursued Alex like a dog on heat all over Zakynthos.

'Funny you should say that,' Bettina mused. 'That was the word the Captain used in his song. Or maybe it was rabid. Something to do with a dog, anyway.'

I put my head in my hand and moaned. A moan that turned to laughter. There was no escaping the troubadour.

Bettina's neighbour Antonia was knocking on my door shortly after I was out of bed on Thursday morning. Apart from a few encounters on the stairs, we hadn't had a chance to socialise. She was acting in a play every night and busy during the day. The play, a social-realist piece set after the war, was a great success and the season had been extended. But today was her day off and she was going to a sculpture exhibition in Piraeas. She wanted me to come, an idea I loved, but I didn't want to stray too far in case Mihalis called. He'd ended up leaving Zakynthos on Monday, Bettina had told me.

'What about the poetry evening tonight then. Do you want to come to that?' she suggested.

'Okay, until tonight I do. Who knows what will happen?'

I went to the Meat Market, ending where I'd begun. I watched people going about their business while I ate. That area of Athens had few tourists and therefore no affectations. An old man playing a folk clarinet reached my table. He stopped playing and, looking towards the sky, began to sing in a rich but mournful voice about the pain of leaving his village. I pulled out a thousand drachmas and gave it to him, recalling a comment my mother had once made about a similar song. 'They're lamenting going to the next village,' she said. 'What about us coming to Australia? We need a whole oratorio, not just one song.'

As I walked home, I spotted a poster advertising the Sub Urbans' concert in Athens. I would have torn it down except it was up too high, but I did retrieve another poster from a wall. It was the Left Coalition's election poster, colourful and bright, with imagery based on traditional Greek puppetry. Some men standing nearby misunderstood my intention and took me to task.

'What have you got against the coalition?' one asked me.

'Nothing,' I said. 'I want to take it back to Australia.'

'Australia! They know about Damanaki in Australia?' they asked in disbelief, referring to the leader of the party.

'Why not?' another countered. 'Damanaki's a distinguished politician.'

I left them to discuss the merits of Damanaki, and with the illusion that Australians were familiar with the leader of a minor Greek political party.

The answering machine was flashing when I got in. I pressed the playback button and Mihalis' voice spilled into the room.

'Fiore, it's Mihalis. I arrived on Monday.' There was a pause and I could hear traffic in the background. 'Perhaps we could catch up tomorrow night? As long as we don't do anything too energetic. I'm sure you've heard. I'll call you again later.'

He'd called! I jumped around the apartment. I put a CD on full blast and danced until Antonia appeared at the door.

'It's nearly four in the afternoon! What are you doing? This is a time for sleep, not dancing.'

I apologised and turned it down, and spent the rest of the afternoon trying on every outfit in my suitcase. The most important decision of my life at that moment was what I was going to wear when I saw Mihalis.

Antonia wouldn't hear of me not going to the poetry night. It was creeping towards seven o'clock when I told her I didn't think I could make it.

'I'm expecting a call,' I said.

'Well, call them instead.'

'I don't have a number, and he said he'd call. I *have* to see him before I go.'

She thought about this for a minute. 'As I understand it,' she said, 'nothing's definite, nothing's arranged, but you're going to stay indoors in case he rings. On your last night in Athens. What nonsense! I've got the night off work, you have a machine – leave a message for him.'

I hadn't thought of that, but it made sense. It's always a shame to stay in when you can go out in Athens. I fiddled with the answering machine for at least half an hour before I managed to work out how to change the message. I left a long story about Bettina being in Zakynthos and told Mihalis I was leaving on Friday and would like to see him. Tomorrow would be all right, I said, but I left the details of the poetry night in case he could make it.

'Now all of Athens will know where to find you,' Antonia laughed.

On the street Antonia didn't stop talking, telling me stories about her friend Lambi, a poet who was part of the show we were about to see, and their days in the Communist Party.

'He got arrested once and told the cop he was fighting on his behalf as well. You can imagine how grateful the cop was.'

People recognised her and stopped to speak to her, saying she'd been wonderful in the play.

'Thank you,' she said. 'Tell your friends.'

A few minutes later, we found ourselves in a cavernous room with blue velvet curtains and an elevated platform where three men and a woman were seated. I was surprised to see so many people in attendance, well over a hundred. I'd imagined some dark, dingy room with twenty grief-stricken bohemian types.

We sat down and Antonia waved to Lambi, who smiled nervously. One of the other men on the platform introduced himself as Ilias, who was chairing the night. The four poets spoke in turn about their life and work and source of inspiration, then read some of their work. Again I was pleasantly surprised, having expected to be bored stiff. I'd thought the best part of the night would be the after-party, but I was enthralled and entertained. At question time an adolescent boy asked the panel why it was that so many poets committed suicide. This led to a discussion about the sensitive nature of poets. A woman asked what their parents thought of them doing such a dangerous job and an old man in a felt hat wondered whether we'd have the poetry we did in the world if

297

there was no unrequited love. Was it a prerequisite for becoming a poet?

'It's a prerequisite for a lot of things,' the sole woman on the panel said, 'madness being one of them.'

'I think there's a more-than-usual degree of unrequited love among poets,' Lambi said, 'because, let's be honest, who'd want to get involved with us? We're such a miserable lot. I could never fall in love with a poet,' he declared, 'not when you could have a football player or a gymnast.'

'The great Irish poet Yeats wrote some of his best poems as a result of his unrequited love for the revolutionary Maud Gonne,' the other man on the panel began. 'One day, after turning him down yet again, she said to him, "You say I make you miserable, but look at the beautiful poetry you're making out of your unhappiness." He made a complete fool of himself over her, but the fruits of his misery are there for all of us in his work, inspiring us and enlightening us.'

The final comment for the night came from the chairman: 'It's not surprising that love inspires so many poets. It inspires all people, artists or not. Because when we love we feel most alive, and it pushes us to do our best.'

There was a thunderous round of applause and cheering. I felt exhilarated and was full of appreciation for Antonia having insisted I come.

'The night's not over yet,' she said as we stood up.

She went off to see Lambi, and suddenly I heard my name

being called in a familiar Zakynthian drawl. I turned to see Mihalis coming towards me.

'You got the message? Oh my God,' I said, noticing the swelling on his jaw. The heroic look wasn't necessarily a good one on him.

'Yes, I've been here since just after it started. Up the back. You're leaving tomorrow?'

We stumbled into each other's questions and answers. I was keen to hear about how he'd been hurt and he wanted to know why I was leaving tomorrow. Antonia interrupted us before either of us could get far, and after introductions she led us to the door, explaining that we were going to a tavern in Lambi's car.

I looked at Mihalis. 'Do you want to go?'

He shrugged.

'Of course he does,' Antonia said. 'We'll have a great time, come on. What happened? Did you get hit by a car?'

Mihalis shook his head. 'A very involved story.'

'Good, tell us in the car.'

Antonia was right. The night hadn't finished and the best was yet to come. Four poets, their assorted loves, an actor, Mihalis and I went to a club that played traditional music. It was a large place, almost full, which surprised me for a Thursday night, and people were already dancing when we arrived. They were doing the kalamatiana and other dances from rural Greece that aren't played in the doghouses or other nightclubs in Athens. I was up on the dancefloor in no

299

time, while the poets reviewed their performance. Once I was back at the table, Ilias asked, 'How do you know those dances?'

'I learnt them at Greek school and parties,' I said, sipping some wine.

'Really?' He took the pipe out of his mouth. 'In Australia?'

'Most of the Greeks in Australia migrated from rural Greece and this is the music they listen to. I grew up with it.'

Urban Greeks, particularly the middle-class educated kind, know very little about migrants and their culture. They get a real shock when they visit Australia, and if they're in an official capacity they make noises about how the diaspora Greeks are keeping up the old traditions, which is a polite way of saying they're stuck in a timewarp.

'But you're from Zakynthos and all the songs they played just now are from Ipiros,' Ilias said.

'The people who lived next door to my parents' shop were from Ipiros,' I told him. 'I used to hear their music all the time and loved it. My parents hated it. They'd go to their parties and complain about having to listen to dirges all night.'

'They had a point,' Lambi said. 'Compared to the melodic music of Zakynthos, it *is* very heavy.'

'Yes, but I like it. My parents identified that music with backwardness. They thought Ipiros people were backward because of their attitude to women and because they were right wing. A lot of the men wouldn't let their wives wear miniskirts, and my mother thought that was terribly old-fashioned. Mind you, my grandmother used to secretly take down the hems of my mother's dresses, iron them and put them back in her wardrobe, thinking she wouldn't notice!'

I didn't sit down much after that, except to take a sip of wine between songs. After a while Mihalis, who was still too stiff and sore to dance, looked at me warily and poured water in my glass. Antonia, noticing what he was doing, admonished him.

'Let the girl drink a little wine.'

'Yes, but she'll get drunk,' Mihalis said.

'So what if she gets a little drunk, it's her last night. She's entitled to a few drinks.' Antonia told him he should curb his chauvinistic tendencies about women and drinking.

'Forgive me,' he said, sizing up his opponent, 'but I've been out with Fiore a few times and it doesn't take much before she's out on the floor.'

'Oh, Mihalis,' I said flippantly, 'that's only because I drank a bomb.'

'What about that night at Markos'?'

'That was because of the testosterone, you said so.' I felt playful. 'Come and dance with me, please.'

'Fiore, it's impossible.'

'But we haven't danced at all this time around,' I pleaded.

'Am I supposed to fill some kind of quota? Besides, we danced together at the ball at the Casino, just before you passed out. Or have you forgotten?'

'No, I haven't forgotten,' I lied. 'But I just like dancing with you.'

'Well, thank you,' he said firmly. 'But there'll no dancing for me, for now.'

We were dropped off at the main square in Kipseli at three in the morning. I insisted on being dropped off there because I was hoping to convince Mihalis to go to a bar somewhere, just the two of us. It had been raining and Antonia thought I was mad. Mihalis gave her a look that said, 'I told you so,' but assured her he would see me home and that she didn't need to come with us. I kissed them all goodnight, told them what a wonderful time I'd had and what great poets they were. I felt like these people were my dearest friends.

Ilias got out of the car and gave me one of his books. Out of earshot of the others, he told me if I were ever in Greece again his number was on the inside cover. I opened the book and there it was. I burst out laughing and he stepped back with a look of nervous terror on his face. His girlfriend was in the car.

'This is an elaborate way to make a pass at me,' I said. 'Do you do this to all the women you fancy?'

'Sshh.' He held up his hands to quieten me, then got quickly back into the car.

Mihalis chuckled as they sped off.

'What are you laughing at?' I asked.

'Your conquests,' he said, shaking his head.

'My conquests! I gave him absolutely no encouragement. And right in front of his girlfriend!'

'I'm not blaming you. He just thought he'd have a go, but he wasn't counting on you making an announcement to the whole of Kipseli. You frightened the poor man to death.' He laughed again.

'Let's go somewhere for a coffee,' I said.

Mihalis looked doubtful. 'Well, if you pass out somewhere, I'm in no condition to carry you home.' I laughed away his concern and we walked down Fokionos Negri until we found a café with booth seating. We sat next to each other, like two American teenagers, alone at last. Flashes of my dream were causing distractions of pleasure in my stomach. I tried to push them away and concentrate on being civil.

'You know the poet that man was talking about tonight – Keats. Do you know anything about him?' I asked.

'Keats? He wasn't talking about Keats. Keats was English, a completely different poet. That man was talking about Yeats, an Irish poet. You don't know him?'

'I haven't read a lot of poetry,' I admitted.

'I don't believe that. You seem so into it.'

'I'm into it when I'm around you, because you talk about it.'

'If only I had this effect on my students,' Mihalis laughed.

'I'm sure you do. The girls probably have crushes on you and the boys see you as a role model.' I was a bit drunk, it was my last night in Athens, and I was ready to say anything.

'Is that what you think?' Mihalis let his eyes rest on mine.

I had to look down, a little self-conscious from my porno-graphic thoughts. When I looked up again his expression hadn't changed.

He leant forward so that his face was closer to mine. 'Yeats was an Irish poet who wrote at the turn of the last century. You should know this stuff, I wonder about your education. His desire for Maud Gonne was famously unrequited. She was an actor and a revolutionary in the cause for Irish inde-pendence. They were close friends and he had the hots for her for years, but she was only drawn to him intellectually. Imagine that,' he said, still not taking his eyes off me. 'The poor tormented bastard.'

I felt uncomfortable. Was he drawing parallels with us?

'Worse still, she used to tease him. Tell him she had dreams of him that she explained as some psychic connec-tion between the two of them. Or that she saw him only as a friend – perhaps like one of those friends you talk about who sleep with you without wanting to fuck you.'

Oh God, I thought. We're really going to fuck. I can't believe that after all these years it really finally might happen. I was looking at him and thinking so much about kissing him that I was only half listening to him. I wished he would touch me, just lean across the table and touch my wrist or some-thing. My heart was beating so fast I lit a cigarette to calm myself down.

Mihalis sat back in his seat, laughing and shaking his head as if remembering an old joke. 'At least Yeats got something out of his failure to convince her to become his lover. What can the rest of us say?' He blinked slowly, sweeping me into the downcast motion of his languishing eyes.

Why doesn't he make a move? I wondered. Of course he wasn't going to make a move. After everything that had gone down between us, why should he risk being rejected again? It was all past history now, anyway. He thought I was a fool. All this teasing with his eyes and furtive glances was just mucking around. I stubbed my cigarette out like I was putting out a fire.

'What's wrong?' Mihalis asked.

'Nothing, what do you mean?'

'You just frowned and sighed.'

I hadn't realised I had been making my thoughts so obvious.

'You must be preoccupied about the trip ahead,' he said, caressing his jaw, which had taken on a purple hue. 'Do you think you'll be coming back soon?'

'If my sister gets married, I'll be here for the wedding.'

He looked wistful. 'Who knows where life will have taken us by then,' he said. He got out of his seat, excusing himself, and made his way to the toilet.

Yes, I thought, who knows? Mihalis might be married, or in another country. It didn't seem too likely that I'd be married. We might be dead. That decided me. It was now or never. I was fucking Mihalis tonight, and to hell with everything. In those few days alone in Athens, helped along by my dream,

I'd developed elaborate fantasies of a moment when all hesitation dissolved, of inexhaustible passion that lasted until the daylight hours, of truths revealing themselves in whispered sighs of relief. A night I could look back on when I was old and reassure myself that some things had measured up. Above all, I wanted a full stop between us. A full stop so that another sentence could start. What sort of sentence that was didn't matter, we could compose it when the time came. Who cared if he thought me a fool? I'd have to make the first move.

But what if he turned me down? Well, it wouldn't be the first time it had happened and it wouldn't be the last. I could live with it. I concentrated on the task ahead. What would I say? 'Mihalis, I want to go to bed with you'? No, too complicated, he wouldn't know how to take it. He'd say, 'To sleep with me like a brother?' or some smart comment like that. The best thing would be to just kiss him. Lean over and kiss him right on the mouth, so he couldn't mistake it for anything else. In some part of me I knew it was going to be all right, but every other part of me was plagued by doubt.

'Mihalis,' I said when he was back, in a tone suggesting a question would follow.

'Yes, my lady?'

Do it now, I told myself. But my eyes drifted to a billboard on the street showing a semi-naked blindfolded woman and a man putting something under her nose.

'What's your opinion of S&M?' I said without thinking.

'My opinion on S&M?' He looked puzzled, and paused

before answering. 'It's something you're either into or you're not. My opinion about it is pretty irrelevant, wouldn't you say?'

I nodded dumbly.

'Why do you ask?'

'I was just wondering . . .'

'Wondering what?' He opened his eyes in a question and suppressed a smile.

'I was reading somewhere that we all have these tendencies in us,' I said lamely. 'To some degree.'

He touched his jaw again and I reached out and touched it myself and didn't take my hand away.

'Correct,' he said, as if I were one of his students giving him the right answer. 'And you're more of a sadist than you know and I'm discovering just how much of a masochist I am.'

He leant forward, pushing me back into the seat, put his lips on mine and we kissed. We kissed with a hunger so consuming that I forgot about his injuries until he let out a yell so painful that the waiter came scurrying. It was only when we looked up into his embarrassed face that we realised we were horizontal in the booth, in full view of the café.

'We don't mind couples kissing and touching, but . . .' He threw up his arms in an appeal to moderation.

'Sorry.' I scrambled into a sitting position, only to find that my cardigan was completely undone. We regained our composure. Mihalis pulled some money out of his pocket and put it on the table. Then he pulled me into him again.

'Let's get out of here,' I whispered.

Drunk more from the anticipation of sex than from alcohol now, we walked the steep hill to Bettina's apartment, stopping every few minutes to kiss and explore our bodies. Foreplay took place in the streets of Kipseli and once we shut the door behind us there was a frenzied blur as we pulled and tugged at our clothes and found ourselves on the sofa. Our passion was interrupted by my insistence on a condom when he was already inside me.

'Listen, you unreconstructed village boy,' I said. 'What are you doing fucking me without a condom?'

He kissed me on one breast. 'Firstly, I'm not a village boy, we've been town people for three generations, and secondly . . .' He paused and kissed me on the other breast, before murmuring something about pulling out. Otherwise known as withdrawal.

'Mihalis,' I said with enormous reluctance as he kissed my breasts, 'I'm not sure about this.'

There was a hunt around the apartment until a condom was found, and we resumed at the same frenetic pace. My dream it wasn't. We were in too much of a hurry, and negotiating a position that avoided causing pain to Mihalis' injuries, mixed with the awkwardness of it being our first time, caused a lot of laughter. But we had the rest of the night. Or the morning, as it must have been by then. We did it again and I had the chance of hearing Mihalis breathless once more, teasing and beseeching, saying my name in phrases of desire I'd never heard before, all the while pulling me closer, feeling me deeper. At one stage I wept. From relief, from pleasure, from pain, from happiness – I didn't know. Maybe from all of them. It was a long overdue fuck and all the sweeter for it.

Afterwards, Mihalis lay on his side with his weight on his arm. With his free hand he pushed my hair off my face.

'You're very beautiful. You should wear your hair like that more often.'

'You sound like my grandmother,' I laughed.

He studied my face for another minute. I was blinking furiously, struggling to keep awake, not wanting to waste a second. He wanted to know why I'd finally decided to succumb to the physical with him. I gabbled something about wanting to say sorry for upsetting him, about always having a special place in my heart for him, about not wanting to leave with him angry at me yet again. 'And I didn't want to lose you,' I said at last.

He sat up. 'What are you talking about? You're leaving.'

'I know.' Sleep, aided by alcohol, was winning the battle with my body. 'I mean, I didn't want to lose you as a . . .' I paused and glimpsed his impatient face. I had been about to say 'friend', but that would completely miss the mark. I couldn't keep my eyes open. I was too tired to explain my feelings to Mihalis. 'Let's talk about it tomorrow,' I managed to say before sleep finally took me.

# CHAPTER SEVENTEEN

The telephone woke me. So what else was new? The answering machine came on before I reached it and the message I had left for Mihalis played itself out. I let the machine take the call – it was Fotis, hoping he and Mario could come and say goodbye some time. He left a number. The light was still flashing, which meant someone else had left a message. I pressed the button.

'Who's Mihalis? It's me, your mother. Why haven't you called us?' She paused. 'I heard from Bettina that you're coming home. It would be nice to know these things. Call and let us know so that we can pick you up.'

Mihalis had gone. I shuffled through the apartment looking for a note. He must have left a note. It was after midday. Twelve hours left. I didn't feel too good. I would have to get this leaving thing over and done with and stop all this sentimental nonsense. I was going back home and getting my life in order. There was no question of staying. I certainly wasn't going to let one night of sexual adventure lead me into lofty ideas for which there was no basis. I found the note on the bathroom mirror. 'Don't leave', signed, 'he who is not a friend'. That was all.

There was no milk in the house, so I went out for a coffee, doing Bettina's trick of pulling my coat over my pyjamas. I looked like a gypsy, and didn't think about it until I stepped into the street and saw that there were people and Vespas and cars and music and arguments everywhere. The handsome butcher was smoking outside his shop near the corner. He stared at my outfit as I walked by and said, 'Good morning.' That's what I like about Greeks. It was nearly one o'clock but it was still morning to them, and lunchtime is three and afternoon is six or seven. They have a way of stretching out the day. The apartment buildings were blocking out the sun and I felt cold until I reached the square, where it was lighter and warmer. I stopped to buy a newspaper and read it over a Greek coffee in an old-fashioned cafenion. An Italian coffee meant walking another two blocks.

I didn't want to ring my parents from Bettina's and leave her with a massive bill, so I used the phone in the kiosk in the square. I dialled the number and watched the units per drachma tick over with alarming speed as soon as my father answered. A trolley passed and someone was buying a newspaper as his voice came over the line.

'Dad, it's me,' I said. 'Fiore.'

'Fiore, what's happening?' His voice was full of surprise and concern.

I gave him the details of my flight and apologised for not calling earlier, saying I'd had things to do in the last few days.

'Yes, we gathered. Your mother said something about a Manolis whom you sounded very keen to see.'

'Greece is very changed since I was here last, Dad' I said, veering away from any talk of Mihalis. 'In ways I never expected. It's going to get very interesting with all the migrants coming in.'

'Why don't you stay?'

'Stay?' I felt confused. This was the last thing I'd expected to hear from my father. 'You want me to stay?'

'What I want isn't relevant,' he said. 'I thought you would stay, to tell you the truth, with you leaving your job and with your sisters over there. Anyway, if you're coming back that's good. We miss you.' His voice faded as more traffic passed me.

'Dad, are you there?'

'Yes, I'm here. So are you coming alone?'

'Of course I'm coming alone, Dad,' I said impatiently. 'Who would I be coming with?'

'I don't know. It's just your mother rang your sister again because you hadn't made contact and she asked about this Manolis and Bettina told her it was someone you'd been interested in for years. So we thought –'

I stopped him right there. 'His name's Mihalis and it's

312

nothing serious, Dad,' I said, aware of the irritation in my voice. I wondered what else Bettina had told them.

'Really?' He sounded as if he didn't believe me.

'Can I speak to Mum?' I asked.

'Nina's dragged her out to see a play. Some comedy. Nina thought she needed cheering up.'

'Why, what's wrong?' But it was just the usual. She'd had words with Bettina.

'To tell you the truth,' my father said, 'we were thinking of coming to Greece.'

Two people standing next to me were talking about the war in the Balkans and the American demonisation of Milosevic. I thought I hadn't heard right. 'What did you say, Dad?'

'Your mother wants to check out the situation for herself,' he said, meaning she wanted to meet Dionysis and sort Bettina out. I chuckled. Good luck to them. They were going to need it. The number on the machine was now in the thousands. An old man was complaining of a late night.

'Dad, we'll talk when I see you,' I said and hung up.

I was thinking about what my father had told me as I packed my case. I was pleased they were talking of coming to Greece. When I returned from my first trip, I'd told them both that they had to go. 'Everyone talks about you,' I said to them. 'Everyone asks after you.' People had expected them to be with me, some looking around as if my father or mother might be hidden somewhere. It was unfathomable to me that

313

my parents had never shown any interest in returning when so many people showered me with love because I was their child. I don't know when I realised that their reluctance was because of us. They worried that a trip back might have unpredictable consequences. It might create longings in them that they could not fulfil. They feared the pull of Greece, and it was a realistic fear. They had seen other compatriots sell up, leave and return again, sometimes with consequences for their children's education. My parents were hesitant about taking a risk that might destabilise their children's lives. It was all about us; my parents had wanted to do the right thing for us. But despite their best intentions, we had ended up a fractured family.

A rap at the door interrupted my packing. Antonia swayed into the apartment, bubbling over with talk about what a wonderful night we'd all had and how Ilias Karayannis had rung her asking after me.

'You Greeks are all sex maniacs,' I joked.

'Look who's talking! You were about to eat that boy from Zakynthos last night.' She looked at me. 'Did you, by the way?'

I nodded and she slapped me on the back.

'That's my girl. And you picked a fine specimen of Greek manhood to spend your last night with. That's the way, leave on a high.'

As if on cue, Mihalis rang to say he was coming. When I hung up, Antonia chuckled at my 'girlie' voice.

'Very cute,' she said in English, kissing me on both cheeks.

314

I thanked her for showing me such a good time in my last days in Athens, but she brushed me off, declaring it was nothing at all. 'Have a safe trip home,' she said. 'And come back.'

As I waited for Mihalis, I disputed the wisdom of seeing him again. Wouldn't it have been better if we'd said our goodbyes last night? I didn't want emotional scenes with words full of promise that would ring in my ears and beckon me back here when there was no basis for anything. I was also nervous about seeing him, in the way you are after first-time sex. When the buzzer went, I checked myself in the mirror before pressing for the door to open. He walked in wearing a dark blue jumper, a black suede jacket and jeans. The dark colours gave him a brooding look, like Heathcliff on the moors.

We were tentative with each other. I had been about to wash the dishes and told him to come into the kitchen. He leant against the fridge watching me as I filled the space between us with irrelevant talk. I talked until I'd finished the dishes and dried my hands, then I folded the tea towel, put it on the table and turned to face him.

'All right. That's done,' I said.

'Fiore, why are you going?'

Now was not the time to be having such a discussion. 'Why am I going? Because I am. Because my life is there.'

'And couldn't your life be here?'

'I don't know.' I sighed. 'Something like this needs a lot of thought. A lot of planning. I can't decide to stay just like that.

315

There's the issue of work and –' I stopped. He came and stood as close to me as he could and softly pushed my hair out of my eyes. A gesture of intimacy that brought last night back.

'Stay,' he said in a voice that was trying hard to retain its authority. 'Stay, Fiore.'

I was crippled with anguish. With his hand on the back of my head, he pulled me in to him and kissed me. Sex was the only sensible thing to do. He pulled a condom out of his pocket and smiled. 'I have come prepared. A lesser man would have given up at that point last night,' he said, and kissed me as I laughed the three steps to the bedroom.

Mihalis was a man of few words after sex. I thought I had exhausted him, but an hour later, when Fotis and Mario arrived, I realised he was sulking. He made no attempt to be social with the boys and followed our conversation looking very disheartened. Fotis and Mario, having noticed something was going on, were up on their feet with their jackets over their shoulders within half an hour.

'We'll be going, then,' they said and I walked them to the door.

'Sorry, guys,' I said when we were outside. 'My friend Mihalis is a bit sad I'm going.'

'Can you blame him?' Mario said. 'These things aren't easy.'

'When will you come again?' Fotis asked.

'Soon, I hope. Who knows? Next year, maybe,' I said,

talking off the top of my head. They offered to hail a cab for me down at the square and send it up. We kissed and they left.

Back inside I looked at the clock. 'Mihalis,' I said, 'it's time for me to go.'

He looked at me with a feeling of disappointment and regret.

Oh, for God's sake, I thought. What did I do with a request like his? It was too big, and too big a decision. I had to think about it seriously, weigh everything up carefully. I wasn't about to make major changes to my life on the strength of one great night with Mihalis. I had to be sensible. It wasn't as if we had a long-standing relationship, he wasn't promising me anything. 'Stay,' he'd said to me. Stay and what?

But what could he have said? I couldn't expect anything else. 'Stay' meant for me to find a life for myself and that the two of us would be in some kind of relationship. What kind of relationship would it be and how long would it last? There was no guarantee. It might last a month, a year, five years, and then it might end horribly. I would regret not only the end of the relationship, but all that I'd sacrificed for it. If it failed it wouldn't be just another bust-up, but a disaster of deeper consequences. No, it would be better for me to go back as planned and think about things in the cold light of a Melbourne day, and make a proper decision. If I was going to live in Greece, I would do it because I wanted to do it, not for Mihalis.

I tried to tell him all this in the best way I could. I was

nervous and anxious and not entirely sure of my position. I became inarticulate, unable to think of the appropriate words in Greek.

'You're so afraid,' he said softly. 'Afraid of taking the risk, aren't you? I didn't know that about you. It's understandable, though. It's easy to choose the safety of what you know, to take the familiar road instead of going somewhere you have never travelled.' He wasn't making this easy for me, quoting cummings, reminding me of that night we'd spent translating him. 'Yet all that front and courage you have,' he went on, 'that's all for other arenas. Out there,' he said, pointing away from himself.

I knew one thing for certain about Mihalis – that I could always rely on him to drag me kicking and screaming into a confrontation with myself. I wanted to defend myself, to tell him how wrong he was – what did he know of the roads I'd travelled anyway? – but as always there was a kind of truth in what he said.

I went to speak but heard the persistent horn of a car in the street below. The taxi had arrived. Stoically Mihalis picked up my bags, carried them downstairs and loaded them into the boot. I got into the car, thinking he'd follow, but he shut the door, stood on the pavement and blew me a kiss. I wound the window down, demanding to know what he was doing.

'I'm going back upstairs,' he said, showing me the key, 'to lock up properly and then leave the key under Antonia's door. Isn't that right?'

'Aren't you coming to the airport?' My heart was about to give way at the possibility that he wasn't. He shook his head. I tried to get out of the car, but it had one of those childproof locks in the back seat. I couldn't believe this. I wanted that last hour with him. I still had things I wanted to say to him.

'Mihalis,' I said in the best schoolteacher voice I could muster, 'get in the car.' It didn't work. By now there were four or five cars behind us that couldn't get past on the one-way street. Horns were honking and people were yelling.

'Are we going?' the taxi driver barked.

'Fiore, I can't.' I looked beseechingly into his green eyes and he looked away. 'Go,' he said to the driver, who was only too happy to obey. I stuck my head out the window, calling to him as the taxi moved off, stricken with sadness and fury that we were parting like this. Tears welled up and poured down my cheeks.

'He didn't tell me he wasn't going to come to the airport,' I sobbed to the driver. 'It wasn't supposed to be like this.'

The taxi driver was a hard realist. 'What difference does it make? Now or at the airport, it's the same thing. You're leaving, he's staying behind. Where it finally happens is hardly the point, my girl.'

I wanted to tell the driver he had it all wrong. That this wasn't necessarily the end. We slowed down as we reached the city centre and I could see cars bumper to bumper up ahead, moving at a snail's pace. My rage with Mihalis swelled inside me. I was putting together a letter to him in my head, which

319

I intended to write as soon as I got on the plane. His parting words demanded a response. Yes, I was afraid. Who doesn't have fears when making the decision to live in another country? And what about him? Look how many years it had taken him just to leave Zakynthos, and he was saying that I didn't have courage. His was just one song, mine was a whole oratorio, as my mother had said. My indignation had soaked up my tears when the taxi came to a complete stop.

What sort of madness is this? I wondered. A traffic jam at ten-thirty on a Thursday night. This city was completely chaotic.

'What the hell is going on?' I asked the driver.

'There's a rally,' he said.

'At this time of the night?' The indignation was growing within me by the minute.

'Why, is there a set time for rallies?' he asked.

I looked out the window at the life on the street. Young men and women in expensive casual clothes strolling with their chests out ready to defy or embrace the night, an old woman begging, groups of girls walking hand in hand, an elderly couple in formal attire, and a mother in her fifties pushing her adult son in a wheelchair. A wall was inscribed with graffiti: COPS SELL HEROIN. PASOK. DINA, I LOVE YOU. People were standing by their parked cars, talking to other drivers or having a cigarette. This was my last glimpse of Athens and the whole beautiful mess made me weep again.

'You may as well cry now and get it over and done with,' said the driver.

'It's not over and done with.'

'What, you're going to write to each other for a while and spend your wage on phone bills? Then what?'

I said nothing.

'Then you'll settle back into your life, get comfortable, and as time passes he will be a nice memory for you. As you will be for him. It's better this way. Keep him for your dreams.'

I pictured the scene as he spoke. Back in my Melbourne life – a life that was work, friends, going out with Jane in the hope of meeting a man, complaining about how we couldn't, and more work. Except this time around I would be dreaming of Mihalis and regretting what might have been. The taxi driver was wrong. Mihalis would not be a nice memory for me, the bastard would torment me forever.

I could hear the chants of the protesters, who were in the next street. 'What's the rally for?' I asked the driver.

'The Albanians.' He chuckled as if this were a joke.

'Really?' This sounded interesting.

'Yes, can you believe it? They come here, take jobs off Greeks because they work for nothing, and on top of it all they want equal rights. Dirty ungrateful dogs.'

'Stop the car,' I said as calmly as I could.

'The car is stopped,' he observed.

'Good, open the boot. I'm getting out.'

'What's gotten into you? You're not going to the airport?'

'No, I'm going to join the rally with the dirty ungrateful

dogs. Just to stick it up people like you.' I threw him some money.

'You stupid idiot,' he yelled, 'why don't you go back to where you came from?'

I couldn't begin to explain to him that with those words I'd never felt more at home.

He dumped my cases on the road, muttering obscenities under his breath. I put my backpack on, and with my handbag and hatbox in one hand I dragged my suitcase on wheels with the other. I turned the corner and the rally was in front of me. There were banners and music and a small crowd of a few hundred people. A good thing I'd come then, as they obviously needed support.

'Hey,' an onlooker said to me over the noise as I joined the march. 'Where are you going with all those bags?'

I smiled and shouted my response in order to be heard. 'Somewhere I have never travelled.'

## LOVE STRUCK

### Melanie La'Brooy

Following an alcohol-induced, relationship-combusting one-night stand, Isabelle Beckett finds herself suddenly single. Caught up in her big city career with an art auction house, her life is an enviable whirl of glamorous gallery openings, avant-garde ironing boards, and once-in-a-lifetime discoveries.

That is, until Isabelle faces the fact that being single in Sydney is an experience for which she is quite unprepared. Forced to contend with hostile taxi drivers, fanged spiders in the shower and the humiliation of being discovered by her latest crush in a wetsuit-tutu combo, she struggles to retain her dignity and belief in romantic destiny. And then, just when she seems to be regaining control of life, Isabelle finds herself on the hit list of a Serial Dater.

A gloriously funny novel about one girl's blossoming love affair with life.

# HOW THE LIGHT GETS IN

## M.J. Hyland

*I have read somewhere that a sheep raised by dogs will
eventually learn to chase cars. But how long does it take to learn
the tricks of another animal? How long will I need to live with
the Hardings before I unlearn the tricks of my own family?*

Lou Connor, a gifted, unhappy sixteen-year-old, is desperate to
escape her life of poverty in Sydney. But when she travels to the
United States as an exchange student, things go terribly wrong.
This is the story of Lou's struggle for survival in the rich home
of her strange host-family, and every detail is observed with dark
humour and a defiance that veils Lou's longing for acceptance.

*How the Light Gets In* marks the arrival of a powerful new voice
in Australian fiction. It delivers a highly charged study of the
emotional intensity of adolescence. In Lou Connor, M.J.
Hyland has created a memorable protagonist, one whose story
is utterly compelling, from hopeful beginning to unexpected,
haunting end.

# FLEECED!

## Lisa Thompson

Considering a seachange?
You might want to think again ...

Melanie Francis is a voluptuous jazz musician and part-time typist on the lookout for love. When a strapping country lad charges into her life, she's convinced she's finally found a man with grunt. Gary Quartermaine has it all – good looks, a sizeable property and, best of all, the ability to take charge. But is there more to Melanie's Denim Prince than meets the eye? Can she live without Carmen Miranda and the Salsa Kings? And what's a city girl to do with an electro-ejaculator?

In her sparkling debut, Lisa Thompson takes us on a romp through the jazz clubs of inner-city Melbourne and the wide open spaces of idyllic country Victoria. *Fleeced!* might just be the story that gives city boys back their pride.